FROM A BIRD'S EYE

FROM A BIRD'S EYE

Chelsea A. Dzingira

to my family and friends,

thank you for helping me realise.

Well, let it pass, he thought:
April is over, April is over.
There are all kinds of love in the world,
but never the same love twice.

F. Scott Fitzgerald

1. DIVISION

Cyan Tufala, a 23-year-old girl, was sitting in a slight coffee shop, in the town of Cesky Krumlov, finishing up her fifth cup of coffee. She was drawn to the café because of its interior. The hanging lights, the multicoloured wallpaper that strategically covered certain parts of the walls and the sizeable arcs in the room were some of the few features that mesmerised her. There was a long couch leaning against the wall that was portioned by wooden tables to create a space for each customer that wanted to sit in and enjoy the ambiance. It was very modern and chic with a splash of olde worlde. Retro Café, being an appropriate name for the little shop because it described the atmosphere perfectly. Cyan thought that the décor balanced itself very well and that was why she loved visiting the coffee shop. It became habitual ever since she relocated to Prague a few months ago. There was a calm air

that Cyan used frequently to sort out her thoughts.
The coffee itself wasn't to be underestimated. It had the ability to melt in one's tongue and pirouette on your taste buds which usually kept customers coming.
Four people including Cyan were still in the café, enjoying the smell of coffee granules and fresh cream, talking and interacting.
She was there alone. Normally she wouldn't be here this late, but she wasn't there on her own accord. She had received a phone call that had brought her here all the way from her apartment.
A waiter, probably three years younger than her, approached her in that moment to ask if she was ready to order actual food or if she was going to sit around and get high on coffee. Cyan could see that he was frustrated, mainly because he wore a bored expression, though his feet were tapping the marbled floor rapidly. He had been serving her the entire duration she had been in the café but slowly became irritated with her when he dropped off her forth black cup. She understood why, she guessed. It was quite late and the only

time he was on his feet was when he was serving Cyan. She could've explained to the freckled young man that she was waiting for someone, who she was actually upset with for being late and thus the only way she could wait for him in the café, their agreed meeting place, was by ordering a beverage and though she didn't like the fact that she was still the café more than he did, she just had to stay put.

The look on his face however, suggested that he didn't really care about anything she had to say unless she was asking for the bill or she was ordering, so she decided to switch things up and ask for a glass of fresh apple juice. After he swiped up the empty cup that Cyan was drinking from, he dragged himself out of the sit-in area and she watched him retire behind the counter. Her focus shifted back to her black wristwatch. It read 9:40 p.m. She would have to leave this place in the next twenty minutes. Where was he? She had been sitting here for almost two hours just waiting and quite frankly, she had become edgy. She had little patience for people who couldn't keep time because it meant that she had to wait. She hated waiting. Were watches not available? The thought of leaving the café occurred to her. There probably wasn't a real reason for her to be here. The shop was about to close anyway. She could just go home and watch crime documentaries with Janine at her apartment. There was still time. Perhaps J was still awake. Maybe the phone call she received from Dave to meet up was nothing of importance. Why entertain this meeting when all it was going to do was open old wounds?

Although all these thoughts raced through her mind, the only reason she hadn't left was because curiosity kept her feet stamped to the floor. It overruled every other emotion she was feeling. She wanted to know why he had called her two nights ago asking to see her. They hadn't communicated in half a year so this was a big surprise. A surprise she wanted to find out about. Whatever it was, she decided that she could spare at least eighteen minutes of her life to hear what he had to say.

The young waiter approached her once more and placed a frosty glass of apple juice on her table. There was a neatly sliced piece of red apple

attached to the rim of the glass and fine sugar that resembled little crystals decorating it. Though he was annoyed with her, he put a little effort in the presentation of her order.
"Your apple juice." he said as he slid the glass towards her.
"Thank you." Cyan smiled gratefully.
"We are about to close." the waiter said shortly. Cyan realised that he was telling her that she had to leave without actually mouthing the words that she needed to stand up and exit the building. Just as she was about to respond to him, she heard the bell above the café door ring as a signal that there was a new entry in the café. Both Cyan and the waiter turned to see who it was.
A man dressed fully in black, who appeared to be in his early thirties, walked in. He was a towering man, almost six feet, who moved with a certain elegance and confidence that one couldn't fake. His sleeked brown hair was combed neatly and his green eyes searched the room until they rested on Cyan. He walked towards the table she was sitting on, pulled out the wooden chair from across hers, removed his black trench coat that had a small

blue bird designed on the top flap, wrapped it around the chair and finally sat down.
"Hello." the waiter greeted the new entry in a monotone voice. He was definitely irritated that he had to serve yet another person, round up and lock up so close to the end of his shift. Cyan genuinely felt for the boy who looked almost too desperate to leave, though the urge to giggle surged through her like a bolt of electricity.
"Is there anything you'd like to drink? We have coffee, tea and fresh fruit juices." he offered flatly.
"I would like a cappuccino, please." Dave answered in his thick London accent. "Go easy on the chocolate powder but add more cinnamon. And add a spoon of salted caramel. Yes, yes. I would like that."
Just as the waiter was about to walk away, Dave exclaimed, "Oh! Can you paint a little design on the foam for me? Make it a spaceship. Or a yacht! Whichever floats your boat." Dave finished dramatically as he batted his eyelashes like a mischievous primary school girl attempting to slip

out of trouble. The waiter subtly rolled his eyes and stalked off.
"I think you've annoyed him further." Cyan chuckled.
"I wouldn't have so much fun messing around with him if he wasn't so grumpy." The man sitting across from Cyan replied.
"I think it has to do with the fact that he had to see my face almost six times in the last two hours." Cyan assumed. "Speaking of the last two hours, I had five cups of coffee waiting for you, David. Where were you?"
"I had to wait until this establishment was quarter to empty so that I could talk to you privately." he replied. As if on cue, the couple sitting two tables away from them stood up from their place and exited the café. It was just them left in the café with a man who was seriously engrossed in whatever he was reading on his mobile phone.
"Dave, why didn't you just choose a more secluded area instead? Like an alleyway or something. Or arrange this meeting for 10p.m instead of 8p.m?" she asked confusedly.

"I heard Retro Café cappuccinos were to die for so I came here to try them." Dave expressed excitedly. "Plus, would you have agreed to meet me at ten? The last I remembered, you decline anything and everything that happens too late at night. I had to bring you in here a little earlier so that you wouldn't turn down this meeting."
Cyan caught a glimpse of the man sitting across from her. It had been months since she last saw him. David O'Connor still looked the same to her except for his new haircut and a fresh face free of all facial hair. He looked younger than her though he was exactly seven years older than her.
"It's very good to see you, Cy." he expressed.
"Right back at you, Dave." she returned. "I see you dropped the goatee."
"I wanted more of a formidable look. The goatee didn't really help with that at all."
"We tried to tell you." Cyan teased. "So, what was so important that you had to fly out all the way from the United Kingdom to Czech just to speak to me?"
The mood quickly slipped from playful to grave and the knot that she was feeling in her stomach

earlier came back. She couldn't help but ask herself why she hadn't left when she had the chance.
Dave pulled out an A4 beige file from inside his jacket and pushed it across the table. It was clasped closed with a metal clip, a black and blue eagle painted in the centre just like the blue bird designed on his coat. She stared at the file for what seemed a while and then jerked her head up. She attempted to read Dave's expression to get a hint of what she was about open but couldn't get anything short of a neutral stare.
"Should I be worried?" Cyan asked.
"Open it." He suggested.
As reluctant as she was, she followed his instruction. She unclasped the clip and flipped the front page open.
Her eyes were met by three pairs of bright, blue eyes looking straight at her. A family photo of three. Two middle aged parents and a young boy. Their picture was taken outside in front of a great, green hedge and a big, white horse as their background. The sun was elucidating light on their smooth fair skins and their wide smiles. They

looked immaculate. And very wealthy. If the stallion wasn't an indication, then the designer clothes definitely were. She stared at the photo for a few more seconds and then looked up at Dave for an explanation.
"That man in the photo is Minister Clement James of Leicester City. That's his family; Susan James and their little boy Lucas James." Dave began.
"Their son was abducted around noon on the 17th of October by two Caucasian males whilst he was still at school. These men, approximately in their thirties, posed as his bodyguards and pulled him out of school early claiming that there was an emergency at home.
Now, Lucas is eleven. He is not dense. He knows the men that escort him to and from daily. Apparently, these two posers had enough information about his family to convince Lucas to leave with them.
His parents realised that he was missing when he didn't return home the time he usually does. The escort assigned to Lucas revealed that he was under the impression that Lucas was finishing his school day at sunset. Minister James called his

school and they were informed that Lucas had already left that afternoon with two other men. His parents reported him missing this morning." Dave finished.
"Are local authorities working the case?" Cyan asked.
"They were at first. Turn to the next page."
Cyan obeyed Dave's instruction and turned to the next page. She gasped in shock. She did not expect to see such a nauseating and disgusting photo.
"They cut one of Lucas's fingers off?" she asked in barely a whisper.
"No, they didn't. Lucas was dropped off a few blocks away from his home this morning with a note tucked in his schoolbag and a grown man's severed finger attached to it." Dave elaborated.
Cyan didn't have the stomach to analyse the severed finger after all that coffee she took so she focused on the photograph that was taken of the note instead. It was one word written on a piece of white paper in black ink. 'TRUTH.'

"I want to ask if they dusted the note for prints but I'm afraid I already know the answer." Cyan said.
"Negative prints for the note as well as from the finger. It's been sent to an advanced laboratory so we'll hear from them in a day." Dave informed.
"These guys dropped Lucas off at his father's house, a place swarmed with heavy security and were careful not be noticed. They are brutal but thorough which makes them very dangerous criminals. That's why the case has been transferred from local authorities to the SSU."
Cyan blinked.
"I don't want to be harsh here," she approached slowly. "But what does this have to do with me?"
Dave looked at her steadily.
"I came here to tell you that there is a position on the SSU Division that is in possession of this case. I want you take it."
The Special Services Unit, popularly known as SSU, was an International Organisation with its Headquarters in London, that claimed highly skilled soldiers who worked tirelessly day and night to protect civilians and eradicate threats to

societies and communities. It was accompanied by the Special Services Academy based in the same city where aspiring agents were trained prior to joining the Agency and dispatched to different parts of the world after graduation.
Cyan attended the academy when she was almost nineteen years old and graduated with flying colours two years later which, looking back, was a big surprise considering the Agency wasn't the direction she had expected her life to take.
In truth, she had planned to attend a good college after high school that would give her a good education and earn herself a decent job. That way, she would be capable of assuming some of the responsibilities around her home and help her mother take care of her two siblings. In the meantime, she worked odd jobs here and there, babysitting and cleaning different shops trying to save for school and to contribute to the few bills she could. So, when her mother brought up the SSU topic to her, she didn't bother hide her confusion and resistance.
She was sprawled on the floor in their little living room in the summer of 2011, catching her breath

from the hectic day that she had had when her mother dropped a piece of paper in her lap. The first thing Cyan saw when she laid her eyes on the leaflet was a huge black and blue eagle stamped in the centre, whose wings were stretched out and long talons raised as if it was prepared to strike.

'**THE SPECIAL SERVICES ACADEMY**' it read below it in big, blue, bold letters. A navy blue that was the same shade as the bird's feathers. A school? That meant that the eagle must have been some kind of mascot. Possibly a logo or perhaps a spirit animal.

''What is this, Ma?'' she had asked.

''Take a look.'' her mother, Patrice, instructed.

Cyan opened the brochure.

A grandiose building, stretching almost over five or six miles, fell in her line of vision. Cyan couldn't tell the exact distance from the picture.

It was painted a dark brown with a matte finishing that if Cyan didn't know any better, she'd have thought that the building was made from cooking chocolate. She chuckled to herself over her little

internal joke and continued gawking at the structure.
It was almost ten stories high, if Cyan was accurate enough, with rectangular shaped shutters decorating the exterior of the building marking every floor. Two castle like towers of the same colour stood on either side of the edifice resembling strong knights protecting royalty, all three buildings with the same black tiled roofing. She was amazed at how high the towers were that she imagined them shaking hands with the clouds. The letters 'SS' and 'UA' were painted on the towers. 'SS' was painted on the left tower and 'UA' on the right tower, all in navy blue paint. It occurred to Cyan that when one approached the school, there was a clear indication of what the school was about. Another clear identification was a towering metal statue of a man wearing military regalia near the left tower. From what she could see on the leaflet, there were a plethora of badges of different shapes and sizes running down the man's suit jacket, a ribbon that twisted all the way from his left shoulder up to his wrist, a sash that he wore down his upper body and a military hat, similar in design to the service caps army commanders wore, that sat neatly on top of his

head. Underneath were the letters, 'SSUA 1996' that served as a standing platform for the man with the obvious, many achievements.
This man must have founded the place or something, Cyan thought. She could tell that the statue was a little old, a little rusty, but it looked well taken care of.
She took a deep breath.
She had never seen such a fancy school before. And when she thought she couldn't be more amazed, she noticed something that should've stood out to her. Admiring the school infrastructure and wondering why she was admiring it in the first place occupied her that she completely missed it. The school sat on a green pasture, neatly trimmed with cobblestone pathways that led to different areas of the school. They emerged from one main pathway that spread for a full mile before reaching the main building. On either side of this pathway, giant-size flowering trees with large barks growing upwards to give air and sunlight to the baby pink flowers resting on their branches. The trees on the left of the pathway locked branches with the trees on the right so high up in the sky as if they were

butting heads to form an arch that would shield anyone who walked through the outside corridor. What a sight.
Cyan wondered what it would look like in the night, all the lights from the buildings pouring their brilliance onto the leaves, the moon adding its natural illumination and the pink leaves drinking it all in, stepping out of their colour and turning into another just for the night. Cyan had no doubt in her mind that the sight was more precious than her imagination could fathom and in the that moment, she almost wished she could see it.
She turned to the next page.
This page had long paragraphs with a bunch of words detailing what the special school was all about. Before she went further down the brochure, Cyan glanced at her mother. What was the endgame here?
"Where did you get this?" Cyan asked.
"Yes. When I bought the paper this morning, I found this flyer tucked in the third page. I had a quick read through and thought maybe you might want to take a look." responded her mother.
Cyan knew her mother like the back of her stubby hand. Her mother always read the daily news

online. She never bought papers because she thought the concept was too old-fashioned.
"Where did you really get the brochure?" Cyan asked again, apprehensively.
"Alright. I received it from the school's representative." Patrice gave in.
"You mean, the representative of this esteemed school came all the way here to Leicester from London to give you their school flyer? Why would they be giving it to you in the first place? You have no connections there." Cyan interrogated. "What are you not telling me?"
"Ever the problem solver." her mother said to herself. "Alright, Cy. I wanted it to be a surprise but-"
"Wanted what to be a surprise, Ma?" Cyan asked slowly.
"I applied to this school on your behalf and they accepted you!" she exclaimed excitedly. "Isn't that great news? The representative, Carl, came to drop off this brochure they give to new students and explained the little intricacies of the school to me in person. This is so fantastic because-"
"Mother! You signed me up for military school? Really?" Cyan asked, evidently shocked.

"Cyan, this school offers a very good education. Maybe, better than all the other tertiary schools you've been applying to! You'll study human behaviour, learn all about exercising discipline and leadership. Real life values that will help you navigate the real world." Patrice explained. "And I think it is the perfect time to start something great in your life."
"But Mama, I had a plan. I was going to look for a reputable college and receive my good education there. It never included being a part of an army." Cyan complained. "Plus, London is far away from you, Nala and Omari, Ma."
"It's not your duty to worry about us, baby." Her mother reassured. "Think about it. After you're done, you become a law enforcer. The cool kind that we only see on the television! I mean, come on Cy-Cy. Take another look at that school and tell me that it doesn't appeal to you one bit."
It sure was pretty but this was as crazy as it got. Cyan knew her mother wanted her out of the house to do something about her future but she didn't think military school was how far she was willing to go. The Organization was called-she looked down at the brochure to take another look at the name again- the "Special Services Unit" and

as far as she knew, there was nothing special about her. She was smart yes, but she didn't believe a girl like her would be accepted into such a distinguished school without a specific skillset that differentiated her from everyone else. Besides, she had no interest in learning with spoiled, snobbish brats.

"Well, thank you for doing this for me. However, I cannot and will not be attending an institution I know nothing about." Cyan declined stubbornly.

"Cyan, you haven't even read the whole brochure. It details all that you must know." her mother chastised.

"Clearly you haven't read it either, Ma. Have you looked at the tuition? It's thrice what you were paying at my high school." Cyan countered.

"So, you were reading the brochure." Patrice smiled. "The school is willing to pay for your tuition in exchange for a period of service commitment. You serve four years of duty after you graduate while self-funding students only dedicate two."

Cyan groaned. "Seriously? I have to defend this country for four years?"

"The whole world! This is an international organization! Please, tell me you see the bigger

picture. When you graduate from this school, your life could change forever, Cy-Cy." Her mother persuaded.
All her life, Cyan knew her mother to be daring. She lived life simply without worrying. She was a free spirit and usually, Cyan loved that about her. But in this instance, her mother's 'leap into the breach' attitude had signed her up to be a soldier in the military and she wasn't loving it very much.
"I'm not sure, Ma. I don't know if I can attend this prestigious institute." she waivered.
"And why not? You passed highest in your form and you have an excellent athletic background. Sooner or later, you're going to have to believe in yourself and see what I see. You will only grow if you jump out of your comfort zone." Patrice advised. "Only then will you realise how strong and capable you are, a young lady who can do anything she sets her mind to."
Patrice Mapondina had a powerful gift. The gift of persuasion. That little pep talk was enough for Cyan to agree to her mother's crazy idea. Plus, they were living in tough times. She knew her mother couldn't support Cyan and her young, twin siblings on her shop teller salary. If she was

going to leave for this school, then she'd do it for her mother.

Cyan heard Patrice sigh and she knew that her mother was about to use her soft voice. One that Cyan rarely fought because it was always mushy, sincere and genuine.

"Cyan, I want you to do better than I did. I know it's not what you had in mind my baby but who knows? You might love it." Her mother had said. "In addition to all that, I'm your mother and what I say goes."

And there it was. The turning point in her little life when her mother convinced her that life was all about grabbing it by the horns and taking charge. Even if it meant carrying ten-pound bricks on her back while jumping hurdles daily as part of a physical education class.

She left for the Academy in the next three weeks, starting her journey at the SSU.

Cyan would've been lying if she said learning at the Academy was a smooth sail. In the first weeks of her term, her performance was just average compared to the top Ivy League students around her. That ruined her confidence and because of that, her grades slipped further down the slope. She was behind in her schoolwork that one of her

professors threatened to take her to the Directors' office, the headmasters of the school. She was passionate about working hard and making her mother proud but she found it very difficult to juggle her academics her and physical classes without neglecting the other.
This was only until she met Aria Trey, a fellow student who later turned into friend, who didn't mind helping her do better. It didn't happen right away but with each week, Cyan became better and better until she passed with distinctions from the Academy.
It taught her everything that she needed to know from mastering colossal firearms and excruciating unarmed hand to hand combat to effective interrogation methods. In short, she could fight as a soldier without disturbing a single strand of hair.
After she graduated, she applied to the Unit Agency to become an official Agent. She received her response twenty-eight days later and in the year 2013, she had the title 'Agent' against her name. Agent Cyan A. Tufala.
The Agency believed that working in teams to enforce the law brought out faster results therefore just like all the other Agents, she was assigned to work in a team with seven other

Agents on homicidal cases. These teams were known as Divisions and they worked under a Supervisor whom they reported to daily. Being a Supervisor meant carrying the responsibility of providing any essentials that his or her Division needed for different crime calls. Private locations where they could work the cases and vehicles for easy transportation being some of the necessities they had to supply when met with certain calls.
Cyan worked professionally for the SSU for four years and it was the most exhilarating experience of her life. She hated to admit it but her mother was absolutely right.
Though it took a little time, she adored being an Agent. If anyone had told her that she'd have a deep affection for the work she did, she'd have thought that they were lying. Work resembled air to her. She needed it every minute to stay alive, to have a purpose. She managed to make her mother happy and, in the process, finding her own happiness.
Cyan later realized that life was full of grey areas. You could love something wholeheartedly and yet, it could still find the gall to hurt you. So, after seven years of being a part of such a prestigious Organisation and playing an important role, she

decided to leave the Agency to tend to her wounds. Never in a million years would she have imagined sitting across from David, months later, having this conversation with him especially when he understood why she left to begin with.
"You want me to go back?" Cyan asked incredulously.
"We need an experienced soldier to be the eighth member of our team. So, yes. I am asking you to come back. I want you to find the guy who did this." Dave responded.
"Dave, there are hundreds of other Agents to choose from. Worldwide. I don't understand why you're here." Cyan said.
"I know. The criminals we are dealing with are highly intelligent and by the looks of it, experienced. I need someone who is willing to go above and beyond. You have proven to be that passionate in the past. And I need all hands-on deck for this one because of how high profile this case is. Only the best, Cyan. You've proven to be that too. That's why I'm here." Dave replied.
"I appreciate that you came all this way, Dave." she responded. "And I understand that this is a critical case but I don't think I can do what you're asking of me."

"I know that you left SSU for a reason and I'm not trying to dismiss that. But I talked to the Directors and they gave me the green light to recruit you for this operation." he informed.
"Dave. I hear you. But no. I'm not going back to the Organisation." Cyan turned down finally.
As a response, Dave leaned back in his chair. The little hope that was burning in his eyes had been extinguished by Cyan's refusal and she could only wonder if there was more to the offer that he was letting on. In that moment, the young, freckled waiter approached their table with a glass brimming of brown and creamy-steamy goodness in a black tray and set it down right in front of Dave. Cyan noticed that the waiter, whose badge read 'Freddie', made a very poor attempt at designing the spaceship that had been asked for on Dave's beverage but he didn't seem to care. Freddie left once again and Dave took a sip of his drink. He closed his eyes and made a moaning noise at the back of his throat. For a second, that glass of cappuccino transported David O'Connor to another dimension.
"I almost forgot to tell you," he said once he opened his eyes. "Joel Müller has taken over as

DEC of Division 38 and it has become a weather storm of a unit.''
Cyan's eyes widened. ''Joel is Division leader? What happened to Thomas?''
''He abdicated shortly after you left. He transferred to Division 24. He says he likes it better there because he doesn't have to carry the weight of dumb jocks anymore.'' Dave reported.
''I can't say I'm surprised. That Division was full of smart alecks. Especially Joel.'' she said. ''What took Thomas so long?''
''He was always attached to the 38th. Even with that big-mouthed cockroach Joel, he saw the bigger picture. He was an SSU Agent before anything else.'' He answered.
''That is what the Agency is all about. We prioritize making this world safer. And that is why Thomas Wyss is ten times the leader Joel Müller will ever be.'' she declared.
''You've always had the guts to put Joel in his place.'' Dave smiled.
''Joel loved to criticize other Divisions on every single thing, which was strange considering his own Division was in shambles.'' Cyan pointed out.
''I had to speak up. I wasn't scared of Joel. In fact, I think he was intimidated by me.''

"He hates being challenged. Especially by wom-"
"Nope." Cyan interrupted. "Let's not even go there."
Cyan thought that they had talked about Joel enough for one night. She refocused her attention to a different topic.
"So, I know you're a Supervisor and asking you this would be weird but I can't help it." she said slowly.
Dave furrowed his eyebrows in interest.
"What is it?" he asked.
"Is Jermaine still sneaking out during work hours to binge on romantic movies in the company van?" Cyan asked.
Dave guffawed loudly. "Do you think he is strong enough to stop? His Supervisor had to install measures to control his obsession."
"He can't resist the power of clichéd romance." Cyan laughed. "And Shannon? Is she still coming up with cool ideas for new gadgets?"
"She's a talented bird." Dave answered. "All the advanced tech and equipment we use is all because of her."
"And uhm, do the Divisions still do takeout and movies in the woods every fortnight?"

Dave did not answer this question immediately but set his coffee down and stared at Cyan instead. It was an intense gaze. Cyan wondered if Dave's silence was a no. Was Fortnight Takeout not a thing anymore within the Divisions? No, that wasn't it. Cyan knew in her heart that all the Divisions based in London and occasionally those from other cities, met in the woods near the Headquarters on a Friday night to spend time together and unwind from the job, laugh uncontrollably like seals until the air in their lungs was no more, watch the cheesy and corny movies that Jermaine loved, sometimes the action movies that Yua loved, sitting around the bonfires that Okoye loved to make and eat marshmallows while stargazing.
A few moments passed and Dave finally spoke.
"You said 'we'."
"What?" Cyan asked confusedly as she snapped back to reality.
"You said 'we'." He pointed out again. He repeated Cyan's words. "'We prioritize making the world safer.' I know that you miss the Organization. I can see it in your eyes."
Dave had never been more right. After Cyan left the Agency, she moved to the Czech Republic. She

wanted a fresh start and she figured a new environment would give her that. She fell in love with the complex designs of the churches, the parks and the gardens with their healthy roses, the bridges and the rivers that looked surreal as if they were plucked straight from a fairy-tale book. And yet, she couldn't stop thinking about what she had left behind. She wondered many nights if she had made the right decision by leaving the one thing that gave her reason and strength. Being an SSU Agent. The one thing she loved freely without bounds.
Dave continued, "Look, I understand that I may be asking for too much. And that I may be disturbing the life that you've built away from the destruction. It's just that, I wouldn't be here if it wasn't important."
Cyan couldn't find the words. She couldn't say no. But she couldn't say yes either. A tragedy was the catalyst to her departure. She wasn't sure if she was fully healed to go back. What if she wasn't strong enough? What if the Organisation was just one big painful reminder of what had happened? What if she wasn't the same Agent she was six months ago? The one with the accolades. The smooth talker. The one who only needed body

language to learn about a person. The one who could handle firearms of any size skilfully just like a baker who knew how to handle their dough. Cyan knew that there was only one way to get answers to all these questions. And she had to admit to herself that she had missed the adrenaline and the mystery solving. This was the truth she couldn't escape. Perhaps this was what she needed to do to get her blood running again. This could be her ticket to face her problems head on and try by all means to move forward with her life.

And, there was no time like the present.

"This one job." Dave pleaded. "And if you still decide that you don't want to be a part of the SSU then you'll be free to leave without any conditions."

"Count me in." she accepted.

Dave let out a breath of relief.

"Trust me." he said. "There is more to this than the kid. You will see later why I asked you to do this."

"When do we leave?"

His lip curled upward.

"At dawn."

*****

A growling sound woke Cyan from her satisfying unconsciousness. It must have been her phone vibrating against her wooden headboard where she had left it before she fell asleep a few hours ago. Nothing else could make such a loud, disturbing noise like the friction between her phone and the headboard.

Cyan wondered who was texting her before the sun made an appearance. She felt for her phone near the bed end and tapped the screen to open it.

Dave.

"06:30", his message read.

Her brain cells began to generate memories from the night before reminding her that she had accepted Dave's proposal and that she was officially employed again. The text was to let her know that they would be leaving for Leicester in the next hour at 06:30am. She understood the urgency of the situation and the need to travel as soon as possible to find the criminals who abducted the boy, but waking up at the crack of

dawn was something she found difficult to get used to.
It was 05:40 already so she willed herself to get out of bed, dragged herself into her small modern bathroom, took a hot shower and put on a pair of jeans, a high neck top and a windbreaker since it was nine degrees outside. Her little carrier bag sat on her made bed with some of the items she had packed after she returned from the café.
Exhaustion claimed her before she could do anything significant so she decided to continue her tasks in the last thirty minutes before it was time to leave.
Packing was the part of travelling she hated the most. It was so easy to forget what was necessary. But as an Agent, she travelled often meaning that she had no choice. With time in the years, packing became less of a frustration as she learnt a small routine to help her remember make her luggage light but with the essentials she needed.
'CTT'. Clothes, Toiletries, and Travel documents. Clothes were always first since they occupied the most space, and they usually consisted of denim jeans, comfortable pants, dark coloured shirts and tank tops, puffer jackets and two pairs of black boots. Next were her toiletries, body products and

hair products. She had amounted to a collection over the years because she was obsessed with different scents and textures. Plus, she loved catering to her warm, tawny skin and her dense coils and curls. To make sure that her hair always looked gorgeous amidst investigations, she always carried all that she needed. Lastly, all her travel documents and her reading glasses. She memorized her routine and what she considered the worst task in the world became bearable because of it.

She was in the middle of an intense search for her phone charger when she heard a knock at the door. The clock on top of her dresser displayed that it was only 06:00 am. It wasn't 06:30 yet so what was Dave doing here so early? He chose today to be punctual? Before Cyan could approach the door, she heard a key twisting in the doorknob. The door was opened from the other side shortly after. Only two people held keys to her apartment and judging from the heavy dragging of feet she was hearing, it could only be her friend, Janine.

"Cy?" Janine called.

"In here!" Cyan shouted back.

A pale girl with long blonde hair, about the same age as Cyan, entered her room. She wore bright red pants accompanied by a grey buttoned-down shirt striped with red, blue and yellow coloured lines. A grey cap sat on her head and knitted on the centre of it was a colourful and cheerful burger. Underneath the burger, a small text read, *'Happy Meals! Where the food dances happiLY in your beLY!'*
"I'm assuming you got the job because of that awful uniform you're wearing." Cyan laughed.
Janine rolled her eyes and plopped on Cyan's bed.
"Give me a break. I need the money." she replied.
"You look like an unmotivated rainbow." Cyan said breathlessly from laughter.
"You know, maybe quitting my boutique job wasn't the smartest move. It paid very well, you know?"
"No, Janine." Cyan said as she composed herself.
"They overworked you and treated you poorly over there. It was the right decision. You will find another boutique job in no time."
"I guess you're right." Janine agreed. She sat up.
"This monkey suit is depressing me. I'm going to make myself some cereal."

She stood up from the bed and dragged her feet all the way to Cyan's refrigerator. Cyan knew that Janine loved to have oats and pieces of dried fruit with strawberry yoghurt whenever she came over propelling her to always purchase that combination whenever she shopped for her own groceries.

"So, Janine." Cyan began.

"Yeah?" she answered from the kitchen.

"What's going on between you and Matthew?"

Janine slammed one of the units that Cyan stored her bowls in.

"Why do you think there's something going on between Matthew and I?" she asked aggressively.

"He was all you talked about a few days ago and now I can't bring him up without you morphing into the hulk. What's going on? Tell me." Cyan prodded.

"Ughh. Okay. I like Matt. I really do. A lot. But I think he is a little clingy." Janine confided.

Cyan left her room and made her way to the kitchen to be closer to Janine.

"Clingy?" she repeated. "Why do you say that?"

"I don't know, Cy. He's always calling me, visiting my apartment, bringing me bouquets of my favourite flowers with a box of my favourite

chocolates. Like, how does he even know my favourite chocolates? The guy is stalking me!" Janine complained.
"Janine, you sound ridiculous. Matt came to me and asked me what you liked and I gave him all that information. He's not a stalker." Cyan clarified.
"Fine. How about the constant calling and texting in the name of checking in? How do you explain that?" Janine interrogated.
Cyan sighed. "Oh, Janine. My poor, oblivious Janine."
"What?" Janine questioned.
"Matthew is in love with you. That's why he does all those things for you."
"I think it's a bit much."
"Oh? Okay. I think I know what's going on here, Hays. You're not used to the good treatment." Cyan surmised.
"'The good treatment?'"
"Yes." Cyan answered. "You, my girl, are not used to good guys like Matthew who shower you with gifts and call you just to find out how you are. You are familiar with the bad boys who occasionally see you as a priority and treat you like a piece of gum stuck on a garbage truck."

"Is it my fault that I find bad boys cute? And I hate it when you psycho-analyse me."
"Well, you need an injection of truth, Janine. I'm just saying. You have something good going with Matt. Don't ruin it. You're a beautiful girl who deserves to be treated like the princess you already are. Let Matt do that." Cyan advised.
"Aw, Cy." Janine pouted. "I guess you're right. He really is a good guy."
"I know I'm right." Cyan bragged. "They don't call me Doctor Love for nothing."
Janine choked on her cereal. "Dr. Love? I don't think anyone calls you that."
"Whatever, hater. Tons of people call me that." Cyan tried to convince.
Janine giggled. "Anyway, Dr. Love. On that note, we should definitely go on a double date then."
Cyan hesitated. "I'm not so sure. A double date?"
"Yes! You, me, Matthew and Jason!" Janine suggested excitedly.
"Jason, Matthew's friend, Jason?" Cyan refused. "No."
"Why 'no'? It'll be fun! We'll go watch a movie and get some Mexican food afterwards. Please, say yes." Janine implored.

"No." Cyan refused. "I don't like Jason in that way. Or even as a person. And I'm not in the mood for any romantic setups right now. So, no."
"Well, I guess you'll be dying alone then." Janine mumbled.
"Alright. First of all, I heard you." Cyan rebuffed. "Secondly, I'd rather die alone than breathe the same air as Jason, thank you very much. And thirdly, I'm fresh out of a relationship so forgive me if romance is buried deeply underneath the dead heap that is my heart."
"Dramatic." Janine scowled. "But I won't push. I'm going to focus all my energy on enjoying this delicious cereal. I made you a plate by the way." Janine pointed to floral plate on the kitchen counter as she threw herself on the couch in the sitting room.
"I'm not sure if you have noticed but I love having breakfast in your home. I feel very comfortable. And very welcomed too. Not to mention that you purchase very tasty cere-."
Janine stopped talking.
"What?" Cyan asked as she added more yoghurt into her cereal.
"What's with the bag on your bed?" Janine finally noticed. "Are you going somewhere?"

Janine had sat on the right side of the little sitting room, diagonal to Cyan's bedroom that gave her the full view of what was inside. She had spotted Cyan's little carrier bag perched on top of her bed. This was the moment Cyan was dreading. She wondered how Janine was going to react to what she was going to tell her. They were so used to doing almost everything together that this was going to be a big schedule shift for the both of them. Was she going to be mad? Hurt? Upset? Cyan didn't know.

But there was no other way to find out other than telling her about Dave's visit.

"Yes, I am J. Uhm, I've been asked to go back to work." Cyan informed quietly.

"Work? As in that spy stuff that you used to do?" Janine asked.

"We are not spies," Cyan sighed. "But I guess you have a rough idea."

"When did this happen and what did you say?" Janine questioned.

"Last night. I can't give you all the details at the moment but it's important that I go back. I hope you're not mad that I didn't tell you sooner."

"Of course not, honey. How could I be?" Janine said softly. "Are you sure about this though? You're ready to go back after...?"
"It's been six months, J. If Nala found out that I stopped working, she would kill me. I plan to do what she wanted me to do." Cyan settled.
Janine reached out and embraced Cyan tightly. "She would be so proud of you, Cy. Even if you counted leaves on trees for a living. No matter what you do, you'll always be her rock. She loves you just like I love you."
Cyan was always sensitive when it came to her sister Nala and because of that, she rarely talked about her. But to hear Janine say that, it reminded her why they became friends in the first place. Cyan thought of the first time she met J. It was within the first few days she arrived in Cesky Krumlov. She dedicated them to finding out more about the city she had blindly escaped to. She would walk up and down the cobblestone streets and admire the tall, picturesque edifices, the vintage restaurants, hotels that were painted in bright colours and the old residential buildings that had been scathed by the weather throughout the years. It was on her sixth day in Cesky that she decided that she liked the sound of living in

Prague so the smartest thing she could do was find a very comfortable place to lay her head every night. The apartment complex she had chosen was minutes away from the city where Cyan felt it was the most convenient. She didn't know much about Cesky so residing in the city where everything was easily available appealed to her.

The apartment she was renting was on the third floor with four rooms; a sitting room, a kitchen, a bathroom and a bedroom.

Upon entering the apartment, the living room, was to the right and the kitchen to the left with an island separating the two. There was another room to the far right beyond the living room that was the bedroom. It was spacious enough to accommodate a couch on one side, a queen-sized bed in the centre of the room on a wooden platform, a wooden dresser and a walk-in closet on the other side. She couldn't stop salivating over the place when Gregory Novek, the property manager of the complex, gave her a tour of the rooms.

"You like?" Gregory asked expectantly. "Small and homey like you asked."

"Very much Mr. Novek. The view of the town is amazing from up here." she replied.
"I aim to please Miss Tufala. So," he said as he led Cyan through the front door and stepped into the hallway, "We will lock the front door until you have gathered all your belongings from your motel to move in."
Before Cyan could reply to that, she heard heavy footsteps and multiple keys jingle to the left of her. She turned to the direction of the noise and saw a tall girl with long blonde hair, tied into a ponytail, unlocking her door that was two apartments away from hers.
"Janine." Gregory called from behind Cyan. His voice caught her attention and Janine turned towards his direction. She smiled at him.
"Oh. Hi Greg. I hadn't seen you there." Janine greeted.
"You couldn't have. You were so focused on your keys. Are you alright?" Gregory asked as he locked Cyan's new apartment door.
"I'm well. I miss seeing you around here." she pouted.
"Of course, you do." Gregory responded dryly. "You just miss the food I bring for you."

Janine cackled. "It's not my fault that your wife loves me and loves cooking for me." She nodded towards Cyan. "Who's the girl?"
"Janine, this is Cyan, your new neighbour." he introduced. "Cyan, that's Janine Hays."
"Hey." They both said simultaneously. They both snickered.
"Greg, did you manage to get the spare?" Janine asked.
"I did. But I can't have you losing keys like this Janine. It inconveniences me." Gregory complained. He reached into his suede jacket pocket, took out a small silver key and handed it to Janine.
"My refrigerator keys!" the blonde-haired girl exclaimed in relief. "I don't know what it is but I'm so clumsy when it comes to my keys. Thanks Greg."
"That's because you have way too many unnecessary keys, Janine." Gregory pointed out.
"A refrigerator key?" Cyan asked no one in particular.
"Yes. A refrigerator key." Gregory answered. "Miss Hays over here, has a lock on every piece of her property. Her refrigerator being one of them. She says it's in case hungry thieves break in and all

they want is food. She calls them grocery grabbers."
"Greg! Why the scepticism in your voice? It's real!" Janine protested.
"Is the lock on your front door not enough?" Cyan asked curiously.
"Look, I tried to give you a good deal on the apartment." Gregory explained to Cyan. "Everything you asked for. Unfortunately, the package comes with a weird neighbour and I'm not paid enough to do something about it."
And after two months of living in the same apartment complex with the weird neighbour, Cyan and Janine became close. They found out that they had a lot in common such as music taste and food so they decided to hang out more. They would spend nights at each other's apartments watching chick flicks and crime documentaries whilst immersing themselves in greasy goods. They would go sight-seeing in the town and when it was nightfall, sit on the park benches and gaze at the crystal jewels in the night sky. They exchanged stories about their lives. Janine told Cyan about her tyrannical, overbearing parents and how she couldn't stay at home any longer leading to her finding her own place in the city.

Cyan told her about her SSU history and why she left. Because of that, Prague had become her home because Janine was there. Janine didn't know it but just her presence alone made Cyan forget everything she was running from.
Looking at Janine now, dressed up in her burger suit, sitting across from her on the couch, Cyan couldn't help but feel emotional. Would it be the same for Janine without Cyan around? Would Cyan herself cope without Janine? Would the amour and shield that had protected her from her own thoughts and miseries these past few months crumble?
She didn't know. All she was certain of was that she was going to miss Janine. Very much. Her job always came with a sacrifice. This time, she was sacrificing a precious friendship for a bigger purpose.
A knock on the door snapped Cyan out of her memories. She guessed that it could only be Dave. It was 06:20 after all.
"I'll get it." Janine offered.
When she strutted to open the door, Cyan heard muffled voices on the other side of the wall and instead of two feet hitting the floor, she could hear four. Janine must've let him in.

Cyan smelt Dave's exotic cologne before he walked in the living room and when he did, he came in floating. He was exquisitely dressed in a black suit and tie ensemble with a neatly pressed, black, trench coat perched on his shoulders. His Patek watch shined brighter than the pendants on her chandelier light and if her carpet had the ability to feel, it would've been aware of the expensive Italian shoe walking on it. One thing Cyan noted about Dave was that he didn't need an occasion to dress well. He believed that dressing well was a lifestyle choice and that it was a part of him, a part of his identity to always present his best self. A wide-eyed Janine was tailing right behind Dave with her eyes so far out of their sockets that if she widened them one more inch, they would've popped out because of it. She looked like a deer that had been cornered by poachers in the pitch-black night with no way to run. She must've been impressed by Dave, perhaps. Janine turned to Cyan with those wide eyes and she had a feeling that Janine was a few minutes away from saying or doing something that would put Cyan in a position where she'd have to explain why she was friends with Janine in the first place.

"I didn't know you were seeing someone, Cy." Janine blurted out. "I mean, he is not what I would've chosen for you. He's a bit older but if that's what you want, I fully supp-"
If Cyan had anything in her mouth, she would've choked on it.
"No, J. No. No." Cyan interrupted. "That's Dave. As in David O'Connor, my boss. He's the one who asked me to go back to work."
Janine was embarrassed. But only for a split second.
"Oh." she giggled.
Cyan hadn't exchanged pleasantries with Dave and yet, Janine had already made herself comfortable on the armrest of his couch.
"Anyway Dave," she purred. "I hear you're this bigshot at the Special Service. Do you need extra hands? An extra spy? Because I could help you."
Dave measured Janine with his eyes. They squinted with careful thought as he took in Janine's offer.
"You might be of use." Dave answered. "Can you operate a vehicle?"
"Yes! Yes, I can!" Janine said too eagerly.
"Good. We'll call you when we need our lunch delivered." Dave grinned. "We love burgers."

Cyan burst into laughter as Janine gasped. She muttered something under her breath, removed herself from the armrest and plonked herself onto the neighbouring couch.
"There goes my dream." she sulked.
"That was unnecessary, Dave." Cyan laughed.
"Can I get you something to drink?"
"No, I'm alright. Thank you, Cy." he declined. "But you can get a leash for that one. What's her name? Jasmine? Jennifer?"
"Janine." Cyan corrected. "And I apologise for her behaviour. I didn't realise that she wanted to be a spy kid until two minutes ago."
"The most eventful two minutes of my day so far." Dave joked.
His brown eyes did a three-sixty sweep of Cyan's apartment.
"So, this is where you were staying for the past six months. Nice." Dave complimented.
"If it was up to me, I'd have painted the walls blue. With a tinge of black." Cyan mused.
"Like a navy? Or a royal blue?" Dave asked.
"Definitely a navy." Cyan answered.
"Too bad Novek refused. It would've looked debonair." Dave said.

Janine furrowed her eyebrows in confusion. ''How did you know that? That she asked our property manager to paint her room?''
''I know everything.'' Dave replied simply.
''So, you pretended not to know my name...''
''Just to tease you a little.'' He smiled. ''Janine Tereza Hays. Daughter of Grizelda Marie Hays and Triford Hays. Twenty-three years of age and a citizen of Czech Republic by decent. You're the last of four siblings. Bort, Frederick and Daniel Hays being the children before you. At the present moment, your mother's last-born son, Daniel, is engaged to a Matilda Dorz, a vegan, who is disgustingly obsessed with recycling. Their small intimate union will be taking place in five weeks and they have chosen one wedding colour to decorate their setting. White. Symbolic of their purest love for one another.''
Cyan wasn't surprised by Dave's immense knowledge of almost everything and everyone but Janine on the other hand couldn't remove her jaw off the floor.
''What...? How did you know all that? My brother hasn't even sent out invitations to his wedding yet!''

"Dave works for the biggest police force in the world so he knows everything." Cyan chimed in.
"I would love to stay here and tell you all about it but I have somewhere important I have to be." Dave said. "It was lovely meeting you Janine Hays."
"Cyan?" he called.
"Yes. I'm ready." Cyan answered, knowing what he meant.
Suddenly, red blotches replaced the paleness of Janine's skin. All her attention was focused on the ceiling and Cyan realised that she was willing herself not to shed any tears. Cyan sat next to her on the couch and clasped her soft hands.
"We'll call every day. It'll feel like you're there with me and I'm here with you." Cyan assured.
"What am I going to do without you?" Janine quavered.
Cyan hugged Janine very tightly as this was the last time she was going to for a while. She pecked J on the cheek and wiped her tears away.
"I'm going to miss you so much." Cyan expressed quietly. "Don't forget to ask Greg to fix the crack on your kitchen ceiling. That little piece of duct tape you put won't hold for much longer. And try to be on time for work, J. Fast food mangers hate

late employees and you're already fifteen minutes late today as we speak. And please Janine, for the love of all that's good, throw away the bloody pineapple in your refrigerator. You know you're allergic. You seem to forget that every time you hear your stomach growling."
"Yes, mother." Janine mocked.
They squeezed each other again. Janine dropped a kiss on Cyan's cheek and finally walked towards the door. Before she completely reached the exit, she turned around and said, "I'll be emptying your refrigerator the moment I come back home."
And with that, she left.
Dave looked dumbfounded but Cyan was surprised that Janine hadn't raided her fridge as soon as she found out that that Cyan would be out of her apartment indefinitely.
"Are you ready?" he asked.
"Yup." She replied.
She retrieved her bag, switched off the lights in her home and locked the door.
They left the apartment and descended the apartment building stairs. As soon as they stepped outside, the early morning noise caused by vendors and shop owners preparing their businesses for the day, hit them like a speed train.

Cyan could tell Dave was quite irritated with the hubbub but it was music to Cyan's ears. If you lived on a volcanic island for six months, you were bound to expect the eruptions.
They didn't walk too far from the complex when they stopped at a black tinted Sedan across the road.
"Our ride." Dave clarified.
He opened the backseat for her and entered in after. The chauffeur seemed to know their destination because Dave didn't utter a word. She started the car and Cyan made herself comfortable as they left the city behind.
They passed all the bright coloured buildings that she was used to admiring, the sophisticated clustered, orange-roofed buildings and the little lakes, reservoirs and ponds. They passed Mr. Charlie's bakery, Dana's outside bookshop and Ermis' hardware shop, all of whom she knew and appreciated.
They had been driving for approximately thirteen minutes when she noticed the sun rising, bringing with it different colours to dye the sky; lavender, orange and flamingo pink, whilst the clouds floated freely in the morning sky without a care in the world. The aesthetic of the mornings always

consumed Cyan. She shut her eyes and felt the low temperatures competing with the timid sun for her attention. The cold temperature pricked her hands and the warmth from the sun penetrated through the car window and stroked her skin. She let the Czech morning consume her one last time, her nose tingling with the smell of fresh bread and coffee.
What a beautiful way to say goodbye.
They drove for another ten minutes until the car stopped.
She opened her eyes. Her pupils adjusted and focused on where they were. The Sedan had stopped in an open field with flowers of all varieties sprouting from underneath it. A large square building, equivalent to a one-story house in size, stood a few feet from them with a wide tarred road paved from inside the building travelling for miles heading to the East.
They left the car and moved closer to the building. Before they entered, Cyan saw a large, cream jet with letters 'SSU' painted in blue on the body of the jet, with a familiar blue bird right next to them, sitting obediently inside. She couldn't be accurate but it looked like a 15 4.8 feet Beechcraft Beech jet. Cyan realized that they had stopped at

a hangar and the long-tarred road was in fact, a runway.
Dave ushered Cyan to the lush jet and she followed him with her bag. The plug door in the centre of the jet opened for them producing a set of stairs for them to climb into the aircraft. Once she was in, she immediately threw herself on the leathery seat near the window. Dave made himself comfortable in the seat across from hers.
"I had forgotten how much you SSU officials love to splurge." Cyan remarked.
"Jets are a good investment. We land at the exact place we need to be." he defended.
"So, are we going straight to Leicester? Or we're stopping in London first? I know that we have to do some paperwork."
"No. Not the Headquarters. You've already been authorized to work this case so we won't be stopping there." Dave answered. "We are going straight to the house. It's on the outskirts of town."
"Alright. So, which Division will I be working under? You hadn't told me that part." Cyan said.
"Division 12." He replied.
Cyan's mouth went dry.
"Division 12?" she repeated slowly.

"Yes, the 12th Division. What? Is there something wrong?" Dave asked with concern.
"No, no. Nothing at all." Cyan replied. "That's one of the most impressive Divisions existing right now. They've added most solved homicide cases in a single year to their record, right? Why didn't you tell me earlier? I probably would've accepted the job a lot sooner." Cyan joked.
"Huh. So, you have been following Agency news."
"It's hard to avoid the exceptional work that they have been doing. They are a formidable force." Cyan complimented.
"This is a high-profile case. It had to go to the extremely willing. Plus, the DEC is a force to be reckoned with." Dave answered.
Cyan was quiet for a few moments before she spoke.
"Nathan is still DEC?"
"Oh, most definitely. One of the best guys we've ever had."
Cyan knew Nathan. She met him when she was still at the Academy and saw him occasionally when teams met for bi-monthly assessments. He was treated as an emperor in and out of the Agency. His grandmother was one of the main SSU sponsors therefore all the Directors' and officials

felt obliged to treat Nathan in high regard seeing as that without his grandmother, SSU wouldn't be what it was today without her.
It was safe to say that Nathan was popular at the Academy. He graduated a year before her making him twenty-four years of age, a year older than she was. It didn't help that Nathan was your typical, classical handsome boy.
He was striking. Tall, broad shoulders, muscular frame, creamy, fair skin, perfect eyebrows, perfect cheek bones, sculpted jaw, wavy hair and blue eyes. All the girls went nuts for him and most, if not all the guys envied and wanted the attention he received. Not only was he SSU's most eligible bachelor, he was also intelligent. He always came up with creative and innovative ways to improve the Agency and everyone paid attention. What was really impressive about him was that he didn't let all the praise get to him. He had a mandate as a member of the Special Services Unit to serve and protect and he always remembered that.
Now as DEC, he led one of the most promising Divisions in the whole Organisation. From the moment she met him, she knew it would happen. It was inevitable. Not because of his background

but because Nathan believed that he would only become the best if he worked hard. And he did. Though she was thrilled to work under the 12th Division, learning that she'd be working under his leadership made her break a sweat. The air was suddenly a little stuffy. Why didn't she ask which Division she'd be working under before she accepted Dave's proposal?
Regardless, she was already in the jet. She'd meet any situations she knew she was going to face, at the bridge.
"I mean, it doesn't hurt that the girls think he is dreamy. They all listen to him." Dave continued.
Cyan cast a sideways glance at Dave.
"Oh, yes. I know all about it." he said. "I'm a Supervisor. Not oblivious."
"He is a natural." Cyan replied shortly.
Dave pulled a beige file from under his seat, similar to the one he had shown her back at the café with the SSU eagle plastered in the centre.
She opened the file just as he began to explain.
"That file contains team hierarchy. Nathan Caldwell being DEC as you know and Evan Patterson as his Second Bearing."
There was a list of names in the file that contained team members of Division 12 including her own.

'Nathaniel Caldwell – Division Expert Chief.'
'Evan Patterson – Second Bearing'
'Harper Blair'
'Jordan-Bailey Ofori'
'William Bradford Jr.'
'Preston Davison'
'Cyan A. Tufala'
'Aria Trey'
Her eyes popped out at the last name.
"Dave!" she shrieked. "You didn't tell me that Aria was transferred to the 12th!"
"I wanted to surprise you." He confessed. "She's pretty excited to see you too. Didn't she tell you anything about her transfer?"
"She didn't give me much when we talked about it. She just said she was moving Divisions but she didn't give me any details. I guess she kept quiet to surprise me too." she surmised.
"She moved about five months ago." Dave said. "I figured she would help you adjust back into the SSU world again since you know, you girls always did everything together. Also, her computer skills are so rad."
"This is great!" Cyan exclaimed excitedly. "And do you do that in front of the others? Attempting to

rekindle the spirit from your youth by using words like 'rad'? Who still says that?"
"I'm the boss. I do and say whatever I want." he retorted.
The pilot stretched his head through the mediator door that connected his flying space and the cabin where Cyan and Dave were seated.
"Is everyone ready?" he asked.
"Always ready, Tommy." he replied. "Cy? Ready?"
"Let's do this."

2. OLD NEW DISCOVERIES

Nathan Caldwell was made aware of Lucas James' abduction case three hours after he was returned home. He had given all his team members case files that contained pictures of the boy, where he was taken, official statements taken from his parents, his teacher and any other witnesses that came forward by the Leicester Police Department. In a nutshell, all the information they needed to find out why Lucas was taken and most importantly, where. In the past day, Nathan and

the team visited the school to recreate the kidnappers' movements in order to find out their motive to abduct Lucas, to speak to available witnesses and most crucially, to speak to Lucas' parents and find out if they had any idea of who could've been behind this plight.
At the present moment, Nathan and three other members of his Division were going over the facts of Lucas James' case.
Lucas was an eleven-year-old boy taken at approximately noon by two Caucasian males, both estimated to be in their thirties. One was average height and one almost six feet, both said to have been dressed in casual wear and dark shades. They interrupted his 11:45 class and one of the perpetrators whispered to the teacher that was presiding over Lucas' English Language lesson, Mrs. Renwich, that they had to pull Lucas out of class because of an emergency back home. Apparently, his great-grandmother, Kale James had been rushed to the hospital after a brutal accident and his parents were asking that Lucas be home with the rest of the family. That consequently resulted in Mrs. Renwich giving Lucas a pass to leave the school premises before the end of the school day.

Ancillary staff that worked outside that afternoon reported that two males left with a sixth grader in a plain, silver van missing its number plates. It was a vehicle foreign to school property. Lucas was not seen again that day until he was spotted twenty hours later, at approximately 07:13am in the morning, a few blocks away from his residence, lying unconscious on the pavement with splatters of blood stained on his clothes without any physical signs of an injury. Everything about him seemed fairly normal except the bloodless, amputated human finger that was packed in the side pocket of his satchel together with a note from the abductors that read '**TRUTH**'. As unconventional as the events were, Nathan went over the information repeatedly to make sense of it all.

While he was sorting the papers he had in chronological order to study them again, he came across a photo of Lucas taken of him recently, given to him by his parents. Long, curly brown hair, sky blue eyes with green specks in them, freckles spread out on his rosy cheeks and a wide smile so contagious it made you want to smile too.

Nathan sighed. Cases that involved children unsettled him because he was left with more questions than answers. Why children? Did heartless people really exist? Did they not understand that children were a no-go area? What gave these perpetrators the boldness to abduct the child of a political giant anyway, knowing full well the intense repercussions of interfering with state families? Not to mention, kidnapping a child in broad daylight and robbing him of his innocence?
Nathan's mind was a windmill, racing, in which most cases, the energy would've been good, but because he had to have a clear mind to break down the facts in front of him, he had to put a cap on his thoughts. He had to focus on the work he was doing in the debrief room with half of the team that was present; Preston Davison, the sharpest individual in the room with an intelligence quotient of 170, Aria Trey, their proficient Technical Analyst and Evan Patterson, his outstanding, esteemed and incomparable Second Bearing. The room they were currently occupying was a large four walled room with a large wooden table in the centre of the room. Eight chairs surrounded this table with beige

velvet couches forming an oval a few feet away from the table. A ninety-inch screen was screwed into the centre wall so as to accommodate effortless viewing of photographs and documents to all the members of the team.
The room balanced three colours. White, black and beige. The walls were painted charcoal while the floors were a sooty marble. The bookshelves at the back of the room were painted a sandy colour while the velvet couches were tan. The hammock on the left side of the room was a bleached white while the fur floor rugs were camel. The screen on the wall was chalky while the table they were surrounding each other on was a cream colour.
This was the room they worked on cases, day and night.
They all had Lucas' file in front of them, a white bedazzled laptop sitting in front of Aria, theories and possible outcomes bouncing off of each other. What was the motive for this kidnapping? Was this the criminal's sick way of staging a protest? An article in the daily newspaper was printed two weeks ago accusing the Minister of soliciting funds meant for the city's development for his own personal luxuries. Was snatching his

son a way of highlighting his incompetence? Could it have been a typical ransom abduction? If it had been, why did the abductors return the boy without making outrageous demands from the James' family for banknotes? That couldn't be it. There was no documented call that they were aware of before the time Lucas was returned thus, the theory null and void of any water. They had to rule it out.
Perhaps, these unknowns had an uncontrollable psychopathic urge for little boys. As sick as it was to think about, they couldn't dismiss that they could potentially be looking at child trafficking. They weren't a hundred percent sure on the unknowns' motives but they were certain that this went beyond any demonstrations or monetary compensation.
"Finding these guys would've been a lot easier if we knew who that finger belonged to." Aria said.
"Tremendously." Preston agreed. "But the finger deteriorated making it difficult to extract the biometric data."
"And we'll only be able to determine who it really belongs to when we receive the lab results in a few hours." Aria said.

"Either way, we have to continue and use the information we already have." Nathan said.
"Lucas was found with a little note and grown man's finger attached to it. Why?"
"Taking the note into consideration, it was presented on a piece of white paper written with black ink in capital letters to make the message distinctive. It is a very simple word that stands alone so as to not distract us from what the senders want us to understand, and yet the fact that that these unknowns want us to focus on the postulation of truth suggests to me that they want to highlight the importance of it. Though there may be a plethora of interpretations and conceptions, one that really strikes me to be likely possible is that they want us to know that they hold vital information, someone's secret maybe, they could expose at any time of their choosing. The severed finger we received may be symbolic of what could happen if the truth made its way out- permanent disrepair of someone's life. Now, because they abducted Lucas James, I'm assuming their targets are his parents." Preston speculated.
"You think they have something on the Minister?" Aria asked.
"Everyone has secrets." Evan broke in.

"Preston and I spoke to his parents yesterday and they swore up and down that they hadn't provoked anyone enough to birth these enemies or even just knowing anyone who would." Aria reported.
"Clement is politician. If anyone had serious enemies he didn't know about, it would be him." Evan responded. "Why use the boy as a messenger in the first place though? If the goal was to send a message, there were easier, less complicated means to do that. An anonymous email, a letter, or even a phone call from a burner phone. Why the drama and risk being compromised?"
"Because it's about so much more than that." Preston answered.
Nathan nodded his head in agreement. "I think it's more than that, yes. Not only was the message simple, but it was very specific. Truth. One word. Abducting Lucas made sure that there was no question about who the message was being delivered to. Plus, the kidnapping was very public. They want everyone to be a witness. It's about humiliation." Nathan explained.
"These men are brave." Aria noted. "Not only did they waltz into Lucas' school, where they could've

been easily identified, but they returned him near his home with this barbaric message."

"They have faith in their abilities. They managed to snatch him up which was the hardest part of the job." Nathan responded. "Dumping him was a piece of cake."

Before she could reply, a ping noise sounded on Aria's laptop to signify that she had received a notification. She focused her brown eyes on the message.

"Lucas is still in the hospital for monitoring but he gave LPD an account of what he remembers."

Her fingers moved at agile speed on her keyboard. "I'm putting it on the screen now."

Moments of silence passed while they all read an account of what Lucas experienced that night, displayed by Aria on the screen attached to the wall.

"So let me get this straight." Evan began once he concluded reading. "He remembers being pushed into a van with a bag over his head. They drove for a short or for a long time, that part is a bit foggy to him, and the car stopped. He was carried out and they went up. A door was opened and eventually he was dropped on a chair and the bag was removed. He couldn't make out much of his surroundings but he was in a very dark room with three silhouettes in front of him, the two men that took him and an older man. He could tell that he was a little older than everyone else because he had grey hair that stood out even in the darkness, and his voice was very husky and hoarse."

"An older man? So, we have three unknowns?" Aria asked.

"Where was he when Lucas was taken out of school?" Preston asked. "Only two men were seen in and out."

"He must've stayed behind. He was probably unable to participate physically in the actual kidnapping." Evan speculated. "Lucas describes him as an old man after all."

"Either that, or he could've paid these two to do all the dirty work while he assumed another position." Preston said.

"A position like what?" Aria asked.

"The orchestrator." Nathan answered.

"That's possible. He calls the shots. Humpty and Dumpty follow." Evan said. "Money is one heck of an incentive if they agreed to go through all of this for it."

"Hm." Nathan sounded

"What?" Evan asked.
"Lucas says they went up." Nathan noted. "Those could be stairs, an elevator or even an escalator. That means that we are looking at two-or three-story buildings within a five-to-fifty-mile radius."
"I'll get LPD on it." Aria said. The sound of her ring filled fingers hitting her keyboard buttons projected in the room.
"Uh, there's more." Aria said. "Lucas says here that there was a fourth man." She read. "He was sitting right next to him in a chair similar to his. He couldn't tell who he was except that he was quite a big guy. A few minutes, he heard shouting. The big guy next to him and the older man were going at it, not giving each other chances to speak, but the older guy's voice was the loudest. Big guy stretches his arm over Lucas' legs, que more noises and then Lucas heard a very loud scream. Like someone had been hurt. Someone poked him with a sharp object and it was lights out. He remembers nothing after that."
"A fourth guy?" Evan asked incredulously. "Could he be a victim we don't know about?"
"That could be since he was seated just like Lucas was. But it's very difficult to tell if he was a victim or a participant like them." Aria expressed.

"No." Nathan refused. "He wasn't a victim. He was definitely a part of this little group."
"What makes you so sure?" Aria questioned.
"This guy stretched his arm over Lucas' legs." Nathan repeated. "It doesn't sound like he was restrained to me. If they were keeping a big guy like Lucas described, then they would've definitely kept some chains on him."
"Additionally, to that, these men were arguing and from what I understood from that account, male number four was one of the primary contributors to the scuffle. If you're held hostage, the only time you vociferate is when you're screaming for help." Preston added.
"What could they have been arguing about?" Aria asked.
"It could've been something personal." Preston suggested.
"Perhaps, it was about the job. It wasn't as clean as it was supposed to be and the old man wasn't too happy about that." Nathan theorized. "They probably made a mistake that we haven't picked up on yet."
"That would apply to the two guys that abducted Lucas. But what about the guy sitting next to Lucas?" Aria asked. "We don't know his role."

"He's sitting." Preston announced.
"His role is sitting?" Evan questioned.
"Pardon?" Nathan asked.
"No. The man next to Lucas. He's sitting." Preston reiterated. "Out of all the places he could be, he is right next to the abducted. And while he's being scolded by the old man, he still stays put which isn't a natural reaction when someone is going at you."
"Unless he's submissive." Nathan argued.
"If he was, then he wouldn't go back and forth with the older man who seems to have a dominant personality. He would naturally retreat and treat his actions as fact." Preston countered.
"So, what are you saying? You think guy number four was rebelling or something?" Evan asked.
"In a way, yes. I think he was protecting Lucas." Preston surmised.
"Protecting?" Nathan asked.
"The way he stretches his arms over Lucas' legs. He was trying to shield him." Preston theorized. "Stay with me, okay? Read Lucas' statement again. After he stretches his arms, there is more arguing. Shortly after, Lucas hears a scream and then suddenly darkness."
They all focused their eyes on the screen.

"Arguing, scream then darkness." Aria repeated the same words in the chronological order under her breath. It occurred to Nathan that Aria was repeating the events over and over to herself so that she could catch what Preston was throwing at them.
"Argue, scream then darkness." Evan repeated.
"What would happen when two men were arguing and a scream followed afterwards?" Preston asked.
"Physical display of dominance." Nathan surmised.
"A fight broke out? Someone was punched?" Aria asked.
"A punch is not enough to make man to scream. In fact, the immediate reaction would be to punch back." Nathan said. "Something else happened."
"The scream could've been someone else though. Like neighbours
or something." Aria theorized.
"These men kidnapped a child. A state child. They would've chosen a secluded area for absolute privacy. That scream could've only been produced in that room they were in." Nathan contested.
"This might be a stretch. I don't know but..." Preston stuttered.

"Go on, Press." Nathan assured.
"We received a man's truncated third finger, right?"
"That was a huge 'get screwed' to us." Aria mumbled.
"Would it be possible that the amputation of his limb happened in that very room?" Preston suggested. "That would explain the scream."
"Limb disassociation is not exactly a quiet activity." Nathan backed. "But that would mean the amputation took place while guy number four was alive."
"There's no record of a dumped body yet." Aria reported.
"And there were blood splatters all over Lucas' clothes yet he wasn't injured in any way. They still had to test it just to be sure." Preston revealed. "Lucas' blood type is A Positive. The blood found on his clothes was O Negative. It's not his."
Nathan eyed Evan. He was holding his writing pen a little too tightly, a habit he had adopted in their teenage years when something bothered him.
"Ev, what do you think?" Nathan asked him.
"There's something I don't understand." Evan replied. "Are we saying that guy number four's

finger was excised in that place? For what? As some sort of punishment?''
''I got a good look at the finger when I was at Forensics. It's sturdy. Definitely fits the description of a middle-aged man. Hairs, patterns and all.'' Nathan described.
''My guess is that the three men had a plan for Lucas, killing him, which would've been the safest option for them. But guy number four probably disagreed to all that because he saw it as the most dangerous. That's why there was so much arguing. Different sets of opinions. He probably didn't want the police to be all over them for murdering a state child.'' Preston reasoned.
''It makes sense. Guy number four's argument was convincing. He planted a seed of doubt within them and the idea of prosecution sounded very unappealing. That's why the decided to let Lucas go unscathed.'' Nathan added.
''Unfortunately for guy number four, his resistance to whatever they had planned to do showed the others his unavailability to really apply himself to the cause.'' Evan continued.
''And so, they punished him by dismembering him and gifting his finger to the very person he was trying to protect. A way to teach him a lesson but

also further their agenda. We might actually be working with guy number four's finger." Aria finished. "Genius."

"Did anyone notice that guy number four wasn't part of the kidnapping?" Evan observed.

"No, he wasn't." Nathan agreed. "I wonder why."

"We are missing something." Evan said.

"I agree." Preston concurred. "Ari, did LPD send you Lucas' medical report as requested?"

"Uhm, give me a sec." she said as she focused on her laptop. "Yes, they did."

"May you display it on the screen please?" Preston asked politely.

A white page filled with unreadable handwriting replaced Lucas' statement on the screen. Must've been the original copy from his doctor. Nathan could barely make out the letters of the first line but Preston didn't seem to have any difficulty reading it because in record time he said, "Just as I thought."

"What is it?" Nathan asked.

"A dose of potent barbiturate was found in Lucas' system." Preston pointed out.

"Barbiturate?" Aria asked.

"Barbiturates are non-selective central nervous system depressants that are at the nexus of

treatments to seduce patients or maintain unconsciousness. Certain barbiturates are used as anticonvulsants or induce thiopental. In this case, it was the latter. They used Amobarbital also known as Amytal, a barbiturate with sedating and hypnotic properties.'' Preston explained.
''Anaesthesia.'' Aria responded simply.
''A more dangerous and uncontrollable anaesthesia. Hospitals don't use drugs like Amytal anymore because it's difficult for patients not to become dependent on them.'' Evan answered.
''Lucas described darkness after a feeling a sharp pain. They injected this drug into his system to knock him out.'' Nathan realized.
''A side effect of the drug is memory loss. That's the reason why we can't piece it all together. He can't remember what the men were arguing about or what they were wearing or what they even looked like. His statement has too many holes.'' Preston said. ''It's a miracle he remembers as much as he does.''
''We had been asking ourselves why they would risk being compromised. They had already prepared a solution to that problem.'' Nathan replied. '' They messed with his memory.''

"And the longer Lucas was awake, the more he would've taken in, the more he would've heard and the more he would've put together." Evan reasoned.
Nathan had to admit that these criminals were a little brainy. They managed to remove Lucas from an institution with more than four hundred children without seeming suspicious or causing a ruckus. That meant that they had been watching him for some time, learning more about him and his schedules so that they were fully prepared to pull off the abduction. In that moment, finding out why Lucas was taken became a hundred times more important because of how the abductors were willing to dedicate their time to study Lucas. They were not any regular criminals. On top of that, they had the whole police force in the palm of their hands, treating them like pawns in their little game.
"All of this just theoretical." Nathan said. "For now, we will wait for the lab results to back up our theories."
As soon as Nathan finished his sentence, he heard the sound of hard rubber hitting the furnished floor. Footsteps of more than one person. He familiarized the sound with the combat boots

Division Units wore as part of their daily uniform when they were on the job. As if they all had one mind, Nathan, Evan, Preston and Aria left the room to enter a massive room adjacent to the debrief room, that combined both the living room and the kitchen. On the right side of the room, grey and cream couches made an oval shape around a mahogany coffee table that sat in the middle with couple magazines on top it. Similar to the debrief room, a black screen was indented on the grey wall expect this one had no access restrictions on it unlike the screen in the other room. On the left side of the humongous room was the kitchen, accommodating a long black countertop beautified with brown lines around it that resembled little bolts of lightning or little cracks in the wood, depending on how you looked at it. Four ebony bar chairs coexisted with the counter and a tan vase of white daisies accessorized them.

All the cabinets, cupboards and drawers, top to bottom, that extended throughout the entire left wall of the kitchen were the same colour and design as the countertop. The sink, the faucet and the refrigerator followed suit. The colours in the house were all in correspondence so it didn't look depressing as much as it sounded. The east wall of the room was made of glass that allowed brightness to slip in and befriend all the dark furniture. Nathan truly enjoyed the view from the glass because it overlooked a steep slope of different trees as the house was built on a hill. Not to mention how attractive it made the house look. The kitchen and television walls could only enjoy the benefits.

Just after the sitting area, there was a short hallway to the right, walls painted in grey, that led to the front door. Before reaching the main entrance, there were two flights of wooden stairs to the right that took them to their sleeping quarters and a bunch of other rooms that Nathan hadn't really explored.

In the room that they were presently in, there was a gap between the sitting area and the kitchen island that was filled by three individuals; one tall, muscular guy with deep rich russet skin, a more slender, pale guy who was the same height and a tan girl with pink undertones, who was shorter than the two boys. They were wearing official SSU gear; jet black cargo pants, compression t-shirts and black combat boots. A black holster was attached on the right side of their cargo pants'

belt accommodating their firearms and their SSU identification badges.
Nathan was standing across from the rest of his team.
"I have a question." Aria said in a very puzzled manner.
"What is it?" Evan asked.
"How does Harper look so flawless? Is she not coming from a field operation?" Aria asked confusedly.
Aria noticed correctly. Unlike the two boys who flanked Harper, dishevelled and ready to collapse at any minute, Harper was very awake and spotless. Her newly cut strawberry blonde hair, inches below her ears, was very neat. Not a single strand out of place. In fact, she was carrying her teammates' operation gear bags they had left with a few hours ago, including her own.
"Have you forgotten? Harper has HTD. High Tolerance for Danger." Preston reminded.
"She could go on a high-risk opp. and still look like she could walk down a runway." Evan added.
"She's an alien." Jordan, the muscular guy, chimed in as he buried himself in the couch.
"Honestly, I can only explain it as female power." Harper shrugged.

"'That's exactly what I'm talking about." Aria complimented Harper as they snickered at each other the way girls did when one complimented the other or talked about their girl power sisterhood.
As he did more often than he liked, Nathan broke up the party as he assumed the responsibilities of the DEC.
"How did the operation go?" he asked.
"Successful." Jordan answered. "We found the two girls alive in the deepest part of the woods. Except for some cuts and minor abrasions, I think they'll be alright."
"And Gambdie Olt?"
"We caught him not too far from here." William, the second guy, spoke. "A few miles away from our house, actually. The idiot chained the poor girls in his truck and attempted to escape on foot."
"That psychopath was in our woods and we didn't even know it. Who knows what he could've done to those girls if we were only a few seconds too late." Jordan said.
"I'm just glad Division 5 asked for our assistance in time knowing our experience and familiarity with these woods." Evan stated.

"It was a smart idea sending you guys to deal with Olt while the rest of us stayed behind to work on the James' case. Job well done." Nathan complimented.
"Thank you." Harper said. "Olt is going away for a very long time. By the time he is out, he won't know what the sky looks like."
"I know it's hectic right now with all the different cases we are working on but I need written reports from the three of you concerning last night's operation as soon as possible." Nathan requested.
"Ugh." Harper groaned. "I hate reports, Nathe."
"I know." Nathan sympathized. "Make sure I have them soon. You know how the Directors can be."
"Will do." William answered. "Any news on the newbie?"
"Her name is Cyan, Will." Aria corrected.
"Whatever." Will replied flatly. "Has she graced us with her presence yet?"
"Will." Nathan warned.
"Fine. Has she arrived?"
"Not yet." Evan responded as he checked his wristwatch. "Probably in a few minutes. It's almost 11."

Nathan had noticed that William had an edge to him whenever the topic of Cyan was brought up. And when they did talk about her, his contributions weren't always the best. He wondered what it was about Cyan that ruffled his little eagle feathers.
He remembered the day Dave mentioned that he wanted to add a new member to the team. A female. It was a few days before they received news of the kidnapping. Dave expressed to them that D12 needed more of a female touch because "Women ruled the world", and that he knew the perfect person. The girls were thrilled just to have another one of them around but when Dave revealed that he was thinking of offering the position to Cyan Tufala, it took a lot out of Aria not to jump on Dave and squeeze him to death. From what Nathan knew, Cyan and Aria had been friends from the time they were in the Academy and still kept in touch after they parted ways for their different Divisions. They were close. Not only were the girls happy to have another female around, but the guys too. He knew that they were tired of Harper and Aria approaching them for solutions to their girl troubles every day. All the

guys except William. He found out the hard way that he knew absolutely nothing about women.
In a nutshell, everyone was happy with Dave's decision for different reasons. Nathan just wasn't sure how successful Dave was going to be on this mission. It wasn't a secret that Cyan left the Agency and why she did so. It had been six months since she was on the field. Was it something she still wanted? He wanted to caution Dave that there was a slight chance Cyan would accept this position on the team but the girls looked excited that he felt like a monster just by thinking about it. So, he decided not to say anything. William on the other hand, took it upon himself to play devil's advocate and make it known that Cyan might not accept the offer and that adding an eighth member to the team was unnecessary. He was adamant in his argument making Nathan realize that Will wasn't necessarily happy about the changes.
Even after all the discouragement from Will, Dave was still passionate about asking Cyan to join their group and truthfully, Nathan secretly hoped that he would get the job done.
Being Supervisor meant acting as a communication liaison between your team and

the board of Directors and that's exactly what Dave was good at. Communicating. His skills were so proficient that if Nathan really put some thought into it, the task wouldn't be impossible for him. He only wondered what it would be like working with her. Would she be a positive update or a negative update? Nathan knew her as a really good agent. Excellent. She didn't receive all those certificates by being average. But would she gel well with D12? If he felt that her joining the team was more of a setback than an upgrade, what would be his next step?

As First, his thoughts were always one step ahead so that nothing was a surprise to him and he was absolutely sure that Evan, his Second, was thinking the same. He just hoped that they wouldn't have to deal with new agent drama because they had a lot of work to do.

Interrupting him from his thoughts, a thick branch with scalloped leaves, knocked part of the glass wall in the living room. The team lived in a huge house in the middle of the woods that Dave arranged for them whenever it was time for them to work on their cases. The advantage of their living arrangement was that they were able to work with no distractions from the city. However, the disadvantage was that they were surrounded by trees and whenever there was a breeze, the conifers felt provoked, releasing all their agitation on the glass wall. Because of the unrelenting mood swings of the trees, Nathan ignored the noise until the same branch violently hit the wall again. Usually, when the nature was uneasy in that way, it indicated that an aircraft was in the area so he willed his ears to search for a quiet wheezing in the air. He listened hard and he heard it.

"The SSU jet." Aria announced.

"Speak of the angel." Evan said as he took a seat on one of the high kitchen chairs.

Nathan got a good look at his teammates. Some expectant, some stoked out of their minds and others with neutral expressions. His own expression was either here nor there. One of his many talents was schooling his emotions. That way, no one could tell what he was really feeling.

"Guys? Hello? I know you missed me!" A deep voice sounded from the hallway.

A well-dressed man in a black suit and tie accompanied by expensive looking shoes emerged from the main entrance and strutted into the room. His skin was a little rosy pink, probably from all the activity with the flight and walking down from the hangar situated a few miles away from the house. But underneath all that, he wore huge smile on his face. He was excited to see them. Nathan had no idea why because Dave had seen them sixteen hours ago.

Next to him stood a tall girl, inches taller than the other two girls but definitely shorter than all the guys. Her hazel eyes were surveying her surroundings, taking in her environment. 101 of the Academy, 'Be alert enough to learn about your environment before it notices you.' She had been out of the game for a while but she certainly hadn't forgotten how to play it.

She possessed caramel coated skin, two shades lighter than Jay's, as if it had been licked by the sun every dawning she opened her eyes. Her sweet, flowery scent waltzed around in the room occupying his nose and her cherry braided hair cascaded down her back, tied into a single ponytail behind her head.

Cherry. A very fitting colour for her that complemented her mien and sang her praises. It was so remarkably her to own a bold colour and walk confidently with it as if it was specifically made for her. He couldn't quite articulate the sublimity of it. But perhaps, he didn't need to. Some realities known weren't meant to be explained.

She had a fit and toned body, which was a requirement for every single member that belonged to the SSU, but a touch of curvy came with hers. A well-proportioned temple she evidently took good care of. She wore black jeans, what he understood as a high neck top from spending too much time with Aria and Harper, a windbreaker and black boots. Whether she was trying or not, she looked exquisite.

"Cy!" Aria exclaimed.

She ran towards Cyan, long black silky hair in the air, and threw herself onto her. Surprised, Cyan dropped her bag but recovered quickly and embraced Aria.

"Oh, Ari! Look at you!" Cyan greeted with her arms around Aria's shoulders.

"Alright, time for a little introduction. Cyan", Dave called.

Cyan and Aria pulled away from each other and zeroed in on Dave.

"Meet Division 12. Aria Trey as you already know, Preston Davison, Jordan-Bailey Ofori, Harper Marie Blair and William Bradford Jr. These are the

strongest, smartest and most skilled group of individuals I know." Dave introduced.
He motioned towards Nathan and Evan's direction.
"Nathaniel Miles Levi Caldwell and Evanildo Isaias Patterson. Our First and Second. These are the captains of our ship." he introduced. "D12, I would like you to meet Cyan Autumn Tufala."
"Hi." Cyan waved.
A chorus of Heys greeted her back.
Jordan turned to Evan. "Evanildo? Your full name is Evanildo?" he tittered.
"I bet all the paper and ink ran out when they tried to write Nathan's names on his birth certificate." Harper snickered.
What had Dave done?
"Full names, Dave?" Nathan asked.
"Thank you, David. Really. Thank you." Evan responded sarcastically.
"Oh, come on, Evanildo. I gave your team a spectacular intro." Dave grinned.
"Last week we were the team that didn't know hard work even if it slapped us across the face and shouted "My name is hard work."" Will recalled.

"I was just a little upset that you guys didn't invite me to your pasta party. So, yeah. I might have said a few things I didn't mean." Dave sighed.
"We're sorry. Will you come to the next one?" Preston laughed.
"Of course." Dave smiled. "Anyway, I have news that's not pretty but it could potentially help the James' case."
"What is it?" Nathan asked.
"Debrief room." Dave suggested.
"Can I put my bag down before we begin?" Cyan asked.
"I'll show you to your room." Aria suggested.
"And I'll take that." Dave offered politely referring to her bag.
"Thanks." Cyan smiled at them.
Dave led the way to the upstairs bedrooms, Cyan's bag in hand, escorted by an eager Preston who was heavily engrossed in whatever conversation they were having. Cyan and Aria were trailing behind while engaging in scintillating and exhilarating conversation of their own.
"I'm going to shower. I'll be back in a jiffy." Harper announced.

"Same here. I need to remove Gambdie's DNA off of me." Jordan croaked and the three of them, including William, made their way up the stairs. It was Nathan and Evan left in the room. Nathan sat next to Evan who hadn't moved from the bar chairs.

"We might have to wait a little until everyone is ready to do the debrief." he said.

"Yeah." Evan agreed. "It gives everyone a chance to rest so that we can work fresh when Dave deposits the new information."

"How do you think he did it?" Nathan asked.

"Did what?"

"How did he convince Cyan to come back?"

"I'm not sure. He probably told her that we needed her, that sort of thing." Evan answered.

"I see." Nathan murmured.

Dave must've worked that charm of his on her. Or perhaps his presence just made her realise what she already wanted. One thing Nathan was certain of was that it was very difficult to escape from the Organisation. It took pieces from you, simultaneously making you feel whole. You didn't feel complete until you were back to where it all started.

Nathan heard fingers clicking in his ear. It took him some to understand that Evan was trying to get his attention.
"Hello? Earth to Caldwell?"
"Huh? Sorry." he apologised. "Did you say something?"
Evan didn't reply right away. He looked at Nathan quizzically as if he was calculating what he would need to do to see what was really going on in his head.
He remained quiet. And Nathan knowing Evan, his silence spoke the loudest. He clearly had something on his chest. Something that he desperately needed to say. Only if Nathan allowed it.
"It's weighing heavily on you, isn't it? Say it." Nathan instructed.
"Say what?" Evan asked.
"We've been best friends for over seven years. I know you more than you know yourself. Out with it." Nathan pushed.
"Okay, then. Only because you begged me." Evan gave in. "Will you be able to keep a straight head with her around? I mean, will you be able to give this case your undivided attention whilst seeing her every day?"

"Who?"
"Cyan."
"What are you on about Evan?" Nathan asked.
"Are you really going to pretend that you have no idea what I'm talking about? You're better than that Nathe." Evan rebuffed.
"Who said anything about pretending? I'm not even pretending." Nathan blustered. "I haven't the slightest clue."
"Fine. I'll rephrase." Evan said. "Tell me the truth. Are you a hundred percent sure that working with your ex-girlfriend is not going to be a problem?"

3. QUESTIONS AND NOSE CANDY

Massive trees of different sizes and heights surrounded the house they were living in. Different colour leaves, some red, some green and some orange, settled on their branches. They were gradually leaving their home, leaf by leaf, like a baby bird leaving its nest. Aided by the wind, they flew far away where they couldn't be seen any longer. Some leaves found it a little difficult to let go, afraid of their fate, and so they remained on the branches, holding on with their entire existence as the wind urged them to move forward. Though the sun was behind the clouds, it rebelled momentarily just to lend its soft rays to the stubborn leaves as a way of assurance that everything was going to be alright. Wherever they ended up, their importance would never be questioned. The branches, conscious and appreciative of the sun's gentle ways, loosened their grip and bid farewell. Pushed by the eager wind, the red and orange leaves left the nest and flew to their future.

Cyan could've watched the cycle of Mother Nature all day. She thought it was precious. Appreciative to the wide glass wall in the living room, she had the luxury of admiring the outside whenever she desired.

The house itself was gorgeous. If there was an award for an unrivalled Supervisor who provided top quality provisions for his or her team, Dave would have a full shelf of accolades.

The house, the hangar, the garage with the latest and fastest vehicles and everything she was yet to see was proof of how well Dave took care of his team. The team didn't need all the extras to produce results. They needed themselves and

their training. But their Supervisor, Dave, went above and beyond for them.
An hour and a half into her arrival, she found herself in a very spacious room that was just after the kitchen. Beige painted bookshelves were situated at the back of the room and held more than a hundred books that ranged from William Shakespeare to Jane Austen to F. Scott Fitzgerald. Whoever purchased and displayed those books had excellent taste, Cyan thought. She noticed that half, if not all the rooms were painted in the colour black including the room they were currently in and oddly, she found it very comforting. Cream chairs surrounded a ginormous table and occupying them were the Agents.
Aria was seated on a chair to the right that overlooked everyone else, her fingers moving as fast as lightning on a white bedazzled laptop.
She had changed in some ways since Cyan saw her last. Her silky, curly hair had grown longer to the small of her back, her olive skin glimmering and a little sparkle on her nose that was new to Cyan. It was a tiny diamond punctured into her left nostril. She spotted a nose stud.
She was easily one of the most beautiful women Cyan had ever had the pleasure of seeing. And it

wasn't just how long her lashes were or how bright her smile was or the colour of her almond eyes. But it was the spirit she radiated. Her protective, sweet and generous spirit.
Cyan wondered what skin regimen Aria was using lately. She wanted to hop onto it immediately. Besides Ari, she recognized a few faces in the room she used to see when she was fully employed at SSU. Jordan's for one. A striking guy from Ghana who always moved with towering confidence, glazed in chocolate brown skin with a broad build jumping out of his shirt. He had a short-cropped haircut and a carefully trimmed and well-groomed beard. As far as Cyan remembered, Jordan was so charming that he received the title of 'ladies' man'. He had never forced his charm on anyone. He was just naturally smooth. Besides, with Jordan's good looks and strong physique, it was difficult for him not to be noticed.
Another person she recognized was Evan. Tall, hanging more to the lean side with warm skin just like hers. He hadn't changed much except for the cloud of soft curly hair that he had shaved into a mini afro of little raven ringlets with chestnut highlights. He loved growing out his hair but

always complained that his *Cabo-Verdiano* mother preferred it short and neat. His English father didn't mind how his son kept his hair, but when it came down to it, he wanted what Evan's mother wanted. By the looks of things now, Evan was living proof that an African mother's demands couldn't be ignored no matter how much you tried.
He was also a fan favourite in the Organisation just like Jordan but it wasn't something Evan particularly paid attention to.
It seemed to Cyan that SSU girls found the African in the man of the Organisation attractive.
Her eyes were taking in every detail of the room, like the vase of blue roses sitting on the windowsill that didn't really fit into the room but still managed to be noticed positively and the bulbs directly above her with the swirling light inside of them. She admired the power that simple items such as vases and bulbs possessed, contributing to the elegance of the room.
Gazing around in amazement, her eyes involuntarily landed on a tall, brawn stacked boy. The long, brown wavy hair that she was used to seeing was trimmed into a shaggy crew cut. The remaining hair, parted in the middle, was

immaculately messy, a few strands springing down to his face. He totally pulled off the cute leader in a boy band look.
His piercing, blue eyes were stuck on his mobile phone and his pink, plumb lip was tucked in-between his teeth. He wasn't sitting like the others but instead, he was standing near the screen with his left side profile facing Cyan. That was where God drew his creamy neck with tan freckles. Cyan remembered that he used to cover them with his hair because he wasn't fond of them but now, he flaunted them like a trophy. He must've developed a new love for them.
He wore a white shirt and a black denim jacket that hugged his arms with a pair of black trackpants and white sneakers.
He had no right to look that good.
And that smell. His smell. Out of all of the different scents soaring in the room, she picked on his first. She must've longed for it.
Cyan took another whiff of Nathan's berry scent. A nostalgic wave smacked her so hard that she had to pinch herself back to reality. She removed her eyes off of him faster than the human eye could blink.
No.

She mentally scolded herself for losing control. She had been trying not to stare at him. She told herself that she wouldn't.
But she couldn't help herself.
Another mental scold.
She promised herself that she wouldn't be distracted by him while she was working the case. So, she wouldn't.
"We seem to have made progress with the James' case as I informed you all earlier. Thirty-six-year-old, white male, Geoffrey Adams was found dead this morning at the Guildhall Musuem." Dave began.
He motioned to Aria, who he was standing next to, to project something on the screen.
Everyone's attention went to the screen hammered on the wall as a picture of a stout man appeared. He was lying on concrete ground in what resembled a courtyard with his grey button-down shirt and pair of blue denim jeans dishevelled to creases. His naturally pale skin was covered in blue almost purple bruises on the lower part of his cheek. Though his damaged body lying flaccid on the ground was an eerie sight, it was not much compared to the hollow hole that

had opened inches of his skin right in the middle of his unbarred, unearthly green eyes.
"He was found in the Museum courtyard at 06:00a.m and according to Forensics, a 6mm passed through his forehead." Dave informed.
"A 6m bullet?" Nathan asked. "Quite a number of firearms use 6mm calibre. Was the casing found?"
"Yes, it was. It was a Rimless bottleneck 7x57mm Mauser." Dave answered.
"A 6-inch Remington Magnum." Evan surmised.
"Those pieces are almost impossible to find because of strict limitations. Specifically for guys like our unknown who go around firing at people in the head." Jordan said. "Where did our unknown get one?"
"He is definitely well connected." a petite blonde-haired girl answered. Harper? Harper, her name was.
"Not only is it difficult to find that gun but when you do get it, you have to pay hefty price for it because of how efficient it is."
"For its accuracy as well." Jordan added. "Do you see how clean that shot is?"
"Triggermen always have access to what is prohibited." Cyan spoke.

"Triggermen?" Aria repeated.
"Are you saying that whoever killed Geoffrey Adams was hired to do it?" Dave asked.
"I can't say for sure but from the little that we can see, I think it points to that." Cyan answered.
"What was it that made you think that our unknown might be a hit man?" Evan asked.
"Because of the way Geoffrey was murdered." Cyan answered. She already felt her blood running just by being a part of the investigation.
"He received a clean, like Jordan said, close range shot directly to the head. It was an unremorseful kill with nothing personal attached to it which is usually typical of an execution kill. The shot was too precise for the killer not to have any skills of a triggerman."
"Besides who, the question is why. Why is Geoffrey in the morgue as we speak?" Dave asked.
"What do we know about Geoffrey?" Nathan asked.
"Okay. So, Mr. Geoffrey here graduated at Coventry University with a degree in Business and Finance at the age of twenty-five in 2006." Aria paraphrased as she read Geoffrey's records.
"Finding a job wasn't easy for him so three years

went by living with and off of his parents. Aged twenty-eight in 2009, he began working at a local insurance company as an intern. He did good work there and gradually climbed the company hierarchy. In 2011, Mr. Frank Wells, company field manager and Geoffrey's predecessor, died of a sudden stroke and seeing as Adams was the obvious candidate, he was promoted to the managerial position. Soon after, he married his long-term girlfriend, Josephine Mund, took in her son from a previous relationship as his own and purchased a house."
"Did he do anything outside work? Any extracurricular activities? Hobbies?" Evan asked.
"No activities. His life consisted of work during the week and spending time with his family during the weekend." Aria told them. "And that's about it. He didn't really have much of a life outside that."
"Sounds like a normal guy." Jordan commented.
"With somewhat a good life." Harper added.
And even though Geoffrey was only thirty-six years old, a young stud Cyan's mother would say, Geoffrey's face was unusually tight with fine lines. The shadows under his eyes were so deep, one could drown in them. Cyan realized that he was

suffering from exhaustion before he died. And not the kind that was repaired by a good night's sleep.
"Normal? Debatable. Good life? Not so much." Aria said. "Last year, while his company was going through tough times, retrenchments and all, Geoffrey found that his wife Josie, was cheating on him."
"Damn." Jordan swore. "How did he find out?"
"Who did she cheat on him with?" Harper followed eagerly with another question.
"Her baby's father." Aria answered.
A series of oous, oh snaps and hmms sounded in the room.
"And to answer your question Jay, he found out through text messages, changes in her behaviour, etcetera." Aria answered. "Not a month a later, Josie divorced Geoffrey and left him for the father of her son. So, not only did Geoffrey lose his wife but he also lost the boy he called his son. You can only imagine how he took all that."
"What happened?" Nathan asked.
"He spiralled. Started showing up to work late, drunk and in a stink of cigarettes. His work became extremely sub-standard." Aria answered.
"That has suspension written all over it." a tall brown-haired boy said. Preston, Cyan

remembered. He was the same guy who introduced the idea of the Organisation hiring scientists earlier to Dave while they ascended the stairs.
"He was actually demoted and eventually fired at the beginning of this year. Apparently, his behaviour wasn't a good brand for the company." Aria reported.
"Wow." Harper sympathized.
"There's something else." Aria announced nervously.
"You mean to tell us that after all that, there's more?" Evan asked incredulously.
"Unfortunately, yes. Two months after he was released from work, his mother was diagnosed with stage four colon cancer."
Cyan felt second hand agony for Geoffrey. His life was hailstorm after hailstorm. There was a dark cloud, rejuvenated by his anguish, that loomed over him in the last years of his life. It followed him everywhere he went to make sure he wouldn't experience even a sliver of happiness or relief. Geoffrey hadn't done anything to upset the universe that his life would turn out this way. Anything Cyan knew of anyway.

"A lot was needed in a short space of time. X-rays, medication and chemotherapy." Aria continued softly. "She passed away a few months ago."
"Aria, would you check his financials? If he lost his income with an ill mother to take care of then he would've been receiving funds somewhere." Nathan pointed out.
"I'll run that." Aria agreed.
"I'm sorry to jump the gun here but what does Adams' shooting have to do with Lucas' kidnapping?" Preston asked curiously.
Dave sighed.
He walked up to the big screen and zoomed in on the picture of Geoffrey. The picture was magnified so that they could see bigger pixels of it. He zoomed in on his limp body, then to his right arm and finally, to his right hand.
Cyan felt unusually strange looking at Geoffrey's hand. She wondered whether it was because she couldn't see correctly owing to the fact that she had left her glasses upstairs in her carrier bag or perhaps it was the fatigue from the plane finally hitting her. She knew there couldn't have been a way she was seeing Geoffrey's little finger and ring finger as the same length. The only difference was that the top of his ring finger was more

crimson red and a creamy colour than all his other fingers. In fact, his whole arm was covered and stained in red like several rivers flowing in different directions.
Blood.
Aria closed her eyes and looked away from the screen.
"What in the...?" Jordan whispered.
"Guy number four." Preston revealed.
"I guess we don't have to wait for those lab results." Aria muttered.
Before the debrief began, half the team that had been working on the James' case discussed their theories with the rest of the team that had left for a field operation, including Cyan and Dave, about an unconventional criminal that was with Lucas the day he was abducted. Cyan remembered Evan calling the man, 'guy number four' because he was the fourth man they had read about in Lucas' statement.
"His ring finger on his right hand was amputated." Dave reported.
Cyan was left speechless. Judging by the silence in the room, she assumed everyone else felt the same. Moments went by until Dave finally broke the silence.

"It's not a coincidence." he said.
"Geoffrey was a victim of his own circumstance." Harper expressed.
"He must've turned to the wrong side of things when he lost everything." Evan noted.
"With no job and a sick mother, he must've resorted to unorthodox means of income." Preston said.
"If that was the case then his bank balance would reflect large, irregular deposits in a short space of time. Or it could even reflect a flat zero balance. Dormant even, as a precaution to being traced; cash or a different account being used as alternatives." Cyan theorized. "Can you access his bank files, Ari?"
"I'm looking at his financials right now and there's nothing at all. There hasn't been a single deposit since his last pay cheque months ago." Aria answered. "It's a dormant account."
"But?" Cyan prodded as she picked something in Aria's tone that suggested there was more that she had figured out.
Aria didn't answer immediately. Her narrowed almond eyes were still plastered on her screen, trying to make sense of what it was exactly she

was looking at. A few seconds later, her eyes widened in realization.
"Well, butter my butt and call me a biscuit." she breathed.
"What is it?" Dave asked.
Nathan, who stood behind Aria, bent down to see what she was staring at on her laptop.
He answered, "There is an account here with a history deposit of fifteen thousand euros in fives within a period of two days. This account belongs to...uh," Nathan paused as he read what he saw. Just like Aria, his eyes were quite wide indicating surprise and realization. "Ben Davies."
"Alright. Who is Ben Davies?" Harper asked slowly.
"Josie's son." Nathan answered.
"What does that mean?" Harper asked once again.
"It means Geoffrey de-activated his own account and opened an account in his stepson's name in order to receive this amount of money. He used his stepson as a cover up." Evan explained.
"Exactly. And get this. His mother died around June and he received this money in May. Around the time that she needed medical treatment." Aria revealed.

"So, in a state of desperation, he asks this money from whoever, promises to return but when time comes to recompense, he doesn't because he can't." Cyan postulated.
"These thugs seem hardcore so the only reason they didn't kill him was if they wanted him to repay them their money in other ways. In labour, perhaps." Harper assumed.
"You know, Geoffrey didn't act like your typical criminal to me." Preston observed.
"Like the way he shielded Lucas. His fatherly instincts kicked in." Jordan added.
"So, it makes sense if being a part of the criminal quartet was something he was forced to do." Harper said.
"So, why kill him now? Could he have been a hinderance to their plans?" Evan asked.
"That or Geoffrey was ready to bow out. Kidnapping Lucas could've been where he drew the line. He was a father after all." Nathan said.
"But that posed problems for our unknowns so their solution was to take him out."
"He was a liability." Harper finished.
"Judging by the shrinkage of his skin and that unmissable red, almost purple, bruise on his cheek, I'd say he had been dead for quite some

time before he was found." Jordan said. "7 hours, maybe."
"Why the museum? Could it hold some significance?" Aria asked.
"It could've been a strategic way of getting everyone's attention." Nathan suggested. "The Museum is a public place."
"Or these unknown suspects could be sick and twisted bastards like we established before." Dave said irritated. "He gifted us with a finger. Anything they do at this point is deluded."
"That doesn't make them less calculative." Evan countered. "They may be sick, which is a fair assessment, but they know what they are doing."
"I agree with Ev. Everything they have been doing up until this point has been a show. Snagging Lucas from his classes in broad daylight, bringing him back but with a grown man's finger and a note as a souvenir and now killing the owner of that finger in the most brutal way possible in one of the most public places in the city. I'd say all this is all directed at someone." Harper reinforced.
"To find these criminals, we have to find their target." Evan reached.
"We theorized previously that Lucas' parents could be the subject. We could look exhaustively

at that and see what we come up with." Preston suggested.
"I don't know if going through the Minister and his wife is a good idea." Dave refused. "This is their case."
"We are not saying they are involved in their own son's case but something in their past could've triggered what is happening to them now." Nathan defended.
"Alright." Dave agreed. "Do it discreetly."
"We'll do that." Nathan agreed. He looked at Dave. "The Adams' case is ours, right?"
"Affirmative. Since there is a connection between the two cases, we are stipulated to work on it." Dave answered.
"We need to find this guy." Jordan said. "Or these guys. We can't have any more casualties."
"I don't think I have to remind you all how important this case is. Now that the SSU is working on the James' case, the Minister is going to be breathing down our necks to find out who traumatized his son." Dave announced. "Find them. I want those idiots behind a cell. Understood?"
"We've got this." Nathan reassured.

Dave didn't respond to that immediately. He searched around the room and when he didn't find what he was looking for, his face scrunched up like a piece of paper in confusion.
"Where is Will?" he asked.
"Right here." a deep voice announced
A tall pale boy with blonde hair and a lean frame walked into the room. Strutted in, more like. Cyan didn't recognize him. Even her subconscious did not register him.
"Dave." he nodded as a way of greeting.
"Hey, everyone! William finally decided that this meeting was actually worth his time." Dave mocked. "What kept you so long, Emperor? Were your servants still washing your feet?"
"Sorry, I'm late Dave." William apologised.
"You're more than late Bradford Jr. You missed the entire meeting!" Dave exclaimed.
"I know, I know." Will said. "I was actually working on the case. That's why I'm late."
"On your own?" Dave asked.
"Yes." William answered. "I just thought it'd be better if I just read through it on my own instead of working it here with...everyone else."
Time was always allocated for Agents to go through cases on their own by their leaders after

the debrief hour if it was necessary, which most of the time, it usually was. Debrief time, however, was never to be missed. It was a crucial hour. This was when facts of a case were relayed to members of a Unit for the first time. Initial thoughts and questions were usually the most important, most honest and the most realistic. A collaborate effort usually brought out fresh, diverse and unbiased ideas therefore making it a priority not to miss DT.

For William to miss it, he must've had another reason, better than wanting to work on the case alone. That was why Dave was so agitated. William's reasoning was more than vague. Actually, the way he articulated the word 'everyone' suggested to Cyan that this William guy was probably avoiding someone's energy in the room. She wondered whose it was.

"Don't miss DT." Dave rebuffed.

William sighed. "I got it."

"Alright. Anyway," Dave went on. "I have supplied everything you'll need for this investigation. This is your house so long as you're working the case. You all know that. A good transportation system has been provided for you. Firearms, ammunition, all the gadgets you

ordered are in the gadget room together with bulletproof vests, shields and other forms of protective clothing.
Once again, ladies and gentlemen, this operation is very serious. Take it that way. I'll need an update soon.'' Dave informed.
''We'll do everything in our power.'' Harper said.
''Everything in your power and more.'' Dave corrected as he placed his mobile phone in his right trouser pocket and picked up a set of car keys that were lying on the table.
''So, that is my cue to leave. You have my number if progress has been made.'' he said as he walked towards the exit of the debrief room.
He left the room and they heard the heel of his Italian shoe hit against the tile floor all the way to the front door.
Cyan heard, ''Treat the newbie well!'' and the front door was slammed shut.
She didn't know if she liked the term 'newbie' very much.
As soon as Dave left, careless chatter erupted in the room. She couldn't keep up with what everyone was talking about but it was as if they hadn't discussed the death of a middle-aged man a few minutes ago.

William, like a thunderstorm, blew out the outbreak and said, "The last time I checked, we were seven on this team. Why are we boarding extra luggage?"
Cyan noticed that William had been in the room for approximately four minutes but the temperature in the room had depleted to the absolute minus.
Aria folded her arms over her chest. "Extra luggage? Who is the extra luggage, William?"
"Don't act dizzy, Aria. You know that I'm talking about your friend." Wiliam retorted. "Dave gave us a very vital case to work on but he still expects us to babysit. Where does he think we'll find the time to do that?"
Cyan couldn't believe her ears. Deadweight was one thing she didn't expect to be called only hours into investigating the case.
She understood a conservative nature within people that feared experiencing new changes. New people. It was difficult to be comfortable around an unfamiliar setting and that fear usually morphed into agitation which Cyan totally understood. What she found difficult to wrap her head around was where William's animosity was coming from.

"What on earth is your problem, Will?" Jordan asked. "You always have something crappy to say."
"My problem, Jordan, is that we are not going to finish this case in time whilst dragging deadweight." William answered. "That's the reason I decided to study this case alone. I would've explained that to David if he wasn't so agitated. I figured that I should hold down the fort while everyone else welcomed the rookie."
Cyan didn't have an easily brushed personality because she believed life was too short to take everything personally. That, and she was too young to develop wrinkle lines.
William, in the few minutes that she had known him, had just become an exception to that. She wanted to take his head and squash it under foot like a grasshopper. How dare he act condescending towards her as if she didn't own any right to be here? As if she had never trained hard to work the case like everyone else.
Cyan then realized that the energy that Wiliam was trying so hard to avoid, was in fact, hers.
"I think that's enough." Aria said.
"Look, I'm just saying." William continued. "Cayana here hasn't been working for six months.

Six full months! I don't know why and I don't care to understand why. But I'm reasonably confused as to why everyone is okay with her being with us when she is just rusty. I bet those fingers don't even remember how to operate a firearm. Do they?"

At this point, Cyan was ready to explode because not only did William mispronounce her name, but he questioned her capabilities. She was more than ready to gauge William's eyeballs out of their sockets. She had a low tolerance for disrespect especially when it was unwarranted.

The only reason she didn't lunge at him was because she didn't want to be labelled as the crazy new agent who couldn't tap her control button when the provocateur was an obvious pompous jerk. So instead, she looked at him dead in the eye and silently challenged him. She wasn't going to give him the satisfaction.

'William!'' Harper exclaimed. ''No one cares about how you feel. If you're unhappy with the decision that has been made, you know the make and model of the front door. Most importantly, you know where it is.''

"If anyone should be shown the door, it should be you Harper. I'm ten times the Agent that you are." William snapped.
"William." Evan warned. "Stop."
That warning from Evan only frightened him in his tracks for only seconds until he decided that he had to continue because no one was taking him seriously.
William sighed. "Evan, I hate conflict, okay? Maybe we can reach a compromise. I'm not thrilled that she's here but I think she can be of use. She can just do what we ask of her. Like an assistant. And she can learn from us while we do what we do best."
If Cyan knew she was going to be offered a secretarial job by one of her teammates, she never would've come.
Though William was extremely rude to her, Cyan tried to reach deep down into her inner calmness, very deep, into her being. Giving out emotion to callous people just like William was just the same as handing someone a gun to shoot you. Emotions were ammunition. People like William fed off from that. She wasn't going to let William disrespect her or anyone else who was defending

her. She just hoped that her voice was just as controlled as her facial features were.
As she was about to maturely put William in his place, Nathan beat her to it.
"Her name is Cyan. Not Cayana." Nathan corrected coldly. His voice as calm and controlled as the ocean while his facial expression displaying extreme annoyance. Nathan's eyebrows were only so far apart while his lip curled upwards.
"In case you forgot that there is only one DEC in this room, I'm going to remind you." Nathan continued. "Evan and I are the quarterbacks of this team. Your job is to receive each and every pass we make to you. In simple words, you adhere to all the decisions that we make because they are only to build this team. Therefore, you are in no shape or form to go against Dave's decisions or our orders."
"I was just saying-"
"Under no circumstances should you ever question the value of any member of this team again." Nathan ordered.
"It's just that in France-"
"You'd better go back there then if you prefer the way they operate." Nathan cut in.

She guessed the team rarely witnessed this side of Nathan because the silence in the room was louder than the outbreak of the chatter earlier. They all wore nervous and expectant expressions except Evan, whose expression showed that he shared Nathan's sentiments.
"The next time you speak out of turn, I won't be as sangfroid." Nathan finished.
William seemed to digest what Nathan had said because his squared-up stance deflated like a popped helium balloon. He didn't utter a single word after the verbal blow he had asked for.
"William, we prefer this kind of Nathan kept in a vault. We don't like it when he is out here with us." Jordan whispered.
Attempted to whisper, Cyan corrected. Everyone could hear him. She was pretty sure that any passer-by on the road could hear him.
"Yeah. I think he scares me." Harper shivered.
That seemed to break the ice because everyone broke out in laughter. Everyone except William, who just folded his hands over his chest.
"Alright. We all heard what Dave said." Nathan addressed. "It's all hands-on deck so Jay, you'll go to Josephine Mund's residence and find out how Geoffrey lived his life at home. It might help us."

"Got it."
"Ev, you'll go with him?" Nathan asked.
"Sure." Evan replied.
Nathan acknowledged that by nodding his head. He resumed, "Pres, you'll meet with the coroner. Her name is Carol Doak. Aria will text you the address."
"Alright." Preston replied.
"Aria, you'll stay here and go through Geoffrey's records." Nathan instructed. "Harp will stay here with you and you'll do fact check together."
"On it." Aria replied.
"Cyan and I will go to Guildhall and process the crime scene." Nathan said. "William, you'll be coming with."
Why? Cyan groaned inwardly.
Orders were orders, she guessed.
"Is everyone clear on what they have to do?" Nathan asked.
A chorus of yeses filled the room including Cyan's.
"Good. Let's go."

******

Nathan, Cyan and William had driven from the house in the outskirts of town to the city where the Museum was situated. They had spent

approximately forty-five minutes on the road until the Guildhall Museum came into view.
The harshest forty-five minutes of Nathan's day. On one hand, he had a sulking William staring out the passenger window, who was evidently unhappy with decisions that had been made concerning the newest addition to the team. And as much as such decisions were final, Nathan always took his teammates' grievances into account. That was the kind of leader he was.
On the other hand, he had a very offended Cyan who also stared outside her own window. And if he remembered correctly, Cyan never allowed her mood to change especially when she was on the job. To her, professionalism took precedence. Unfortunately for Cyan, Nathan knew her in ways not many did. He could read what she tried to hide. For instance, the way she always inhaled deeply whenever there was a gush of wind. It usually meant that she was using her all just to keep it together. At first, Nathan was a little surprised when he noticed that Cyan was not reactive to what William had said to her until a strong gale hit against their car and he heard her take several deep breaths. That was when he knew.

Nathan thought adding Cyan to be the eighth member of D12 was a well-thought-out decision. In fact, she was a really good addition. Why it was so difficult for William to accept the change was anyone's guess. And bizarrely, this situation wasn't as horrifying as some of the other issues he had to deal with in the past as DEC.

At one time, Jay and Harper didn't see eye to eye for days because of a ridiculous squabble they had had that escalated into something even more ridiculous. Their fight intensified where out of character insults were the order of the day even though the two were supposed to be best friends. The team had to intervene because their fight affected the efficiency of their work as a Unit. Harper would walk out of the room as soon as Jordan entered it and Jordan wouldn't go on operations if it meant that she'd see Harper's face at any point of it. This consequently resulted in D12 being two men short. After the whole team involved themselves in Jordan and Harper's business, the two friends made up and everything was swell again. The intervention was quite quick because both parties missed each other and the hide and avoidance had worn them out.

Nathan made a mental note to find out what it was they really fought about.
His memory took him to another time Aria slept one night in a jail cell for physically assaulting another Division member who apparently insulted her. Aria reported that she had heard from a third party that a girl named Dionta, who was a member of Division 1, had insulted her computer and data work, commenting on how below average her skills were and that the best thing for her was to go back to her home country Cuba, where she could use her substandard skills to cure the technological deficiency there. This information, upon falling on Aria's ears, resulted in Dionta receiving a hot slap to the face from Aria.
The sequence of events didn't really shock Nathan. He knew that women took it too far at times. He was just shocked that his timid Aria was capable of swiping someone across the face.
As DEC, Nathan had to answer for that insubordinate behaviour to their Superiors and help them understand that this incident didn't reveal or reflect anything about Aria's character. She would never scratch another Agent's face without cause. After using his charm on the

Directors', Nathan managed to convince them not to fire Aria but to let her go with a warning instead.
After that debacle, Aria found that the third party that had initially approached her about Dionta gave her false information with many unnecessary additions. Dionta hadn't said any of it. It was a DeAndre, another Technical Analyst, who expressed his dislike for Aria's profession since they worked in the same field. 'Work' was a general term meaning 'Technical Analyst' and not anything else that specifically related to the effort and projects that Aria did professionally.
It was safe to say that Aria had overreacted a little.
Nathan laughed inwardly and asked himself whether the members of his team were unique characters or if he was just simply heading a dysfunctional team. Nevertheless, he felt proud and quite relieved to say that the back and forth that happened in the debrief room was not the worst he had dealt with.
When the Museum appeared in his peripheral vision, he let out a breath of relief. He could finally breathe real air again and not awkward oxygen.

He parked their car right next to the other blue and white cruisers outside the entrance.
"We are here." he announced and descended from their black Ford truck.
The museum was a large white building marked with grey stripes down the entire structure with its bottom half stone-layered. It was surrounded by a black fence and average length black poles that were a few feet apart. It was a plain structure that lacked any outstanding details except for fading grey rectangles that were built into the building resembling prison windows, as well as the triangular asphalt shingle roof that had smaller triangular roofs positioned horizontally indicating different rooms. It looked exactly like what it was. A very old museum. In its aging, Nathan thought that the building was fairly captivating. But then again, perhaps it was just him. He always believed in the 'less is more' thing.
They reached the black metal gates that were labelled 'GUILDHALL MUSEUM' on them. They opened to a towering stone-layered Cathedral to their left and a brick-layered building to their right. Nathan led the way to their right and entered the museum through the opaque automatic doors.

Upon entering, they were introduced to a wide room that had colourful banners sitting at the corners of the room, waiting to present on the museum to whomever walked in. Objects such as ancient wooden shoes, drinking jars and combs were displayed in transparent glass cases with different banners sitting next to the display, explaining the history of the museum.
The desk and chair where the receptionist would've been was empty.
It was very chilly in the room, Nathan thought. He reflexively searched for the air conditioning system which he found attached on the left corner inches below the ceiling. He then noticed a camera stapled on the right corner below the ceiling.
''Will, go through the security footage. See if you can get any visual.'' he instructed.
''On it.'' William answered as he moved towards the empty chair and the grey desktop.
Nathan and Cyan left him behind and proceeded straight down a narrow hallway. They had taken only a few steps when they found a white chipped wooden door to their right with a sign written 'GUILDHALL' attached to it and exited the reception area through it.

The other side of the door revealed an empty outside space surrounded by the rear end of all the museum's buildings. It was the courtyard they saw on the screen back at the house. Yellow crime scene tapes printed, 'DO NOT CROSS' bordered the area where Geoffrey Adams was murdered. White tape outlined the cobblestone ground on the exact position he was found that morning. Uniformed police officers were scattered in the courtyard questioning witnesses, taking pictures of the crime scene and others scouring the area for any kind of evidence.
As he was taking it all in, Nathan felt a light pat on his shoulder that motivated him to turn around. He was met by a man in a beige police uniform who was old enough to be in his fifties. He had a black buzz cut, marked with white hairs and a clean-shaven face. Typical military style. He had attached to him his badges, his holster, his firearm and his police radio.
"Agents." he greeted. "I'm Sergent Bruce Hill. Our department answered the call."
"Sergent. I'm Agent Nathaniel Caldwell." Nathan introduced. "With me is Agent Cyan Tufala and Agent William Bradford Jr in the reception area."
Cyan nodded her head in greeting.

"Mr. O'Connor informed me that his agents from the SSU would be coming." Sergeant Bruce mentioned. He whistled in the direction of four police officers who were taking part in different evidence search protocols. Their heads perked up but only one ran towards Seargent Bruce with a black bag strapped down across his torso.
"Sergeant." the police officer responded in deep breaths as he stopped. He wore the same beige uniform as his superior but with less decorative badges.
"Officer Fills, these are the Agents from SSU. Agent Nathaniel Caldwell and Agent Cayenne Tufama." Sergeant Bruce introduced.
Nathan felt Cyan tense up beside him. He knew she hated it whenever her name was mispronounced. The Sergeant couldn't have made it any worse by calling her the name of a spice.
"Cyan Tufala, Sir." Cyan corrected.
"Uh, yes. Sorry." Sergeant answered gruffly.
Officer Fills' eyes widened with surprise. Nathan saw that exact look on a few police officers he had met when he was introduced as an SSU Agent or whenever he flashed his badge. He guessed he understood why they all reacted that way. SSU was a unique unit. It specialized in homicides,

international terrorism and drug trades operated across borders, making it one of the most exhilarating Organisations to be a part of. Anyone who was focused on doing something big for the world wanted to be a part of it because it was extremely impressive. It moulded the best Agents in all aspects; strong physically and sound mentally. Emotions weren't easily tamed but the Agency did try it's best to help Agents make it there.

What outsiders didn't know was that the Agency churned you inside out like dirty laundry in order to make sure you were ready to handle the harsh realities of the world. Only a few could withstand that pressure. If only Officer Fills knew what it took to be in this impressive Organisation; to forget yourself and apply your whole being to the job. Most, if not all SSU members experienced this sacrifice at some point in their career.

Fills handed the bag to Sergeant Bruce. The Sergeant opened it and took out three, small transparent plastic bags. Evidence bags. One contained a black leather wallet, the other contained a smartphone and the last bag carried the shell casing of a bullet.

"We found his wallet and his mobile phone on him. Nothing was taken. He wasn't robbed which means, as you know, this wasn't any ordinary murder."
Nathan took out two pairs of black rubber gloves from his pocket and handed the other pair to Cyan. They both put them on and retrieved the transparent bags from Officer Fills; Nathan with the wallet and Cyan with the phone.
Nathan opened up the Geoffrey's worn out leather brown wallet. The first thing he saw was a small family picture tucked into a little outlet in his wallet. Him at the back, a slender blonde woman and young boy with a head full of hair next to him. Bright faces and bright smiles. Nathan surmised that whenever Geoffrey opened his wallet, the picture of himself, Josephine and her little boy would've been the first thing he saw.
Nathan expanded the wallet a little further and found his identity card and his driver's license. He found his bank cards and a few frozen yoghurt vouchers which pretty much summed it up in that area. He opened the compartment that money was kept in. All Nathan could see was petty cash. Pounds here and some pennies there. Just when he thought that he couldn't get much from the

wallet, his eyes made contact with a small transparent sachet. In it, was white powder, the shade of snow.

Before he took it out to confirm what it was, he heard Cyan groan loudly.

"Why does Geoffrey have a thousand passwords on his phone?" she asked.

"Do you have a password on your phone?" Nathan asked.

"Yeah." Cyan answered certainly.

"Then why wouldn't a criminal have one?"

"Good point." Cyan shrugged.

"We can take it to the LPD lab to remove the password." Sergeant Bruce offered.

"Thank you but we'll take it back to our quarters and have our Technical Analyst take care of it." Nathan declined.

'Of course. Actually, I'd like you to pay particular attention to the casing of the bullet." Sergeant Bruce said as he pointed to the third transparent bag that he was holding.

Cyan moved her head closer to take a better look at the casing.

"Rimless bottleneck." she analysed. "Were tests done on this?"

"Yes. The tests came out positive for a 6-inch Remington Magnum." Sergeant replied.
Nathan exchanged glances with Cyan.
"So, we were correct about the firearm." Cyan said.
"Where did you find the casing?" Nathan asked.
Sergeant Bruce led the way to the white tape that boarded the shape of Geoffrey's body inside the 'DO NOT CROSS' area. Bruce pointed to a spot just outside the white tape where Geoffrey's head was.
"Right here." he answered.
"Are you sure the shell was found right here?" Nathan asked.
"Hundred percent. We didn't remove it." Sergeant Bruce replied.
'Hm." Nathan scrutinized.
He noticed Cyan eyeing him curiously.
"What are you thinking?" she asked him.
"The bullet was found here." Nathan began as he walked around surveying the area around the bullet. He was careful not to get Geoffrey's semi-dried blood on his black boots. "And the blood is more or less in one place meaning he was shot and killed in this exact spot. He wasn't dragged or dumped post-mortem."

"Why leave his body here?" Sergeant asked. "The unknowns didn't even try to hide it."
"We think these unknowns are targeting a specific person and all these events they've caused are to get their attention." Nathan answered.
"They also believe in the concept of truth judging by that note they left, so we can assume that anything they've done and will do in the future will be out in the open. Full transparency." Cyan added. "They don't believe in secrets."
"What was our victim doing here so late anyway?" Officer Fills asked.
"He could've been brought here by the shooter. Threatened by him." Sergeant Bruce suggested.
"I'm not sure about that because his 2004 Honda Civic is parked out in the front." Officer Fills contested. "According to the miles on his car, he arrived here between the hours of midnight and 2a.m."
"What was Geoffrey Adams doing here at midnight anyway? Isn't this place closed after 9p.m?" Sergeant asked.
"I'd also like to know.'' Cyan responded. "It's worrying that he would be here at that time."

"Very worrying." Nathan agreed. "Him being here at the museum at that time probably has a lot to do with why he was shot."
"Are you implying that he was a criminal?" Officer Fills asked.
"We are not yet sure of his motive for being here at uncouth hours of the day but it doesn't look good for him." Nathan responded.
"Who found the body?" Cyan asked.
"The receptionist found him lying here when she arrived for her morning shift." the Sergeant answered.
"Is she still around?" Cyan asked.
"Officer." Sergeant Bruce said to Officer Fills.
Fills understood what he had to do because he left for a minute and came back with a pale lady. Red eyes, smudged make-up and hair strands everywhere. Her white blouse and black skirt were creased and a towel was wrapped around her shoulders to cover her.
She was beyond distraught.
"Lisa, these Agents would like to speak with you." Sergeant told the receptionist. "They want to know more about what you saw this morning."
She didn't answer. The police presence was probably making her nervous, Nathan thought.

"Thank you, Sergeant. We will take it from here." Nathan said.
"Yes. We'll leave you to it. If you need anything, just shout." Sergeant Bruce offered.
Cyan waited until Bruce and Fills were out of earshot to talk to Lisa.
"Hi Lisa. I'm Cyan and next to me is my friend, Nathan." Cyan introduced sweetly. "Sergeant Bruce told us you found Geoffrey this morning."
Lisa's eyes were still glued to the ground.
Cyan continued softly. "We know that this is very hard for you honey but we are going to ask you a few questions. Is that okay with you?"
Lisa nodded.
"Alright. What time did you arrive for your shift today?" Cyan asked.
"7." Lisa answered quietly.
"When you walked into your office, what did you do first?"
"I put my handbag under my desk and then I checked my emails."
"What did you do next?"
"I made some coffee. Strong coffee. After that, I sat on my chair to drink it."
"Why did you make strong coffee?"

"I was feeling a little nauseous. I had a bad burrito the night before." Lisa said hesitantly.
"Is that what prompted you to go outside?" Cyan asked. "Fresh air?"
"Yes. I went into the courtyard for some air and that's when..." Lisa choked. She began to shiver.
"It's alright. Take your time." Nathan soothed her. "Take a deep breath."
She inhaled, exhaled and continued. "I found Geoff here, lying on the ground with his eyes open. I called out his name but he didn't answer. So, I walked towards him because he wasn't moving and when I got closer, I realized that he had been shot."
Geoff?
"You shortened his name to 'Geoff'." Cyan repeated. "Did the two of you know each other?"
"Yeah, it was hard not to. He was my friend. We worked together."
Nathan heard himself take an uneven breath. How did they miss the fact that Geoffrey worked in the same museum that he was murdered in?
"Geoffrey worked here? At the museum?" Cyan asked.
"Yeah. He was a part-time janitor. He would clean up and lock. He always told me that his finances

were tight and that he needed this job to generate income. Sometimes, he would bring his sculptures to the museum and ask Admin to sell them for extra cash.''
''Okay, thank you Lisa. You did good.'' Nathan thanked and Lisa wobbled away.
In that moment, a cold, powerful gush lifted Nathan's denim jacket, causing it to perform somersaults in the air. He noticed that Cyan's thin braids were also moved by the wind, dancing around her until her gentle hands took her hair tie from her wrist and arrested them into a ponytail. She had let down her hair at some point during their trip but the wind had proven to be an irritation.
He couldn't help but watch her. She didn't have to do much to get his attention. She could've been doing as little as tying her loose hair into a ponytail and it would take everything in him not to stare. Because he hadn't seen her in months, he felt deprived of her that any chance he got to slip in a look, he'd take it.
Silly of him to think that it would be easy. That it wouldn't be this difficult to be around her and not crave her touch.
He guessed some things hadn't changed.

"Do you think it makes sense for Geoffrey to work here whilst being a thug on the side?" Cyan asked.
"Yes, it would. To present a normal appearance, I suppose. Plus, if we are correct, I don't think he was receiving much money from his side jobs. He was working for his debt therefore he needed another form of income to subsidize." Nathan answered.
"So, he was a legit worker here." Cyan said. "That doesn't answer why he was here at odd hours even for a worker. Why was he here?"
"I think I might be able to answer that."
Nathan turned around to see Will holding a tablet in both his hands. He must've used the white door that Nathan and Cyan had used to enter the courtyard. They hadn't heard him with all the ruckus that was going on.
"I managed to get Aria to access the security footage on the computer and upload it onto this tablet." William informed. "You need to take a look."
Nathan's eyes fell on four grids on the tablet William was holding. He realized that the four grids on the screen represented four different cameras placed in different places in the museum. His eyes focused on the camera on the bottom

right corner that showed the courtyard. Activity was low in the beginning to the point where Nathan grew impatient.
"Bradford, what exactly are we looking at?" he asked tightly.
"Just look." William chided.
An alive Geoffrey Adams appeared seconds letter in the first grid that showed the museum entrance. He approached the front doors, reached into his pocket and retrieved a small key. He unlocked the doors and they opened for him. He was wearing the same clothes he was found dead in, a shirt and jeans. Except in the video, he looked less dishevelled and less...dead. The doors opened for him and he walked into the first room, checked if there was anyone around and proceeded to advance to the next room. He opened the glass display case of jars and combs, the one Nathan and Cyan had passed on their way to the courtyard, and his hand reached out for the large jar. From the jar, he pulled a wide ward of cash and put the jar back in the display case. Adams' body froze. His head perked up showing that he had heard something. The entrance camera showed a tall figure wearing a pair of pants and a t-shirt with a cap that obscured his

face from the camera. The doors automatically opened and he stepped in.
Adams took off with impeccable speed and opened the door to the courtyard. He closed the door a little too hard and attempted to lock it with the key he had used to unlock the automatic doors. He didn't do it in time because the suspicious figure pushed through the door and entered the courtyard. Adams held up his hands to ward him off as the other man advanced towards him. The video footage was soundless but it looked as if Goeffrey tried to talk to that man who was after him. Pleading, to be exact, because his palms were stuck together in the same way one would if they were praying or begging.
The other man took out his rifle and pointed it at Geoffrey.
At this stage, Geoffrey was shaking uncontrollably and in a blink of an eye, the other figure pulled the trigger and Geoffrey's body fell to the ground. He put his firearm back in his belt and went back the same way he came. The first grid showed him leaving the entrance doors and that was the last of him.
"So, this mystery man followed Geoffrey here. There's no other way he would've walked

confidently in the museum knowing it was unlocked. He saw Geoffrey unlock the doors." Nathan pointed out.
"It was as if Geoffrey knew exactly what was going to happen because he didn't wait to see who had entered the museum before he ran towards the door." Cyan said. "He already knew who it was."
"The running, the pleading. Poor Geoffrey did something that landed him here in this courtyard. Dead." William commented.
"And the money Geoffrey took out of that jar? What was all that about?" Cyan asked.
"So, while I was watching the footage, there was an officer watching it with me. Once we saw where Geoffrey pulled out that money, we checked if there was any more in the other display cases." William explained.
"Let me guess. There was more money hidden in different artifacts in the display cases." Cyan suggested.
"No." William refused. "Actually, there was..."
Nathan felt a vibrating sensation inside his denim jacket. The sound of his ringing phone cut William short.

"Sorry." Nathan apologised as he opened his denim jacket to retrieve his phone. The caller ID told him that Evan was calling and so he answered.
"What's up?" he answered.
"Jordan and I are done at the Davies' household. We are about to leave." Evan informed him.
"Did you get a chance to speak to Josephine?"
"She's inconsolable at the moment. But she doesn't have the slightest idea of who could've been behind this."
"Yeah, pretty inconsolable for a love rat." Jordan mumbled in the back.
Nathan heard a loud pat and an "Ouch!" from Jordan.
"Well, she is entitled to her grief regardless of what she did in the past. Geoffrey was a part of her life. She will pull through eventually." Nathan replied optimistically. "Anything helpful from her?"
"She did say a few interesting things." Evan said.
"Hold on. I'm putting you on speaker. Cyan and Will are here." Nathan told them.
"So, Josie told us that ever since her ex-husband started experiencing troubles at his job, he was an absolute mess. He was bummed out that he

wasn't making enough to provide for his family so he picked a new hustle. Sculpting." Evan reported.
"We learned that Geoffrey was a sculptor from the Museum's receptionist. We didn't know he started this sculpting thing before he lost his office job." Cyan said.
"Apparently, he just did it as a hobby but decided to make a habit of it after his income was cut." Evan answered.
"He sold his sculptures for a bit of money." Jordan continued. *"But given where Josie Joe is living now, I'd say that it wasn't that much."*
"She also said that after Geoffrey found out that she had been unfaithful, one night, he came back home high like the sky. It was just cannabis, apparently." Evan said. *"But when she eventually left Geoffrey for the father of her child, she said it was because Geoffrey was becoming erratic and unstable. Yeah, 'unstable' was the word she used."*
"He was using?" Cyan asked.
"It wouldn't surprise me." Will said.
"Why wouldn't it?" Evan asked.
"Not only were wards of money found in numerous parts of the museum but little sachets

of powder were found in one of the artifacts in the display cases.'' William explained.
''Powder, powder?'' Jordan asked.
''No way.'' Cyan breathed.
''How many?'' Nathan asked.
''Thirty.'' William answered. ''Pure, A-grade. Ninety-five percent.''
Nathan thought back to the little sachet of powder he found in Geoffrey's wallet. He wasn't sure it was really powder at first but with all these revelations, it was confirmed.
''I guess that would explain the sachet I found in his wallet.'' Nathan reported.
He opened the wallet that he was still holding and took out the little transparent plastic.
''Those were definitely for sale because he couldn't have been using them all without killing himself.'' William pointed out.
''We can add another skill to our DOA's resume.'' Jordan said sardonically
''It explains why Geoffrey was here so late.'' Cyan realized. ‘''He was part of a drug scheme in the museum."

4. PASSIONATE COURAGE

"A what?"
"A drug trade."
"In the museum?"
"In the museum."
"Hold on a second. What makes you think the drugs belonged to Geoffrey? Maybe they didn't."
"They were found in his wallet and in more of the sculptures that he brought in to Administration to sell."
"Wow."
"Yeah. Wow."
Cyan was seated on the middle couch between Aria and Harper in the living room, explaining to them the findings that Nathan, William and herself had discovered after processing the crime scene. The two boys had dropped her off at the house with Geoffrey's phone so that Aria could crack the passcodes as fast as possible while they returned to the Museum to speak to the Curator. "Knowing the daily operations of the place would be helpful in order to discern how Geoffrey squeezed in an opportunity to run his side business." Nathan had explained before he left.

"You said you found product in the sculptures?" Harper, who had been sitting on Cyan's right, asked.
"Yes. The receptionist said that Geoffrey brought in some sculptures he had made to the museum. Admin offered to purchase some and sell some on his behalf because apparently, he was pretty good. Unfortunately, in three of his sculptures, sachets of product were found." Cyan answered.
"So, he made those sculptures with a specific motive. Either, he built his sculptures around the drugs or he simply slipped them inside." Harper said.
"How sure are we that he actually made them? He could've bought them off somewhere like Amazon and inserted the drugs inside." Aria suggested.
"I thought about that." Cyan acknowledged. "But companies like Amazon sell more of Fine Art than 3D Art. And they wouldn't accept less than perfect pieces because they receive commission upon goods sold. It would ruin their brand if they sold messy art."
"I thought you said the Museum thought that Geoffrey's art was pretty good." Harper said.

"It was quite good. But it was very asymmetrical. The carver lacked mathematical precision that would present the sculptures in a more balanced technique. Then I realized that the person who worked on that piece of art didn't really have the experience of an artist. Rather, an amateur, who participated in sculpting more out of convenience than passion." Cyan argued.
"Like for instance, a guy who worked in an office job for years who suddenly picked up sculpting as a way to make ends meet." Aria surmised.
"Of course." Harper agreed.
"Exactly. And humans have a way of telling on themselves without saying anything." Cyan resumed. "The sculptures that were identified to be Geoffrey's were comprised of two concepts of life. Physically, these were hearts and family models. Of course, they were all different designs but it was just that. But symbolically, his sculptures represented love and households. And what do we know about Geoffrey? He was family oriented. He loved his wife to the point that he allowed her betrayal to break him. Whether he did it consciously or not, he used sculpting as a way of releasing the way he felt. Those pieces are definitely his."

"I definitely see where you're coming from. But where did he get A grade pure coke? We all know he didn't have the connections or the resources to purchase or even supply. The most he could've been was a retailer." Harper said.
"I think he was a mule. A low-level and low-risk distributor. He probably received the drugs from the supplier, inserted them in the sculptures and then and notified the buyers to go to the Museum and purchase the sculptures with drugs in them." Aria said.
"I'm intrigued." Harper breathed. "And impressed."
"You and me both." Cyan admired.
'If there is one thing I know about drug trades, it's that there is a strong system of hierarchy. Especially here in Leicester. We have the retailer, the local wholesaler, the national wholesaler and the importer. Geoffrey's supplier would've been a local because of the intensity of their trade." Harper said.
"My guess is that they were all in this together. Geoffrey and the three men who took Lucas. They all ran this operation. It could potentially be the debt that Geoffrey was paying off." Aria said. "I just don't understand how it's all connected."

"All three men could've been distributors like Geoffrey." Cyan agreed. "But from the information that we received, there seems to be an established hierarchy in that group already. The man that Lucas identified as old drips of dominance. He wouldn't be found anywhere in the street dealing product."
"He could be the importer; the most important and wealthy part of the syndicate." Harper said.
"Well, what we come up with is all circumstantial unless we open this phone." Aria said.
"How's it going?" Cyan asked.
Aria was on the edge of her seat with her bedazzled laptop on her lap. There was a black cable that was swallowed by Aria's laptop on one side and Geoffrey's phone on the other.
"I wanted to find a way to remove the passcodes from Geoffrey's phone without erasing the data so I went the ADB route. Android Debug Bridge. I had to set it up on my PC and enable the USB debugging on Geoffrey's android phone via developer's option in the settings menu on his phone. Then I had to connect the devices with this USB cable so that I could open a command prompt on my PC and issue a command to allow the debugging to happen. Once I was in, I had to

issue another command to disable the security. It should be rebooting now and, in a few minutes, we'll see what's inside." Aria explained.
"So, in other words, you did it? You opened the phone?" Harper asked expectantly.
"That's exactly what I just explained, Harper." Aria answered dryly.
"Alright, Cleopatra. There's no reason to be so snooty." Harper complained.
"What? I'm not being snooty." Aria refused.
"Yes. Yes, you are. You're being snooty."
"You know who the real snoot bomb was today?" Aria posed. "William."
"Ugh." Harper groaned loudly. "Every time I hear about William Wannabe Shakespeare, I just want to take a one ply and blow him away to another Organisation."
Aria scoffed. "In another life maybe. The Organisation will blow *you* away if you do that. His parents are way too valuable here at SSU."
"Why is that?" Cyan asked curiously.
"William's parents are old money rich. Like, breakfast buddies with the Queen rich. Absolutely generational wealth rich. They are one of the biggest sponsors of SSU along with Nathan's grandparents." Harper answered.

"I'm almost familiar with all the Agents that work for the English Base with Sponsor parents but I've never heard of a William with generational old money parents. Wouldn't I know about him if his parents were SSU sponsors?" Cyan asked.
"After the Jan Jalesmycie incident six months ago-"

Aria cleared her throat so abruptly that Harper stopped mid-sentence and wide-eyed Aria. Aria attempted to send silent signals with her eyes to her, rigidly shaking her stiffed neck. Cyan realized what was going on and internally sighed.
As often as she spoke about her sister was just as often as she spoke about the Jan Jalesmycie Incident that transpired six months ago while she still worked at the Organisation. The two were so intricately intertwined in ways that made Cyan's body ache.
Harper was probably unaware of the profound effect of events that day had on her and she couldn't blame her. Not many did.
Did Cyan want to hear anything related to the incident that made her leave in the first place? No. But she'd gladly accept any information that explained William's attitude and behaviour toward her earlier, however it was given out.

Cyan subtly winked at Aria as a way of thanking her for trying to protect her feelings. She appreciated the way Ari tried to warn Harper without triggering her. However, she had to allow a baffled Harper continue with her explanation.
"What happened after the incident?" Cyan asked as if she hadn't noticed the awkward exchange.
"Uhm, well." Harper continued hesitantly.
Cyan knew that Harper could feel the temperature change in the room though she couldn't exactly pick on what made it so. She continued nonetheless. "After the incident, quite a few Agents left. Approximately five to six soldiers. Not a handful in my opinion but the Agency felt as if they had lost the lotto, especially when a good Agent like yourself left. Some Agents transferred themselves to different Bases and some completely abandoned the Organisation. So, to fill that void, the Agency searched for three new Agents who were well-versed, exceedingly exposed and extremely talented to join the English side. That's how they recruited William and moved him from the Agency Base in Paris to the one here. He was one of the three."
Aria's almond eyes stared at Cyan. "Cy, the only reason you don't know about him is because he

was the Agent that took your place. The Organisation thought that he could fill the hole you left. He took over your shifts and worked with your former Division before he decided he wanted to be permanently tied to D12." Aria explained.
Cyan felt the saliva dry in her mouth. She was working with someone who had replaced her? It stung a little. And it annoyed her how much it affected her because she was the one who left. But she knew the Organisation had to continue running. Crime had no days off. It was just that at times, you believed that you were irreplaceable. Situations had a way of reminding you otherwise.
"I still don't understand why he was so rude to me. He's the one who replaced me and not the other way around." Cyan sighed.
Aria inhaled softly. "Did you ever consider that William acted like an expert prick because he finally met the big shoes he had to fill? He had a moment of insecurity."
"I guess." Cyan agreed thoughtfully.
"We are so sorry about what he said to you though." Harper apologised.
"Don't worry. He's not the first and he definitely won't be the last."

"I just want to sock him sometimes." Aria expressed.
"And that's saying a lot because Aria rarely feels like socking people." Harper pointed out.
A rhythmic notification sound projected in the room and Aria grabbed Geoffrey's phone for an update on what she was doing.
"Guys." she called. "The phone is on."
Harper moved to the edge of her seat. "What's on it?"
Aria tapped on the screen several times, scrolled down, scrolled up and tapped a few more times.
"There's not much in here." she reported. "No text messages, no pictures and no apps. He was smart enough to cover his tracks."
"There has to be something." Haper contested.
"There is, actually. There is a number here in the call logs that appears more than the others." Aria said.
"How often?" Cyan asked.
"The calls are quite sporadic but three times a week from what I can get here." Aria answered.
"What's the country code?" Harper asked.
"+44." Aria answered.
"Local." Cyan noticed.

"Why would he erase everything on his phone but keep his call logs? Wouldn't it make sense to delete the call logs and keep everything else?" Harper asked.
"Importance, perhaps?" Cyan asked.
"Aria, can you find out who that number belongs to?" Harper asked.
"Yeah, I can. Give me a second to go through the Database." Aria answered.
"Are there any other numbers he called besides the one you've mentioned?" Harper asked.
"Yeah. A few." Aria answered as she tapped her laptop buttons. "Alright. So, the first number, +44 731 578 126, belongs to Josephine Mund. The second number, +44 612 450 001 belongs to his father, Thomas Adams. The third number, the frequent caller, +44 174 932 332, is registered to a Pedro Gallo."
"Repeat that. Did you say Pedro Gallo?" Harper asked expectantly.
"Yeah. Pedro Gallo." Aria answered slowly. "His name does sound familiar, doesn't it?"
"It does, yeah." Harper answered. "He's the manager of that popular nightclub in the city, Quarter 25. We had him, back in August, for drugs

but he slipped out of our cuffs like overcooked spaghetti."
"What did you get him for?" Cyan asked.
"He had a possession charge." Aria answered.
"Do you still remember what you found on him?" Cyan asked.
"Yeah. He had Coke on him, Ecstasy, some steroids, Amphetamines, magic mushrooms and Heroin." Harper answered.
"And he slipped through all that? How?" Cyan asked.
"We handed him to local authorities after we caught him. After two days, he posted bail and received a fine of £500,000." Harper answered.
"He should've spent at least seven years behind a cell." Cyan said.
"It was outside our jurisdiction. We had done our part by catching him and handing him over to local authorities. There was nothing else we could do besides work on other cases." Aria answered.
Harper jumped as if her couch had sent an electric shock up her nervous system. "Oh, yes! Yes. Uhm, we also caught Gallo with Caffeine and Amobarbital."
It was Cyan's turn to move towards the edge of her seat. "Amobarbital? Are you sure?"

"Yeah, I drove the product back to HQ myself." Harper answered. "Why?"
"That was the same drug that was found in Lucas' system." Cyan responded.
"What? I thought it was Amytal." Aria countered.
"It's the same thing. They just have different names." Cyan explained. "When one talks about Amobarbital, they are referring to Amytal. Just like when you talk about tomato sauce and ketchup. They are essentially the same thing."
"Now we know why Geoffrey and Gallo were in contact." Aria said as she leaned back on her couch.
"Pedro was Geoffrey's local supplier." Cyan resolved.
"That's another part of the puzzle solved." a male voice announced from behind Cyan.
Cyan whipped her head sideways to see who the voice belonged to. Evan, Jordan and Preston were standing in the living room, a few feet away from the couches. Cyan must've been too engrossed in the discussion to hear them come in. They must've have arrived simultaneously since they had gone to different places.

"So, Geoffrey was the one in contact with the supplier? Isn't that a lot of responsibility bestowed on a newcomer criminal?" Aria asked.
"Look at it like this; they only let Geoffrey do most of the heavy lifting and the dirty work so that he'd be the only one implicated in the end." Evan explained.
"And he is dead now." Harper said flatly. "They just couldn't wait."
"His death was quite something." Preston commented.
"What did the coroner say, Pres?" Jordan asked.
"Before I begin, can I just point out that Carol Doak analyses cadavers in the basement of her house? I mean, she lives in a pulchritudinous neighbourhood with brick-layered establishments, grass plots and crisp air and yet in her cellar, she accepts cremation orders and used body parts of the dead for investigations. Isn't that weird?"
Jordan raised an eyebrow. "Would you rather she analyse cadavers in the middle of the road?"
"I don't know but-"
"Pres. The coroner's report." Evan reminded.
"Oh, right. Sorry. Forensics confirmed that Geoffrey took one bullet to the head. That, we all saw." he began. "The projectile passed entirely

through his head and left entrance and exit wounds known in the medical word as a perforating wound. The bullet damaged his internal carotid artery that provided oxygenated blood to his eyes, cerebrum, scalp and his external one as well that allowed blood to supply another part of his cerebrum and his thyroid gland."

"So, what does that mean in simple English? What was the cause of death?" Aria asked.

"He bled to death." Preston answered. "His major blood vessels on the sides of his neck had been vitiated."

"If the receptionist had arrived a little earlier for her shift, we could've been telling a different story." Harper assumed.

"Not necessarily. Given the velocity and range of the bullet, he was already dead the minute that firearm was pointed at him." Preston said. " He also suffered blunt force trauma caused by strong knuckles connecting with his mandible explaining the contusions we saw on his face."

"Was it broken?" Evan asked. "The jaw, I mean."

"Nothing a wire couldn't fix." Preston answered.

"And his toxicology report? Anything unusual in his system?" Evan asked.

"Except the cannabis he smoked and the small traces of coke found in his body, there were no detrimental toxins found."
"The small traces mean that he could've just tried drugs to be familiar but not enough to be an addict." Cyan said.
"I suppose so." Preston agreed. "His death was quick and simple. Nothing overly dramatic and unnecessarily gruesome. It was simply a mission-oriented kill. There was nothing personal about it which speaks to the context surrounding Geoffrey's murder. A liability was all he was." Preston concluded.
"So, these guys kidnap children, deal drugs and kill people. What don't they do?" Jordan commented dryly.
"What won't they do? They seem to be doing everything inside the criminal handbook." Cyan added.
"What's next now?" Aria asked. "We can't let them get away with anything else."
"Nathan and William are still at the museum waiting for the Curator. Talking to him might give us a lead. Perhaps a list of people Geoffrey sold his sculptures to." Jordan submitted.

"The buyers wouldn't have exposed their real names." Evan argued.
Jordan furrowed his eyebrows. "No, they wouldn't have."
"There is something we could do." Harper said.
"What is that?" Evan asked.
"Let's just go to the club." she proposed.
"Excuse me?" Aria asked incredulously.
Cyan had to admit that she was quite shook herself. How was partying going to help with the investigation?
"Pedro Gallo works at Quarter 25, right? We should go over there and extort information from him. Since he is the supplier, he'll lead us straight to the importer." Harper explained.
"Do you think he'll talk to the feds?" Aria asked.
"We'll make him talk." Harper replied simply.
"We'll stick out like a sore thumb in there. Our natural scents gun oil and shoe polish." Preston expressed.
"Unless we switch things up. Look the part." Cyan suggested. "We have a tangible lead. We know what Pedro does and where he is. We should go for it."
"Exactly." Harper agreed. She turned towards Evan. "Ev? What do you think?"

"It's quite a risk but we should chase any leads we have." he answered. "Tonight."
"But it's a Tuesday. Won't we find the clubs empty?" Preston asked curiously.
"Oh, my geeky friend. That's when the clubs are the fullest. It's way more fun winding down during the week." Jordan smiled." I might just meet my future wife tonight."
"Jay." Evan scolded. "Strictly work."
"I'm kidding." Jordan snickered.
"Wait. When you say, 'look the part' what do you mean exactly?" Aria asked nervously.
Cyan stood up from her couch and scrutinized Aria who was seated on her couch.
"Tell me, do you by any chance own a cocktail dress and pair of six-inch heels?"

*****

Cyan and Harper had assembled in Aria's room an hour after it was decided that going to club was their next plan of action. Harper had made it known that it was going to be difficult for Aria to find something "club-like" to wear so it was in her best interest they meet in Aria's room and go through her closet to see if they could rally some of her clothing to create a decent outfit. Cyan immediately agreed with this idea because she knew Aria hid her God-given gifts under baggy sweatshirts and oversized pants, which was allowed, in Cyan's opinion. She loved to wear that too. But there came a time in a woman's life where her figure had to be shaped by a body-hugging dress. At least once. Aria's time was today.

Looking around in Aria's bedroom, Cyan noticed that it was the same décor and set up as hers, a medium sized room with a lush bathroom and a shower, a wooden dresser and a queen-sized bed that herself and Aria were currently sitting on. The walls of the room were an amalgam of light and dark brown hues, a completely different scene from the rooms downstairs. She had posters pasted on the wall that her bed sat against, of old school classics such as The Notebook, Mean Girls, and 10 Things I Hate About You. Some of Cyan's favourite movies.

She also had a poster of large body of water, that was the colour black, on her wall. It was definitely out of place compared to the bright and colourful posters next to it. It was so worn out that attempting to remove it off the wall was no longer an option because that resulted in the tearing of it. Her body being at a one-hundred-and-eighty-degree tilt, Cyan squinted her eyes at the black sea and realized that it was more of a painting than a poster. It was the same painting that she used to see in Aria's dorm room when they were still at the Academy. Cyan remembered Aria explaining to her that her favourite Cuban artist, Yoan Capote, was the passion behind the piece. It clarified the aging of the painting. Cyan had known about it for as long as she knew Aria.

A loud screech from Harper brought Cyan back to the realities of why she was in Aria's room to begin with.

"Aria! What the world is this?"

In Harper's right hand, she held a long multicoloured cardigan that she eyed with disgust. It was designed with a purple dog that had a chocolate brown nose and chocolate brown ears that were disproportionate to its body. It had a thin tail and very thin paws, disproportionate to its body as well. The dog was standing upright, instead on all fours with its tinted teeth out in a smile, posing for a picture.

Cyan giggled as soon as she made sense of what she saw.

"Is that Courage from that cartoon? What is it called again?"
"Yeah. Courage The Cowardly Dog." Aria answered. "Harper, put that back please. It's limited-edition merchandise."
"I wouldn't mind wearing that." Cyan complimented.
"Thanks." Aria smiled.
"It doesn't change the fact that you have nothing to wear *tonight*. You can be a weirdo later." Harper said as she emphasized the word "tonight."
"You two look like you're about the same size. Maybe you can lend Ari something." Cyan suggested to Harper.
"Why didn't I think of that? I definitely have something." Harper realized.
"I guess it's sorted. I won't look like a slob." Aria said dryly.
"I actually like your style." Cyan assured. "It's just that you need to look different tonight for the purposes of fitting in."
"Yes. Cy is right. We'll style you, do your hair and makeup. Oh! This is exciting!" Harper exclaimed. "Do you have an outfit, Cy?"

"I think I do." Cyan answered. "I'll just improvise when it's time to go. Have you decided on anything?" she asked Harper.
"Of course, she has." Aria interjected with a sneaky smile. "I'm sure she's going to dress all nice to impress Jordan."
"Aria!" Harper shrieked. Her cheeks transformed from tan to a rosy colour faster than the speed of light. She was clearly embarrassed.
"Jordan!" Aria exclaimed in a sing-song voice.
"Gee, Ari. Shhhh!" Harper quieted.
"Jordan-Bailey? You like Jordan?" Cyan asked under her breath in order to respect the little dignity that Harper had left.
"Yes, she does." Aria answered.
"What? No. I don't. I don't like him. Stop that." Harper ordered.
Cyan and Aria guffawed. They clearly enjoyed this side of Harper. Ravelled, nervous and tense.
"You're overcompensating." Cyan observed. "You do like him!"
"You should've seen her face when he said that he'd find his wife at the club tonight. She looked like someone had spat in her dinner." Aria mocked.

With that, Cyan and Aria broke out in more chaotic laughter.
"Okay, fine. I might feel something for him." Harper admitted.
Cyan composed herself and asked, "Does he know?"
"He doesn't see me that way." Harper replied quietly.
"Did he tell you that?"
"He didn't have to."
"You can't know for sure if he's into you or not if you don't make a move." Aria chimed in.
"I mean, she can do little things here and there to get his attention but at the end of the day, Jordan should approach her." Cyan said.
"Really, Cy? Come on. It's 2017. Girls can approach boys." Aria countered.
"Of course. But the last I checked, Jordan entertained all sorts of women." Cyan answered. "The only way Harper will know if he is absolutely serious is if he approaches her first."
"Would you do it, Aria?" Harper posed. "Would you approach any of the guys here first?"
"Yes. Well, no. Not really. I mean, I don't really-"
"Hmm." Cyan sounded cynically. "You like the chase, don't you?"

"Well, so many girls chase after Jordan that my chances are close to zero. He sees me as his best friend." Harper pouted.
"That may be a good thing." Aria presented. "He won't cross that line with you because your friendship means a lot to him."
"Probably." Harper sulked.
"Any guy that gets to breathe the same air as you is very privileged." Cyan said.
"Yes, he is lucky." Harper repeated as if it was her first time believing it.
"Of course, he is lucky. He doesn't know how blessed he is by being in the same room as you." Aria added.
"Exactly." Cyan backed.
"I appreciate you guys." Harper thanked.
In that moment, a knock on the door interrupted the girls' discussion.
"It's open!" Aria yelled.
The wooden door was opened from the other side and a rosy-cheeked Nathan walked in.
"Oh, hey. When'd you get here?" Aria asked.
"A few moments ago, actually." He answered as he leaned casually against Aria's dresser. "What are you girls doing?

"Going through Aria's wardrobe." Harper answered as she sat on the bed on Aria's right side. "Anything useful from the Curator?"
"He didn't show up to the museum." Nathan answered. "So, we visited his place. It was clean of almost everything he owned."
"He ran?" Aria asked.
"Looks that way." Nathan replied.
"He is hiding something." Cyan said.
"Or he is directly involved in the case." Harper added.
"We've put an amber on him. He won't travel far before we catch him." Nathan informed.
"Now that a potential lead is in the wind, we really need answers from Pedro." Harper said.
"About that," Nathan said as his eyes narrowed pensively. He slightly shifted his weight off of Aria's dresser. "I'm not sure outsourcing information from a drug dealer in his territory is a good idea."
"He won't talk if we bring him in officially." Harper responded. "But we can sneak up on him tonight, catch him off guard and watch him slip."
"I'm still not sure." Nathan expressed. "What if someone recognizes us? We don't even know the

interior plan of Quarter 25 to manoeuvre unnoticed."
"Nathan, I thought you said I was the best Analyst in the world." Aria broke in. "Surely you know that I've got those ends covered."
"And I have a connection in the club that'll make sure that there are no bumps on the road." Harper assured.
"'Connection'?" Nathan repeated as if the word was hot on his tongue.
"I might know a few people who work there." Harper answered sheepishly.
Nathan didn't ask any questions after that and nodded his head at Harper.
He turned in Cyan's direction, who was still seated on the bed, and motioned towards the door.
"May I have a moment?" he asked her.
Cyan wondered what it was that he wanted to speak to her about in private but given the formal connotations in his voice, it probably had to with an impersonal issue.
"Uh, sure." Cyan answered.
She removed herself off of Aria's bed and walked through the door that Nathan had opened for her.
He led her down the corridor and down the stairs past the front entrance, the living room and the

kitchen area. Still following him in silence, they aimed straight for another large room that she hadn't noticed when she first arrived. It was such a place that if you weren't aware of its existence, you wouldn't have seen it.
The first thing that caught Cyan's attention when she walked in was the long spiralling chandelier that was hung from the ceiling. Iron wire was attached to the ceiling holding the chambers that kept the little crystal bulbs inside. The wires were so meticulously and strategically placed that the chambers they held formed a spiral that resembled a deformed 'C' shape facing backwards. It was as if the lights were curling outward. To make it better, in every single chamber that was hung, a tiny blue crystal sat neatly inside and illuminated the room. The crystals were of different shades of blue; navy, royal, sapphire, sky and even turquoise. It reminded Cyan of child prodigies with unique, strange talents who blazed their light divergently but still dazzled nonetheless.
She didn't know she was holding her breath until she looked at what the room contained. Gadgets of all shapes and form filled all the spaces on the shelves as well as on the humongous marble

table, similar to the one in the kitchen, in the centre of the room. The likes of cameras, license plate readers, drones, coms, trackers and many more technical equipment that Cyan had no knowledge of loaded the room. She saw desktops as well, tablets and a few satellite and disposable phones. Vests, boots of different sizes, helmets with flashlights attached, shields with the letters 'SSU' painted on them and ammunition filled up the shelves at the back of the room. This must've been the gadget room Dave mentioned earlier before he left. It truly lived up to its name because all the gadgets that she'd ever used in the past and all those that she'd never seen before were staring back at her.
"Cool gadgets." she complimented.
"I'll tell Dave you said that." Nathan replied.
Of course, it was Dave's idea to have a whole room full of equipment. Cyan knew him as an over-the-top person. It was evident in the clothes he wore and the cars he preferred to drive. And now, it was more evident than ever in the room they were currently standing in.
"You wanted to talk to me?" Cyan asked.
"Yes, I did. I just wanted to formally welcome you into our team and give you this." he said as his

calloused fingers handed a small rectangular metal plate with a preying eagle engraved in the middle. There were two holes punched in at the left and top right corners where a short chain penetrated so it could be worn around the neck. It was an official SSU badge with her full name engraved on it.

Her official SSU badge. It was a replica of the one she used to carry before she threw hers away. Another one must've been made for her.

The one she was holding in her hands was slightly different. There was another metal plate attached under the one she was given. The two plates were magnetized at the edges with an opening clip in the front.

"Open it." Nathan said.

She slid the top plate open to find tiny rubber buds. They resembled wired earplugs. Coms.

"Your com pieces. These are little earpieces that have a microphone embedded in the transmitter to enhance communication efficiency with whomever is connected. In this case, our whole team." Nathan explained.

Cyan chuckled quietly. "I worked in the SSU once. My absence didn't give me amnesia."

"Right." Nathan responded. "These are designed to respond specifically to you. You have two just in case you lose one."
Cyan nodded. "Of course. Got it."
Immediately after, a heavy wave of silence fell over them. This was the first time they had been alone in a room without the case contributing to their conversation. It seemed to Cyan that if they weren't discussing Lucas or Geoffrey, they had nothing to talk about.
She realized then how awkward she felt being in his space, near him, that she took a step back. She wasn't deathly close to him but perhaps the huge gap she had created between them would give room for her thoughts to circulate around objectively.
It would've never occurred to Cyan that Nathan paid attention to her step back by his expression. It was indifferent and disengaged, void of any visible emotion. But the way he subtly cleared his throat indicated to Cyan that he did notice that the air they were currently inhaling was uncomfortable.
This was insane, Cyan thought. Surely, they could engage in a conversation without acting like strangers.

Cyan broke the silence. "You didn't have to."
Nathan furrowed his eyes. "Didn't have to what?"
"Defend me the way you did. You know, when William was going at me. I was going to handle it."
"No, I didn't. But I had to remind him who makes the decisions around here. It had little to do with protecting your feelings." He replied monochromatically.
"Oh." Cyan responded faintly. "Okay."
She didn't expect such a response from him and quite frankly, the conversation had run its course. All she wanted to do in that moment was leave so she turned around to the direction of the door and walked out the way they came.
"Cy." Nathan called.
That stopped her in her tracks.
She turned around to face him.
"We can work together, right? On this case, I mean. Things aren't weird between us?" Nathan asked. "Since we, you know..."
"Dated?" Cyan filled in. "You can say the word. Your tongue won't explode into flames."
There were times in the past Cyan would be unreasonably short with Nathan. Most times she had motive, sometimes she didn't at all. She would've just missed him and craved his company

whenever he wasn't around. Instead of going back and forth with her, he would just look at her with gleaming and blazing eyes. Eyes brimming with affection and understanding.
Those were the same eyes looking at her now. Perhaps he understood why she was crisp with him. She felt as if that unlocked the door to a conversation they had left untouched for a very long time. An opportunity rose for her to finally express what she had been feeling these past months.
"We were together, yes." Nathan agreed. "But we couldn't continue."
"'We couldn't continue.'" Cyan repeatedly softly.
"No." Nathan replied just as quietly.
"And you thought the best way to let me know was through a text?" Cyan asked in a dangerously low voice. Now that they were on their way to the core of the issue, Cyan could feel her body fevering with anger.
"You were in Prague, Cyan. That was the only way I could tell you." Nathan replied. He attempted to move closer to her.
"Don't." she ordered.
He instantly stopped where he was.

"We dated for more than a year." Cyan evoked. "We had plans to work under the same Division. I even met your family."
"I couldn't forget all that even if I wanted to." Nathan returned.
"Then why, Nathaniel?" Cyan's voice cracked. "Tell me why you left with no warning."
Nathan shut his eyes and crunched his teeth the way one would when they were trying to distract themselves from a situation they were dreading to approach.
"It's complicated." he said curtly.
"Uncomplicate it." Cyan pressed.
Nathan sighed and dropped himself on a stool that was near the marble table. His hand raked through his cotton hair several times in that minute which showed Cyan that he was nervous. And he was rarely so.
After they split, Cyan believed that their breakup affected her only. Looking at Nathan now, it was possible that she could've been wrong.
"Do you remember when my Division made that arrest earlier this year in March? We caught that group that sold illegal tanks and ammo across the border." Nathan said in a low voice.

"I remember. That was a very big arrest." Cyan replied.
"You wanted us to celebrate." Nathan continued. "It was our joint leave anyway so you wanted us to travel to London."
Cyan chortled. She pulled another stool that was casually standing on the other side of the table and positioned it that when she sat down, she was sitting directly across from Nathan.
"I was obsessed with French cuisine at the time so to celebrate you, I reserved a table for us at Hélène Darroze at The Connaught. It was a modest yet sophisticated place. Easy colours. Your kind of thing. I even bought a fancy black dress and a pair of these silver pumps." Cyan reminisced. "I was so excited."
"I didn't show up."
Cyan didn't answer that immediately because he was right. He hadn't shown up on that night. Cyan was left hanging in a strapless black number and a face full of make up in her apartment. She tried to call him several times to no avail. She reached a stage where she stopped trying to get hold of him because even if he showed, they wouldn't have made it to the restaurant for their reservation on time. Drowsiness decided to put her out of her

misery and she ended up falling asleep in her expensive outfit with her fur coat covering her and her disappointed heart.
Cyan saw him four days later at Headquarters after their few days off. When she asked him where he had been, he brushed her off. He pecked her quickly and rushed to the offices. She never brought it up again.
"No. You didn't." Cyan replied shortly.
"I was such a jerk to you. I'm really sorry." Nathan apologised.
"Where did you go that day?" Cyan asked.
"I spent the day with Ev and his dad before our date. We cleaned his old man's vintage cars which was cool. We had fun." Nathan said. "It was when I returned to my place that I began to feel weird. Evan's dad practically raised me, but I started thinking of my own. Where he was, why he abandoned me and if he ever thought of me. If he'd be proud of me if he knew I was part of the SSU. It messed me up, Cy. I didn't know the man and I hated him. Yet, I still needed his approval. So, before I knew it, I grabbed my car keys and ended up at my mother's grave. I didn't know what I expected to find there. Answers on her stone, maybe.

After that day, I wasn't myself for a long time. I know you noticed because you walked on eggshells around me."
Cyan was careful not say or do just anything around him because the smallest incidents agitated him. Cyan's mind took her back to the time when he stormed off after she teased him about how he was his grandmother's favourite boy. She tried to laugh off the awkward atmosphere that his unresponsive mood had created, only for him to roll his eyes and walk away. Not to mention the way he spent less and less time with her. He always had something to do. A case to work on. A meeting to attend. Reports to proofread; which was all ironic to Cyan because it seemed as if the fire that was ignited by his work had been snuffed out of him. Meetings were assemblies he attended only when he felt like, which was unheard of because Nathan was always present for anything and everything that was work related.
After she left for Prague, she was convinced that he didn't want anything to do with her considering that he just let her go in the state that she was in. Her mind told her that their already strained relationship wouldn't survive her move

but she didn't expect a one-line text message from him confirming what her heart wasn't willing to bear.
Nathan's piercing blue eyes stared at the floor.
"I became anxious. Couldn't sleep at night. I would hear the thoughts when I closed my eyes and in my deepest slumber, I couldn't stop thinking.
You've ever experienced that? An invasion in what's supposed to be your most peaceful place? It's the worst." Nathan chuckled. "Because then I had nowhere to run."
He paused to glare at the crystal lights.
"Ironically, the same thoughts that kept me away from sleep were the same thoughts that kept me in bed." he started again. "Waking up every day felt heavy, like a heap of rocks pushing me down further and further, forcing me to break there. I started asking myself why I did so much for the Directors because I stretched and manipulated myself in ways for them that I didn't think were humanely possible. I attended every meeting, every gala, flew to all the charities and assumed all the cases they wanted me handle.
I did all that trying to make sense of my own life. Trying to grapple why my own father would

abandon me when I all I had was him. I mean, I couldn't hide from the pressures of the Agency, what they expected me to do and who they wanted me to be.
But uhm, I wanted to call you. I wanted to tell you that I was feeling unhappy. I just didn't know how to.
How could I explain to you that the reason I couldn't be with you was because I was so exhausted? I couldn't give my fullest self to anything or to anyone, especially you. There was a lot you were dealing with that offloading on you felt so wrong. And I kick myself every single day because I wasn't there, Cyan. I wasn't there when you needed me. And it wasn't because I didn't want to. I just couldn't. Heck, I couldn't even stop you when you left.
You deserved more than I gave you, Cyan. Seriously, more. And sending that text was the only way I could part from you. One of the hardest decisions I had to make but it was the only way I could do it, Cyan. I didn't want you to burden you so that was why I had to end things with you."
Cyan's shock sewed her lips shut. She was rendered speechless. She expected to hear that he left her in pursuit of something better.

Someone better. She remembered being so broken and angry simultaneously that she had completely written him off in her life. Though, the littlest things like his favourite ice cream flavour, reminded her that she was still irrevocably in love with him.
She felt her heart constricting, conscious of the fact that she didn't know he was going through a trying time. She was livid at herself that she couldn't protect him from all the heart-shattering events that took place in his life that stole his happiness and peace. But mostly, she was beside herself with rage for not noticing when his mental health declined. It was her job to look after him and she didn't even do that correctly.
Nathan chuckled nervously. "Before you ask and I know you will, I'm over it. I talked to someone. And I know you hate me for not checking in on you after you left."
"I don't hate you." Cyan responded quietly. She was afraid that if she said more, the build-up of tears would fall like an avalanche.
"I know you didn't want to talk to me after I ended things so whenever you and Aria called each other, I'd be there with her just to hear your

voice." He revealed. "I know Janine took care of you."
At that, Cyan stared directly into Nathan's eyes. Her warm hand cupped his right cheek. She wanted to say so much to him, but she couldn't bring herself to open her mouth without unwanted tears falling down her cheek. She stroked his defined face and he leaned into her touch as if it was something he had yearned for. This moment expressed more than her words could ever have.
I'm so sorry. I wish I knew. I'm sorry. I missed you so much.
She felt his calloused hands assist her up from her stool and within seconds she was in his soft embrace. She placed her head on his chest and hugged him back. He stroked her braids in a downwards motion in order to synchronize her uneven breathing. Right away, she truly remembered that home was never attached to a place. But to a person.
"Nate! Is my badge read-"
Cyan heard Evan's shoe thud in the gadget room and she pulled herself away from Nathan so quickly that one of his jacket's buttons scraped her palm.

She didn't care. She had more pressing matters such as Evan seeing her devastated on Nathan's chest.
"Oh." Evan said awkwardly. "I can always come back later if you're busy."
"No, come in. What did you need?" Nathan asked. He had already returned to being DEC as if their heart to heart had never happened.
Cyan admired that. She had always envied people who could switch through emotions with no difficulties. If she looked at herself in that present moment, she was sure that all she would see was distress on her face.
"Uhm, my badge." Evan mentioned carefully. "Is it ready?"
Nathan walked to the East wing of the room and reached up on the second shelf from the top. He retrieved a metal badge that was identical to Cyan's and handed it to Evan.
"Break it again next time and you'll fix it yourself." Nathan threatened.
"Whatever." Evan mocked.
Cyan took their back and forth as a sign to leave the room.
"Thanks for the badge." she said as she brisk-walked to the door.

"See you later." Nathan waved with a small smile. Cyan could only glance at him before she left the room. She sighed to herself when she was out in the corridor.
"Are you ready to hear my 'I told you so'?" Cyan heard Evan say to Nathan.
"Shut up." Nathan answered.
Cyan wondered what that was supposed to mean but instead of dwelling on it, she shrugged it off and decided to ascend the stairs that led her to her room.

5. PARTYING IN VI-PRISONER

After a productive fifteen minutes of showering off the day's activity from her body under scorching hot water, thirty minutes dedicated to her make-up, another ten minutes to her hair and an additional ten minutes of dressing up for their operation, she looked back at the reflection in her vanity mirror to see a familiar woman looking back at her. She wore a pitch-black, short slip-on with thread straps and a long, leather, sweeping trench coat. Although it was Fall season, the desperate wind was still on a rampage to shred any bare arms and legs it would find on sight, provoking her to pair the minidress with thigh-high black boots that gripped three-quarters of her leg. Turning around to earn full view of her outfit, she noticed that though she was almost fully covered, the satin dress was still a good distance away from the beginning of her boots, accentuating her curves as she had planned it to. Cyan hated the cold. And she knew she was going to feel it seeing as that she deliberately wore a short dress having checked the weather on her cell phone. But she believed that the end results of wearing a piping-hot dress were more important. If one planned to look good then personal feelings about the weather didn't matter.

She clipped on her gold hoop earrings and put on her gold necklace, that carried the 'C' pendant, around her neck. Half her braids were tied up in a high ponytail whilst the rest of them lounged leisurely on her back. Their crimson colour complimented the blood red lipstick she applied that Cyan couldn't have been happier with the shade of extensions she had chosen. The tiny hairs at the start of her forehead were brushed in a perfect swoosh design and the particles of her

sweet, amber fragrance dispersed with every movement she made. Cyan beamed at herself. She had almost forgotten how stunning she could be.
Her cell phone made a ping sound and she went over to where it was on the bed. She dragged the notification's bar to see that a text message from Janine had popped up.
"Bad news; I lost my key again. Good news; I threw out the pineapple."
Cyan chuckled at that.
She texted back, *"Bad news; Greg is going to hate you. Good news; you can a take break from going to the bathroom every few minutes."*
She checked the time at the top, right corner of the screen. It was 20:30p.m in Leicester and 19:30p.m in Prague owing to the one-hour difference. The chances were that Janine was off work now, recuperating with a good television show and an unhealthy snack. Alternatively, Cyan was dressed in the skimpiest outfit to blend in a crowd of unruly partygoers in order to drain information out of a drug dealer.
How different their nights were.
Still zoned in on the time, Cyan remembered that they were all supposed to be on the road by nine

to be at the club at ten, so she decided to pack some of her lady essentials in her purse, insert her badge in the inside pocket of her coat, apply order in her room and closed all the windows. She glimmered at herself in the mirror one last time and exited the room.
Descending the stairs two at a time in hopes that she was not late, Cyan skimmed through the stairs in her heavy boots a few minutes faster than she would've if she was taking one step.
She entered the living room where she was greeted by the hustle and bustle of young adult Agents in casual-fashionable wear, moving with determination and purpose in their strides. Bullet-proof vests were loaded into gear bags, firearms were undergoing screening and selection, devices such as laptops and notebooks were packed into their casings and straight into bags while careless chatter acted as the background music, adding to the aesthetic to the preparations.
She noticed that everyone was dressed differently than she'd seen earlier, which was expected since they were all going out, but the Agents of Division 12 were no longer in the room. If Cyan didn't know any better, she would've thought that this

was a group of twentysomethings readying to lose themselves in the night of drinks and music.
She acknowledged that the boys looked pretty fantastic, being that they didn't spend an immeasurable amount of time working on their appearance unlike the girls whom she couldn't see anywhere in the room.
The guys had infused a twist to their hoodie and pants outfits and added a flare to them. Like Evan. He wore a black turtleneck that hugged his lean body with a pair of beige cargo pants and white sneakers to pair. Tiny silver hoops dangled from his ears, going hand in hand with the silver chain around his neck. He was laughing with Jordan near the big screen who wore a grey hoodie, a white flannel and black jeans. She also noticed Preston who was sitting on the edge of the couch, inserting comms into his ears. He was in a Courage the Cowardly Dog t-shirt, black jeans and denim jacket. She made a mental note to find out where Preston bought the purple dog so that she could purchase one for herself.
Behind Preston's couch stood Nathan, packing black SSU vests with the eagle insignia on them and the number of their Division in a gear bag. He wore a pair of cream pants, a plain, white round

neck t-shirt and a cream short-sleeved button down. He married that together with his white sneakers to compliment his snow outfit. His hair was parted sideways and just like Evan, he wore a silver chain around his neck.
As if some unknown entity told him to look up from what he was doing, Nathan's head jerked in her direction and he spotted her. Cyan hadn't realized that she had been holding her breath when she tried to inhale a quick one to calm all the raving butterflies in her stomach. She wanted to approach him and tell him that he looked very good.
But she decided against it. She didn't know where they were or what they were thus not wanting to make decisions or take actions that would assume otherwise. He stopped packing the vests and unmindfully threw the bag on the floor to his feet. If Cyan was unsure about how she looked that night, she would've easily found confirmation in Nathan's blazing eyes that widened in amazement when they stopped on her. He explored her slowly, like a poacher that had set eyes on an extinct species for the very first time. Cyan was not a fan of eye contact. It made her self-conscious. But the feeling of holding Nathan's

gaze was addictive. It made her feel marked and momentous, and for what seemed like an interminable moment, Cyan couldn't see anyone else.

Because Nathan's stare grew much like a small fire in the woods, Cyan quickly pried her eyes off of him. It had something to do with her face increasing in temperature.

Not caring what it was that her eyes landed on next, they latched onto a pair of Nathan's white shoes. Then another pair of white shoes belonging to Preston and eventually she managed a half-circle turn to clock if Evan and Jordan wore white shoes as well.

They did. Cyan giggled at the image of the boys discussing their footwear like excited high school girls because they all wore a similar pair.

All of them, except one.

Cyan's boot heel hit the wooden floor to the speed of her step as she walked over to the television area where Evan and Jordan were standing, near the counter that held firearms with their respective equipment adjacent to them.

"I didn't want to say anything but I think a university professor snuck into your house." Cyan

commented sarcastically as she approached the boys.
"What do you mean?" Evan asked confusedly.
"I think she is talking about the head of academia over there." Jordan clarified.
Evans's eyes travelled the direction Jordan's finger had led them to. They found William perched on one of the bar chairs in the kitchen polishing his brown derby shoes as he talked to them. The sight of William slowly losing his mind before Cyan's eyes was not nearly as disturbing as compared to what he was wearing.
"He knows where we are going, right?" Evan asked curiously.
"It depends. Does the club have a senior citizen's section? Because he'd definitely blend in with the other polo shirts and khakis." Cyan replied.
"I bet he has never been out to a bar before." Jordan gambled.
"I bet he has. But all the women he asked to dance obviously rejected him, pushing him to declare revenge on all the good-for-nothing girls by wearing the worst outfit humanely possible in efforts to punish them and anyone else who has the misfortune of looking at him." Cyan responded in one breath.

Evan laughed. "That's very possible."
"Now that I think about it, that's likely the explanation." Jordan joined in on the laughter. "Looking good, by the way."
"Thanks Jay." Cyan smiled. "So do you. Both of you."
"Thanks." the two boys said.
She refocused her attention to the Glocks that were spread out on the counter. She picked the last firearm, sitting at the edge of the table. It was a Glock 17. It was her signature firearm for all the years she was at the SSU and she didn't mind reintroducing herself to it again. She made sure no one was in her peripheral vision and drew the weapon at the glass wall as if it was her target. Her right hand gripped the firearm, supported by her left hand that clutched her right wrist, with her index finger on the trigger. It felt familiar, easy to operate. Comfortable too.
She collected the Glock with its magazine tube, the respective bullets that came with it and inserted them into the inside of her trench coat pocket.
"Damn." Jordan swore.
Cyan looked up from what she was doing. "What?"

"William just added a knitted scarf to his ensemble." Jordan announced. "He can't go outlooking like that."
Evan and Cyan glanced at each other for brief moment.
"Have fun." they both said simultaneously as they briskly walked away from Jordan.
After successfully convincing William to change his country club outfit to something more appropriate for the occasion, Nathan and Evan took it as indication that everyone was ready and brought the cars they would be travelling in to the front. There was a minor miscalculation with that notion when Harper ran back into the house, twice, to change her lipstick back to lip gloss and her lip gloss back to lip stick. Her reasoning was that she didn't know whether to look naturally glamorous with the lip gloss and give her outfit all the attention or to look extravagantly glamorous with the lipstick and allow her face to do all the talking. Obviously, the boys did not understand a word she said so they just groaned and waited for her until she made up her mind. When Harper was sure that her outfit and the lip stick could co-exist in the same world, the boys jumped in with

Nathan while the girls hopped into the second vehicle driven by Evan.

Before they began to move, Evan pulled his phone out of his front pocket and connected it to the car's Bluetooth system. He tapped on it for a few seconds and the song 'C'est La Vie' by Claudia Valentina blared from the sound speakers. Cyan quizzically gaped at Evan for the reason that pop was the last genre he expected him to play. As far as she knew, the guys were into hardcore, speaker-breaking music. Cyan quickly closed her wide mouth and reprimanded herself for stereotyping him.

He began to sing along to the song, Aria and Harper following his lead.

Cyan thought back to when they were jumping into the vehicles. It made sense why no one racked their head over which car they wanted to travel in. It was as if it was obvious that Evan drove with the girls and Nathan with the rest of the gang.

Cyan joined in the sing along to the familiar song and allowed the catchy beat and the singer's hypnotic voice to loosen her up. They were going to a party after all.

*****

Cyan didn't realize that they had arrived at the night spot an hour later because Evan's amazing playlist distracted her from the distance. Subsequent to descending from their vehicles and suffering the icy chill outside, the Division found themselves in a dark establishment illuminated by the bright, primary colours of strobe lights. Nathan dispatched them to different areas of Quarter 25 to cover all its angles; Jordan, Harper, William in the crowd, Cyan by the bar, Aria in the car in order to hack the security cameras while the rest of them assumed the upstairs area of the nightspot.

Not wanting to spend another minute on the dancefloor, Cyan followed orders and shoved her way through to the bar. Apart from the many "excuse mes" and the "I'm sorrys" she dropped on her way there when her body collided with other fellow bodies, she didn't have much difficulty navigating her way to the bar, given half the light that brightened the club emanated from its counter. It shed light on a fair-skinned bartender running from either end of the counter

to make sure the numerous customers relaxing there were kept happy.
It was overcrowded. If it wasn't a drink being ordered, it was the ladies flirting with the busy barman or the guys trying to make conversation with the ladies who were interested in the barman.
Cyan internally grumbled and wondered if she would be able to procure a seat that would give her a good view of the club, preferably where no one would bother her with futile conversation. Or perhaps just a seat. She couldn't afford to aim too high.
She scanned the area for an available stool and almost jumped in the air with relief when she eyed an empty seat on the far, right side of the counter. She briskly walked towards it, almost running speed, to claim it before anyone could sit on it. It wasn't the best seat in the house but it would have to do.
The plan was to keep an eye out for Pedro. Once found, anyone who had eyes on him first would lure him outside and force him to talk.
Simple. Easy; if Quarter 25 wasn't perfectly packed with hundreds of belligerent ravers who were louder than the blaring music. The task was

easier said than done. But they knew that travelling to the city.
Cyan figured if she was going to sit at the bar, it would be best if she acted believable and ordered a drink like a normal club-goer. She signalled for the bartender and asked for a Piña Colada; sweet and milky. She ordered a non-alcoholic, since she was on duty, but hoped she wouldn't be pushed to switch to the alternative depending on how the night went.
"Operation find Gallo's criminal behind in motion." Jordan said through the coms that Cyan had shoved in her ears.
"Everyone in place?" Nathan asked.
"Copy." all the members of the team answered.
"Nathan, it's too hot in this crowd." William complained.
"Don't worry about him, Nathe." Jordan assured. *"We are good down here."*
There were probably one in a million chances that Cyan and William would ever agree on anything and this was one of those slim but likely chances. Unlike the relenting weather outside, the club was blistering hot. This was aided by the fact that the club was full past its capacity, sweaty bodies generating heat by dancing to the music mixed in

by the disc jockey. She couldn't see much of the place, except the bar area and what the strobe lights allowed her to see. Occasionally, a blue light would land on the DJ booth to her right, accommodating a fedora-wearing man who was switching it up with the beats, or a yellow light on the bouncer that was stationed in-house. But everywhere she looked, she saw men and women holding an alcoholic beverage, toasting and cheering to the ceiling every time a popular song was played. 'Animals' by Martin Garrix was included in the playlist and Cyan's ears almost melted off because of all the happy screams on the dance floor.

She readjusted her attention to her creamy drink and allowed the cool sensation to perform tricks down her throat. She removed her coat, hung it around her stool and authorized the cool air to graze her bare arms and legs. The freshness of the air was too compelling so she untied her braids, letting them fall lazily on her back. She felt much better. Cooler.

"Oh. Cyan, don't look. But there is a six o'clock staring at you." Harper gasped. *"How I wish it was me in your seat."*

"What?" Cyan asked.

"I want Mr. tall, dark and handsome to look at me the way he is digging holes into you."
"Harper-"
"Shh, shh! He is walking towards you!"
Cyan didn't want to be approached. By anyone. She just wanted to scout Pedro without any interruptions. Cyan then remembered that she was in a club, the hub of interactions and pointless conversations. She couldn't avoid it even if she wanted to and wished straight away for the night to be over.
A large thud on the empty seat to her right pulled her out of her thoughts. A muscular man had confidently thrown himself on the free seat next to hers and moved it subtly towards hers. He tried to be subtle. He was a buff man on a stool smaller than him that Cyan was surprised at the tiny stool for not taking him down with it. He possessed rich, syrup skin, free of any facial hair and head void of any, not even a single strand. His full lips were moisturized thoroughly, straight teeth protruding underneath them, reminding Cyan of the heartbreakers that your parents and friends warned you about. His wide eyes travelled Cyan's body with his tongue out, panting like a ravenous animal.

Cyan cocked her head to the side and whispered into her coms, "I don't want to talk to him."
"Oh, come on, Cy-Cy." Jordan joked. *"Give him a chance. I'm sure he is the guy your mother would love to meet."*
"Ha-Ha-Ha. Jordan." Harper mocked. *"Cyan, don't listen to him. This guy is a fire hazard. Talk to him."*
"Fire hazard?" Preston asked.
"It just means he's really cute." Harper clarified. *"He's cute, isn't he?"*
"Uhm, I don't know how to answer that question." Preston replied unsurely.
"I don't see it." William answered honestly.
"Is it possible for everyone to concentrate on the task at hand?" Nathan asked. *"We are not here for a match-making enterprise."*
"Right. Sorry." Cyan apologized, as did as her other teammates.
"Charles!" the man next to Cyan bellowed, causing her to slightly spring out of her stool. The pale man from the other side of the counter dropped all he was doing and ran to their side.
"Whiskey." the man ordered. "Orange juice for the lady."
"On it, sir."

Cyan didn't want to look at the man next to her but her confrontational side decided to glance at him anyway. She was met by his persistent stare that Cyan asked herself where all his confidence emanated from.
"Orange juice?" Cyan asked him.
"Is there a problem?" the man whispered seductively.
"Cyan, don't." Nathan cautioned.
Cyan ignored him and replied to the man next to her, "I think there is."
"It would make me the happiest man in the world if you enlightened me." he smirked.
Cyan laughed at the mistake this man had made. He mistook her calling him out for flirting with him, only that she tried to understand what it was about her that made him think that she couldn't take on a drink that was implicitly, supposedly for men exclusively.
"You don't think I can handle a whiskey?" Cyan asked.
"Perhaps citrus is quite weak for a woman of your stature, I admit." the man chatted up. He analysed her again from her forehead to the tip of her heel. "But you'd have to show me if you can handle a big boy's drink."

"I have to prove to *you* that I can drink alcohol? What, women can't do anything these days without the approval of men?"
"That's just how the world works." the man shrugged.
"Cy, I love that you are willing to go toe to toe with this man about the societal issues we are plagued with in this world but remember that you're on duty. Don't forget why we are here." Nathan warned.
Nathan was right. She would've gone toe to toe with the man sitting beside her. But she had to thicken her skin so as to not respond to everything he said. She had a job to do.
"Shayne." the man introduced himself. He stuck out his hand towards Cyan in hopes to receive a handshake. Cyan gave him half a smile to acknowledge that she heard him.
"What's yours?" he asked.
"Agnes." Cyan replied automatically.
"That's a beautiful name." Shayne complimented. "What does it mean?"
Cyan shrugged her shoulders. Perhaps her indifference would encourage him to choose different woman to bother.
It didn't.

"Where do you come from?"
She would've been honest with him that she came from a small city called Mbabane in the country of Swaziland, south of Africa, but she didn't think he deserved to know anything about her so she replied, "Many places."
"That's...cool."
And that was the moment silence invaded their conversation. As far as Cyan was concerned, she was more than happy to let it because she had made it clear from the beginning that she didn't want to talk to him. Although, some part of her was glad that she did converse with him because if she hadn't, she wouldn't have noticed that there was something off about him. As appealing as he thought he was, there was another layer to him that wasn't as captivating as he presented it to be. She couldn't quite understand it but the more he talked, the more she noticed a peculiar air around him.
"So, listen. I think you're hot and I don't want to waste time talking." Shayne said. "I have a private room upstairs that we can both have fun in. Preferably without our clothes on."
"Can I remove my coms?" William asked dryly.

It took Shayne shorter than Cyan expected to reveal his true motives behind the small talk. Revolted but not surprised, Cyan ignored Shayne's advance and allowed the screams of the crowd over the song 'Leg Over' by a Ghanaian artist, Mr Eazi, mixed in by the DJ, reply to Shayne instead. From the corner of her eye, she could see that Shayne's corrupt eyes measured her exposed legs and wished she could dig a hole somewhere and hide from his blatant and shameless looks. Never had she been disgusted by another man's gaze like she was by Shayne's. She wasn’t used to it. It almost persuaded her to grab her stuff and stake Pedro elsewhere.

She was about to dramatically gather all her belongings and look for another area to monitor the club when the VIP band wrapped around Shayne's wrist caught her eyes and she set the thought to leave aside and came to terms with what she had to do.

Cyan sat up straight, rendering her dress shorter, swallowed the vomit that was rising up and batted her eyelashes at Shayne.

"Your room, is it big?" Cyan asked suggestively.

"Of course." Shayne answered excitedly, understanding that his target was finally responding to his pursuits.
"Then why don't you take me there after we've had a few drinks? Not at this tacky bar."
"I'll take you wherever you want." Shayne promised.
"VIP?" Cyan confirmed softly.
"Wherever." Shayne smirked.
"Ew. Perv." Harper expressed.
"Only if my friend is invited too." Cyan demanded.
"Yeah, whatever." Shayne agreed as he gulped the rest of his drink and sloppily pecked Cyan on the cheek.
"I'll meet you by the stairs." he whispered in her ear.
Cyan pulled off a gesture that resembled a smile until Shayne disappeared into the crowd. When she was sure that he was out of sight, she exhaled deeply, more out of disgust than relief, and silently thanked her friends for encouraging her to join the drama club when they were still in high school.
"VIP, then what?" Nathan asked.

"Shayne is our ticket to get eyes on Pedro." Cyan responded. "I think the VIP section is likely where he'll be."
"But we are upstairs already." Evan contested.
Cyan heard the live click-clack of high heel shoes and felt taps on both her shoulders. She turned around to face a Harper who was breathing heavily. She must've lost her breath trying to push through the bodies in the crowd. Cyan also wondered if Harper was psychic because when she told Shayne she would be bringing a friend, Harper was exactly the person she was referring to.
"You're not upstairs enough, Ev. Only a pair of heels and a cute outfit will take you where we are going." Harper explained. "Cy and I will go in there and talk to Pedro."
"Fifteen minutes." Nathan instructed.
"We'll be back in fourteen." Cyan assured.
With that, the two girls met Shayne by the stairs near the DJ booth waiting for them. He led the way up the thick flight and took them to an area that was quieter too, melodies that resembled jazz but not as elegant to match the atmosphere of the nightspot. There were velvet couches all around them with pear-shaped tables holding

metal buckets filled with ice. The lights were quieter too, exhibiting non-blinding colours. It occurred to Cyan that they were in more of a lounge reserved for important persons only. A handful of men slouched on these velvet couches, surrounded by dancing women in pieces of cloth that covered only the important areas. Cyan had less than appropriate remarks for them but thought wisely and swallowed them down.
"So, ladies. What time are you leaving?" Shayne asked.
Harper chuckled. "Oh, we don’t know. Maybe ten minutes before midnight."
"Oddly exact." Shayne laughed.
Cyan didn’t remember any of them specifically discussing their time of departure at any point before, during or even after they made their trip to the city. It was pretty obvious that they were going to leave after they completed what they had come to do, which led Cyan to believe that Harper was trying to communicate with her without alerting Shayne.
"Ten minutes before midnight" Harper had said. That meant twelve o'clock. Cyan subtly turned north-west from where they were currently

standing and understood what Harper was referring to.
In that direction, an oval booth leaned against the wall, circling a long velvet couch. On it was a man with too much oil in his hair, slumped nonchalantly across the purple sofa as if his only worry was ruining his shiny suit with creases. Cyan couldn't see much of him because he was surrounded by a thick cloud of smoke that emanated from his Jamaican cigar. There was too much smoke for Cyan's short-sighted vision but they were heading in that direction anyway that she didn't wreck her head over what Harper was trying to say to her.
As they walked closer to the booth, the olive-toned man whipped his head at the sound of Harper's heels and abruptly sat up. Cyan was taken off guard by this action but she guessed he was mesmerized by her. Cyan couldn't blame him. Harper was dressed to kill. She wore a fitted, strapless top made of black leather and coupled that with black, leather pants and glassy heels. Her straight, strawberry blonde hair was a stark contrast to her dark outfit, intensifying the fascination of whomever was lucky enough to look at her. Not to mention the blinding jewellery

around her neck, her wrist and her ankle that added lavishness to her outfit.
The man eyed Shayne with pride and said, "I see you have brought some friends."
He stood up from his divan like an impressed African prince and stretched out his hand towards Harper in attempt to introduce himself. Harper placed her slender hand in his palm and he kissed it.
"My name is Venustiano Vicente." the man succulently introduced. "But you can call me Pedro."
Cyan couldn't help but deride inwardly at him. He was completely enthralled by Harper that his memory failed to remind him that she had arrested him for drug possession not long ago.
"Would you ladies like to join me for some 2001 Guiseppe Quintarelli in my office?" Pedro asked.
"What's the occasion?" Harper asked sceptically.
"I've laid my unworthy eyes on two beautiful women." he smirked.
"But I-I thought we were all hanging out here." Shayne stammered.
Pedro eyed him as if he was the last insect on a spotless floor he had to crush before he went on his way.

"Not now." Pedro dismissed. "Go and check if the barman is mixing the drinks correctly."
Cyan guessed that Shayne wasn't very happy with what he was instructed to do because he rolled his eyes and stormed away the same way they came. She was silently grateful that Shayne was sent to babysit the bartender because she didn't think she could endure another minute of standing anywhere near him. Pedro was already leading them into a dark, narrow hallway that he didn't witness Shayne's little fit.
They didn't walk for very long until they reached the end of the hallway and turned to a small room on their right. Pedro ushered them in, like the perfect gentlemen he was pretending to be, and walked in after them.
With no delay, Cyan felt different. Before they left the lounge, she was expectant. But standing in Pedro's office, she felt very edgy. She blamed her sixth sense for always being aware. Her apprehension was assisted by the lack of noise in the upper part of the building they were in. It was way too quiet up here. She couldn't hear any club music or a collective of screams from hundreds of drunk socialites or even Wiliam's obnoxious

commentary in her ear about why clubs only existed for the intellectually deficient.

Wait.

Exactly.

She couldn't hear William through her coms anymore. She also couldn't hear Nathan and Evan theorizing about Lucas' unique abduction. Even Jordan's heavy breathing was gone. Cyan whipped her head towards Harper to see if she was experiencing the same silence she was. Based off of the same confused look Harper wore on her face, Cyan realized that it was not just happening to her.

Harper tapped her ears subtly and mouthed, *"Coms?"*

Cyan had an idea of what was happening but the thought was only solidified when she heard a loud click behind her. She turned around to see that Pedro had locked the door. Why would he do that if they were planning on enjoying themselves with glasses of wine?

Cyan and Harper had walked into a trap.

As if a switch had been turned on in Cyan's mind, her body weight shifted in the direction of the door, she retrieved her Glock from her coat pocket at lightning speed and aimed it swiftly at

Pedro. She knew she couldn’t fire at the smug bastard because he was unarmed but she hoped that facing the inside of a dangerous barrel held by a very dangerous Agent would urge Pedro to explain what he planned on doing. In the corner of her eye, she saw that Harper was in the exact same position as she was.
Pedro raised his hands in a defensive manner though his facial expression was evened to the point of no expression. Him raising his hands in that manner was more of an involuntary action than a scared reaction.
"There's no need for all that." he assured calmly.
"What are you trying to achieve by locking us in here and tampering with our coms?" Harper grilled.
Pedro howled in laughter. "Did you really think you could come up here, try to seduce me and think I wouldn’t recognize you, Agent Blair?"
"What do you want?" Cyan asked.
"To chat." Pedro answered as he dropped his arms to his sides.
"And why would we want to waste our breath on you?' ’Harper snapped.

Pedro smiled a small smile. "Because I know why you're here. And I can help you with the information you need."
"Can you believe him?" Harper asked Cyan incredulously.
She hated that she did but something in Pedro's physical behaviour told Cyan that there was some truth to what he was saying. He wasn't trying too hard to convince them that he wanted to offer assistance to them, given his long RAP sheet, but instead maintained steady eye contact with them without faltering.
Cyan slowly lowered her firearm.
"Harp, lower it."
"He is only going to say filth. We can't listen to a thing he says!" Harper exclaimed.
"I know you're aware of my dealings with Geoffrey. But I want what you want." Pedro said. "I want to know who killed him."
Cyan focused on Harper. "I don't trust him either, Harp. We'd be fools to. But right now, we need him talking more than we need him quiet." she reasoned. "We need to know what he knows."
After what felt like a long moment, Harper finally lowered her weapon.

"He'll say what he needs to say once Nathan and Evan are in here." she said.
"By all means." Pedro smirked.
He unlocked the door and opened it for Harper to exit. Harper measured him from head to toe with distaste before stalking out of the room.
Something in Cyan told her that they would regret giving a drug-dealing menace a chance to help them with their investigation. But they had little say in the matter.
Pedro seemed to be enjoying the little game he had them playing that he made himself comfortable behind his oak desk. With all the gun-aiming and trust issues brewing, Cyan hadn't had the chance to survey his office. Ancient wallpaper, ancient rug, and ancient picture frames; his office looked as if a medieval knight had thrown up the Renaissance Era in it with 15th Century duplicate paintings of Mona Lisa and Venus garnishing his office. She wondered why Pedro found paintings of naked women of the Renaissance fascinating enough to incorporate in almost every inch of his workspace. It was disturbing. She subtly glimpsed at him to gain some answers on this. Maybe his body language would reveal something to her.

Watching him, Pedro gave the impression that he was an open book with his charisma and allure but his personality was the opposite. He was reserved. A beautiful woman was standing right in front of him in his office and not once did he engage in any small talk nor chat himself up in any way.
She could've tried to decipher more but then their eyes met. He was probably trying to analyse her just as she was doing to him. She quickly looked away and cursed herself for not leaving with Harper. She knew she had to stay and keep an eye on Pedro because he was as slippery as he was charming but it didn't make it any easier being in the same room as him.
He smiled at Cyan which seemed to be what he was all about; sly smiles and mind games. He opened his mouth to say something but thought against it and shut his mouth as quickly as he opened it.
Instead, he placed his short legs on his table, relaxed into his chair and said, "Wine?"

6. TECHNICAL DIFFICULTIES

William complaining about the heat in the club was carbon-copy to complaining about enjoying Oreo cookies without full-cream milk to dip them in. Dairy was indulgence. What Will complained about was a luxury compared to being crammed inside an immobile car outside a cold parking lot. Of course, Aria was inside their vehicle where it was warm and toasty but she was still cooped up in a rectangle made of steel and aluminium indefinitely.

It wasn't her choice, really. It was the job position she chose. Working as a Technical Analyst meant that she couldn't work directly in the field unlike her Division mates. Drawing out her weapon whilst simultaneously examining data was impossible. It wasn't logical. She knew because she once tried.

But if she was entirely honest with herself, one of the main reasons she adored being an Analyst was its restriction to be on the field. She preferred to work on the side-lines, far away from all the adrenaline and the pressure. What's more, she didn't have to look at the dead bodies.

She learned that she wasn't a fan of so much as glancing at a dead person when she worked her very first case after graduation. Division 6 was dispatched to a flat complex that had been set on fire by a vengeful arsonist. The operation was successful as it could be; they managed to clear out ten dead bodies that had been charred beyond recognition and extricate the few that were still alive.

No matter how hard she tried, Aria couldn't forget about the firefighters dressed in asbestos suits who formed a convoy, pushing and dragging out stretchers heaped with black body bags out of the complex.

One stretcher. Two stretchers. Three stretchers. Four stretchers. Five. Six.

Aria felt overwhelming sadness as the bodies passed by her, the smell of smoke and burnt flesh that escaped from the cadaver pouches giving her an excuse to walk away from all the madness. She felt choked, by both the sorrow and the queasiness, and she hoped that holding onto the brick of the building would give her a much-needed break to control to the nausea that was rising due to the polluted air.

Aria remembered feeling very hot. She thought the ponds of sweat were caused by being around a viscous fire. But when she removed her leather jacket and unfastened the bulletproof vest underneath it, her body temperature dropped to a refrigerating chill. Goosebumps formed on her uncovered arms and her teeth began to chatter against each other. Her face and her neck were wet, all the liquid, she realized, coming from her eyes.

She was crying.

And in no time, two of the grilled-cheese sandwiches she took that morning traced their path back to her mouth and exited in a sickening mesh of different colours and textures.

Ew, she remembered thinking. Her guts were already on the ground for everyone to see. It was only her first day and her teammates knew more of herself than she did.

She felt hands gently suspending her long hair on top of her head as she tried her hardest to allow all the toxic vomit exit her system. Jason, one of her teammates, had noticed her absence and approached her to find out what was going on with her. Aria couldn't efficiently formulate the words to tell him that she wasn't feeling so good

so she unwillingly pointed at her vomit. Luckily, Jason was part of their medical team so it only took him seconds to diagnose her with an anxiety attack.
After cleaning up Aria's mouth, he instructed her to straighten her arms to the sky to calm her down. A few long breaths with Jason's help and she was breathing normally.
In essence, that was what her career at SSU consisted of for almost two years.
She couldn't stomach it all; the nausea, the body rot and the bleach that cleaned the body rot. She was saturated. Because she was the type of Agent that couldn't be around the deceased, her Supervisor decided to demote her to Distress Gatekeeper, which was just a fancy term for someone who responded to emergency calls. It was the same time she truly acknowledged that she couldn't do what her teammates could. She couldn't depersonalize the victims and work through without batting an eyelash. Being a normal Agent like everyone else was not in the books for her. And it only made matters worse when all her teammates treated her exactly how she felt; useless.

Why continue working there, someone would ask, if all the Organisation brought were puke and tears?
She met Dave. He advised her to harness the skills embedded in her and utilise what she already knew. He even planted the seed of her as a potential D12 member and months later, she couldn't have been happier. Her choice to transfer to the 12th Division in her fourth year at the Organisation changed the trajectory of her life.
For once she felt understood. Nathan gave her the opportunity to prove that she was a great asset to his Division just by being herself. And whenever she had difficulties of any kind, Evan was always there to practice breathing exercises with her.
Nothing could've prepared her to create space in her heart for the best leaders and friends many yearned for. She had finally found a family.
Akin to a flower growing in the right soil with the appropriate nutrients, as a member of Division 12, Aria blossomed alike a flourishing rosebush.
Focusing her passion on being an Analyst was one of the best choices she made for her career. She applied herself and it resulted in her improving her manoeuvres such as hacking any security system in under sixty seconds or less.

Just as she had done to Pedro's system.
Two system units were balanced on her laps, projecting the interior of the club in four parts of her screens- telling her that there were only four cameras in the nightspot. She had already spotted everyone; Nathan, Preston and Evan conversing in the area up the stairs, occasionally rejecting advances and approaches made by any species that wore a skirt. Jordan and Harper were bopping their heads to the music downstairs on the dancefloor while William leaned against the dancefloor with a dreadful look on his face, repelling those who thought they were strong enough to approach him. Cy was sitting at the bar; a white, foamy drink in hand, flanked by an unfamiliar man sitting beside her.
Aria knew Cyan for a very long time and though she couldn't see the man's face, she definitely knew that he was not her type. She was more into cute DECs with impeccable leadership qualities, phenomenal hair and a stellar personality. Aria wondered what was going on between them anyway. Seeing Nathan after all that time must've been a little difficult for Cy. For Nate too. Whenever they were ready to talk, she would be

there for them. As for now, any thoughts she had, she kept to herself.
Concentrating on the camera that filmed the bar area, Aria noticed that events there undertook a heaty turn. Cyan's body language changed from resistant to unusually coy and Aria wondered what all of that was about. She instantly reached for her coms in the drinks compartment of the car, where she had put them when her ears became a little itchy and shoved them back in her ears.
"...meet you by the stairs." Aria heard the man say as he left the bar.
"VIP, then what?" Nathan asked.
That was followed by Cyan and Harper justifying their last-minute plan to seek out Pedro in the upstairs section to the rest of them. It made sense to Aria for Cy and Harp to follow the smoke whilst the trail was still visible and Nathan comprehended that too because he gave them the go-ahead.
With her thumb and index finger, Aria moved them a significant distance away from each other to expand the camera block that displayed Cyan, Harper and the man they had used to gain access to the lounge section. Aria didn't want to say it

and she certainly didn't want to think it but the lounge area resembled more of a strip club than anything. Half-naked women danced on important men in suits while being rewarded with showers of money and champagne. Cy looked around the place registering what Aria had also seen. But she still maintained synchronised step with Harper and the man that flanked her.

They didn't walk far until they stopped at a booth where a man reclined lazily on a purple couch. He was smoking so much that Aria couldn't see his face even when she attempted to zoom in. When the girls stopped at the booth, the man excitedly stood up from his seat and greeted Harper by pecking her knuckles. When he lifted his head to express his gratification to the second man, Aria noticed the familiar face of Pedro Gallo. He sent Cyan's impromptu date away and led Cyan and Harper into a narrow hallway in the opposite direction. Without notice, the screens on Aria's laps went dark after Cyan and Harper followed Gallo to wherever he was leading them.

The hallway wasn't covered by any camera. It was a blind spot.

Aria sighed and slid down the leather seat. She had lost eyes on two Agents and seeing as they had entered the lion's den, they needed all the backup they could get. Aria could've given them that by tracing their every move. But she also knew that Cyan and Harper were more than capable of holding their own since they were well-equipped. She just hoped that there were no surprises hiding in the bushes.

Aria flung herself up in her seat.

"Guys." she called into her buds. "Can you hear me?"

"Yeah." Jay answered.

"Yes." William answered.

"*We can hear you*." Nathan answered. "*Why*?"

"Do you hear that?" Aria asked.

"You mean the loud music and the drunken cheering we've all been hearing since we arrived here?" William asked flatly.

"Nothing I haven't been hearing before." Evan answered.

"*I don't hear anything*." Preston said.

"Exactly." Aria answered. "We can't hear the girls anymore."

There was a silent moment of realization that occurred. Not seeing Cyan and Harper was one thing but not hearing them was a disaster that she

didn't want to deal with. Their connections were lost and Aria's stomach was a pit full of nerves.
''I don't hear them.'' Evan confirmed. *''What's going on?''*
''Their signals were interrupted.'' Aria answered frantically, fingers running over keyboards attempting to reconnect the disconnected coms.
''That means Pedro figured out who they are.'' Nathan deduced.
''That means Pedro figured out who we all are.'' William surmised. ''Aria, lock all your-''
Aria didn't receive the chance to hear the end of what William's sentence because the passenger seat door was abruptly opened by a man Aria didn't recognize. She wanted to yell at him for disrespecting her privacy but her lips were immediately sown shut when the man pulled out a pistol out of his jeans and pointed it at her.
Aria went incredibly still with panic.
She closed her eyes and opened them again to make sure that she wasn't in a bad dream. When it sunk in that she was directly across the barrel of a pistol, her heart began to pump at a million beats per minute. Regardless of her frenzy and confusion, she still applied protocol under duress;

she kept her eyes away from the firearm and put her hands up admitting surrender.
"Aria? Aria!" she heard the boys call her.
She was tempted to send a signal to notify them that she was in danger but her attacker's posture told her that if she did something stupid, he wouldn't hesitate for a second to pull the trigger.
Grabbing her own weapon was out of the picture.
She picked comfort over common sense when she threw it in the back seat after it dug in her side.
She never wanted to strangle herself so badly.
The man stealthily moved closer to her and checked her ears. His cold hands violently removed her coms from both her ears and threw them on the tarred ground. He lifted his leg and his leather cowboy boots crushed them into unrecognizable pieces. After he was done destroying Aria devices, his calloused hands dug holes into her exposed arm and dragged out her out of the vehicle.
Under the horrible circumstances, she was silently grateful that she did not allow Harper to talk her into wearing heels because upon being dragged out of the Ford, she lost her balance and sprained her ankle. Her face met the ground and the tiny stones pricked their way into her skin. She tried to

get up but she fell down again because it felt as if a stack of needles had stabbed her ankle all at the same time.

The pain was excruciating.

The little canon, however, was placed directly over her spine so it motivated her to forget about the amount of pain she was in and move a little faster. As someone with little choice in the matter, she willed herself to push the pace with her good leg, forcing her throbbing right leg to limp more steps. And as if the pistol hadn't aggravated the predicament enough, the cold weather brushed ferociously across her smarting ankle, making it the second enemy she had made that night.

They passed the main entrance and walked to the rear of the club. Her provocateur pushed her to the back of the building where they found another door similar to the one in front. The man kicked the door open just like Chuck Norris and hauled Aria into the darkness that was at the pariah of the club. Aria couldn't see much because the lights were off but she noticed that the man was very familiar with where they were, pulling Aria by the strap of her dress and ascending the creaking stairs with her.

A strong wave of alcohol and sweat punched her brutally in the nose making it difficult for her to breathe. She was not ignorant to the queer scents of nightspots but the smell she was currently inhaling was disastrously lethal. Clearly immune to the dark and the off-putting smell, her other half kept it moving in the dark space, passing silhouettes of men lying across the floor. From the little that Aria could see, these silhouettes were sitting upright against the walls popping pills or snorting white powder.
Most were doing both.
"Oh, look. Pedro's lapdog." one of the silhouettes slurred.
"Shut up." Aria's abductor sneered.
"Isn't it pathetic how Shayne does the boss' dirty work for approval?" another silhouette from the floor bunch laughed.
Shayne.
Without letting her go, Shayne, who held her hostage, punched the drunk man across his face with his pistol. His limp body fell off the chair he was sitting on and thudded on the floor right in front of Aria.
She almost shrilled. But she realized she would be next if she made a sound. She gripped the thin

material of her maxi dress to focus her feelings of fright that were manically creating hysteria within her and silently prayed to still be alive by the end of the night.
Shaking off his acts of violence nonchalantly, Shayne casually fixed his shirt that rode up his torso and proceeded with Aria down the smelly hallway.
"What exactly do you think you're doing, young man? Holding that poor lady like a piece of meat." another man from the dark corners asked. It occurred to Aria that this man was either unafraid of Shayne or he hadn't seen what had been done to one of his friends.
Aria snuck a glance at Shayne. Menace and darkness masked an otherwise handsome face. He smirked.
'Checking if the bartender mixed the drinks correctly."

*****

"I never thought I would have the pleasure of hosting the Special task force in my little office." Pedro taunted.

Cyan, Nathan, Evan and Harper were crowded in Pedro's bijou office, eager to hear what information he claimed to have. Everyone seemed calm and collected, attempting not to set Pedro off by giving him the impression that they needed his help. That would only result in mind games they didn't have time for. Harper, on the other hand, didn't hesitate to show Gallo that she was very upset with him after being locked in his office.

"Don't waste our time." Harper flared.

Pedro chuckled softly. "You need to control that temper, little girl. It might benefit you in the future."

"You know what we are here for, Pedro. Let's dive right into it." Nathan reminded.

"Straight to the point. I like it." Pedro leered. "You know that I run an expensive drug business here. How do I know that you won't take me out of here in handcuffs after telling you everything?"

"How do we know that you're not giving us false information?" Evan asked.

"Because the same person that killed Geoffrey is the same person I import drugs from and I want him gone." Pedro divulged.

"And here I thought you offered to help because you felt terrible about Geoffrey's death." Harper replied in an acidic tone.
"I do. We worked together." Pedro responded dryly. "But he is six feet underground and I am still alive above the earth. I have to rid myself of inconveniences by any means necessary."
""'Inconveniences"?" Cyan repeated.
Pedro sighed. This was the first time Cyan witnessed raw emotion replace the permanent smug look on his face. It changed quite a few things. For one, Pedro must've been really desperate to co-operate with the police. Clearly, he needed them more than they needed him, which said less about Pedro and more about the threat they were trying to deal with.
"I made some injudicious business investments in the past." Pedro started. "I was out of money and I couldn't keep myself or the club afloat. This wealthy guy offered to bail me out and I accepted his help. There was a catch, obviously. I was to sell his drugs in my club as well as distribute it to willing sellers that wanted to make a pound."
"I'm assuming you didn't refuse his deal given the current predicament you're in." Cyan guessed.

"Of course, I didn't say no. I was dead broke at the time and he gave me sixty percent of all the earnings. That sounded like a delicious amount of money to me." Pedro defended. "Maybe if I knew and understood the crap I was putting myself in, I would've made a different decision."
"You sold your soul to the devil." Evan chipped in.
"He is more than that. And I can't get a refund because that would result in my death." Pedro complained.
"He sounds scary." Nathan commented flatly.
"He is nuisance too." Pedro added. "He harasses me. He helped me out of a problem once and now he thinks he owns me. I can't run *my* business the way I want without him ruining everything. You see that cheap vodka at the bar? It's not liquor I'd ever supply to my customers."
"Is that why we are here? To give you back your freedom?" Evan asked.
"You know, you're lucky I'm even helping you." Pedro scoffed. "That man is dangerous. So dangerous that many want him gone. Permanently."
"Well, do you know who this mystery guy really is?" Cyan asked.

"He has been in the game for as long as the Big Ben has been around. He is a Cane Corso. Do you think he'd be stupid enough to tell me his real name?" Pedro asked incredulously. "I only know that he calls himself George Campbell. Could be his real name. Maybe not."
"Alright. And have you met this George Campbell in person?" Harper asked.
"Only once. Man in his forties with really weird, grey hair. Wears very expensive suits." Pedro described.
"That is more than half the demographic in this country! That could be anyone!" Harper exclaimed. "Sorry to break it to you but your semi-vermin information does nothing for us."
"Harper." Nathan called firmly.
He seemed to calm Harper down with his unwavering stare and helped redirect her irritation towards Mona Lisa and Venus. Cyan could understand Harper's feelings of mistrust for Pedro. Sadly, Pedro was the closest source to the information they needed to know.
"I'm a small fish." Pedro burst out.
"Come again?" Evan asked.
"I am a small fish." Pedro repeated. "You're wasting your time grilling me when you should be

finding out who George really is. He is the bigger fish you need to sauté."
"How did George and Geoffrey-"
"Geoffrey?!" Pedro laughed hysterically. "You're still worried about Geoffrey? He was a means to an end. You know what that is? It means that Geoffrey was weak and received what was coming for him. The bigger problem here wears real fur and a 'GC' tattoo behind his ear."
That seemed to spark Nathan's interest.
"GC? Are you sure?" he asked.
"Yes, I am sure. I know I only laid my eyes once on the guy but I'm sure he had those initials printed behind his ear." Pedro replied.
"Anything else?" Nathan asked.
Pedro took one quick glance at his Monalisa replica before answering. "No."
"Huh." Harper scoffed. "You could've added more effort into that lie."
"There's more, isn't there?" Evan noticed.
Cyan agreed with Evan and Harper. Pedro was definitely hiding something.
"My deal?" Pedro asked smugly.
There was no answer.
Cyan had a feeling she was thinking the same thing her teammates were thinking; they would

be in hot water if the Organisation found out they had brokered a deal with a criminal involved in a high-profile case. It went against their values as an Organisation. She didn't think it was worth it. To her, the Directors were scarier than this George character because they had the power to revoke their Agent statuses. There had to be another path to this information.
"We won't take you in." Nathan announced.
Cyan gawked at him, alarmed. What did he think he was doing? There was nothing Cyan wanted to do more than drag Nathan out of the room and shake all the destructive decisions out. If Pedro's loose mouth bragged that they had let him go, they were all as good as dead. Or worse; unemployed.
Registering Nathan's stone-cold expression, Cyan understood that he was aware of the repercussions. There was a stronger force that was motivating him to get answers by any way.
In a flash, Cyan heard a loud noise behind her. She slightly moved out of her seat to see what had interrupted them. The door had been thrown open by Shayne. His exaggerated and noisy entrance didn't frighten Cyan as much as what she saw next.

Aria was held close to him by the straps of her long dress, a pistol puncturing a hole in her neck. Her eyes were almost fully shut but Cyan could tell that she was still breathing by the slow rising and falling of her chest. Her face was scrunched up in pain and Cyan did a quick run-over of her body to see where she had been injured. All of Aria's weight rested on one leg and Cyan noticed that Aria's right ankle was savagely swollen. What had Shayne done to her? Vigorous fear filled Cyan that she didn't notice she was already on her feet with her weapon out.
"Another step and Shayne severs her little spine." Pedro threatened calmly.
It was as if they had met two different characters that belonged to Pedro. The scared Pedro that desperately needed their help and another Pedro that meant what he said by "any means necessary."
Everyone's panic was suppressed by what he said because they knew he had nothing to lose the moment he resorted to tell them about his oppressor, George; especially when he thought he no longer owned what belonged to him. Pedro was an already burning flame. Any gas poured on him would result in an explosion that could tear

all their lives apart. If they didn't want Aria with a bullet through her pharynx, they had to handle the situation delicately.
"What do you think you're doing?" Nathan demanded icily.
"The answer is simple, really." Pedro goaded. "I didn't trust that I'd walk out of here a free man so I had to think on my feet."
"Do you understand what you're doing?!" Cyan exclaimed "You're holding an International Agent against her will. That gives you more than seven years in a cell."
"You better make sure that doesn't happen, sweetheart. Otherwise, her head will end up like the ligaments of her torn ankle and she won't be able to tell the difference." Pedro threatened. "I'll tell you more of what I know about your case once I'm sure I can walk free."
"Don't let him walk." Aria muttered.
"Shut up!" Pedro yelled. "Shayne!"
Shayne removed the pistol from her neck and slammed it against Aria's head. She screamed in pain and Shayne forced the deadly piece of metal in Aria's mouth to shut her up. Her eyes budged out with fear and admittedly, Cyan, Nathan, Evan and Harper had become unimaginably frantic.

"Fine! Okay!" they all shouted at different counts.
"You'll walk out." Nathan agreed.
"Let her go." Evan followed sternly.
"Good choice." Pedro smiled innocently.
"Damn you." Harper spat.
Shayne pushed Aria away from him as if she resembled trash to him, in time for Evan to catch her quickly before she fell and potentially hurt herself. Seeing Aria, hurt as she was, sparked a fury so great in Cyan that she found it very difficult to control it. She wanted to pounce on Shayne and hurt him just as he had hurt Aria. She wanted to swipe the smug look off his face and pin him to the ground. It appealed to her so much in that moment that her hands began to shake uncontrollably. Nathan subtly stood behind her and soothed the small of her back to calm down. She guessed he noticed the smashing and gnashing of her own teeth and took charge of the predicament before it spiralled out of control more than it already had.
"What else?" Nathan asked Pedro.
"You know Rock In Diner?" Pedro asked.
"The American restaurant on Saxon?" Evan asked.
"Precisely. I heard Campbell's minions talking to each other one time. He used to own it with two

of his buddies back in the day.'' Pedro reported. ''Apparently, they expanded the restaurant's capabilities. Drug dealing, laundering, gambling and possibly a brothel to generate income.''

''So, what happened?'' Evan asked.

''LPD received an anonymous tip about their illegal restaurant and they were all arrested.'' Pedro said.

''The minimum one can receive for all those charges is fifteen years.'' Harper recalled.

''George did twenty.'' Pedro said. ''If my math is correct, he was arrested in 1993 and was released in 2013.''

''So, he is out.'' Nathan said. ''Has been for a while.''

''We'll check his prison records and track down his real name.'' Harper said.

''It's not going to be that easy, love.'' Pedro decreed. ''I think, for your sake, I should repeat that George Campbell is a very powerful man. He wouldn't leave traces of his old life for people like you to pick and analyse. Don't underestimate him.''

''Surely, you must know about him.'' Harper prodded. ''How do we find him?''

"How would I look in those goth uniforms of yours? Because I might as well join the SSU since I'm doing your job for you." Pedro laughed.
"Don't piss me off." Nathan growled. "Answer the bloody question. How do we find George?"
"Okay, look." Pedro gulped. "I told you all I know. It's hard to know about someone when they can't be tracked. But you don't have to actively search for him to find him."
"Elaborate." Cyan said.
"Check out the diner." Pedro suggested. "You might find clues there."
Nathan narrowed his gaze. "Pedro, if I find out that you so much as breathed a lie-"
"Calm down, pretty boy. I'm telling you the truth." Pedro said. "Nothing hidden in the dark stays there forever."
"Don't expect a thank you." Harper snapped as she stormed out of Pedro's office.
Evan carried Aria across his chest and followed Harper out. Nathan gave Pedro one last look and stalked out of the office after Evan, leaving Cyan to walk after him.
The noise slowly crept up on Cyan's ears as they reached the end of the narrow hallway. The music, the jeers in the crowd and the familiar stink

of alcohol and sweat told Cyan that they were back in the lounge. She didn't know how long they had been in Pedro's office but the night was just as young as they met it when they entered the club. Ravers were still dancing and smoking as if their lives depended on it.
Compared to the vivacious characters they had to push through to leave the club, Cyan and the rest of the Division were the opposite. They were vexed. Rightfully so. A member of their family had been attacked. There was no other horrifying feeling such as watching torture happen right in front of you. You felt the pain, not only because your family was a part of you, but you felt helpless. All you could do was stand idly and let the best parts of you disappear.
Cyan couldn't explain it but it was as if someone threw a burning matchstick to her already existing fury. She was more upset now than she had been when Shayne violated Aria. All she could feel was rage. For once, she didn't control it. Professionalism wouldn't take precedence tonight.
One thing led to another and she detoured her route. She threw her purse on the floor without regard for its future purposes and stomped back

to the narrow hallway. She had only one thing in mind; going back to that office. She heard Nathan call out her name but his voice drowned in all the music and the screams. He couldn't catch up to her in time because she moved with shocking speed back to Pedro's headquarters.
Before she entered his office, she heard Pedro and Shayne laughing their tails off as if what they had done was material that belonged to a comedy special. That only infuriated her more, enough to enter his territory and make her presence felt. The two men were having too much of a good time to notice that Cyan was back in their space and consequently used that to her advantage. Shayne had his back to her, standing a few feet away from Pedro's desk. So, she used the bridge of her heel to strike the sensitive area of his shin. Viciously. Shayne groaned blaringly and dropped down with a heavy thud to the ground. He tried to reach for his gun, supported by his pants' belt, but Cyan grabbed it in time and kicked it harshly outside the office. She obliterated his other shin to completely immobilize him on the floor and pulled his burly arm to dislocate it out of its socket.
Shayne screamed.

His arm was probably never stretched in such a barbaric way before, resulting in Cyan yanking it again so that he could familiarize himself with the pain. She pinned it on the rear end of his neck and depressed her heel on top of his hand, that faced upwards, as destructively as she could, forming a neck-hand-foot sandwich. Not forgetting Gallo, Cyan briskly retrieved her Glock from her coat and drew it at him.

"Please! Stop! I can't breathe!" Shayne shouted. His face, squashed and trampled on the floor, was almost a blue-purple colour. His breath was rapidly leaving his body.

Cyan depressed her foot on his neck harder.

"Just put the gun down." Pedro pleaded. "Let's talk, okay?"

It was almost as if Cyan had blacked out and lost all sense of reason. She didn't want to talk. She was seething. All she wanted was to settle accounts with Shayne for what he did. He thought he could get away with breaking her friend's ankle but he was dead wrong. He had made an unforgivable mistake.

Without removing her glower from Pedro, Cyan loaded the Glock.

The clicking sound scared Pedro out of his seat, unlike earlier, when she met his sarcastic reaction after pointing her firearm. This time, she was dealing with the real deal. Never had she heard a grown man whimper so loudly, tears and snot running down his face. She must've really terrified him.

"Cy." a familiar voice called. Nathan.

She didn't dare remove her stare off of Pedro nor her foot off of Shayne.

"Cyan." Nathan called with more urgency. He became visible on her right side where he knelt cautiously.

"I'm going to remove your foot off of him now, okay?" Nathan said slowly as if he was attempting to calm down a dog that had his favourite shirt in its mouth.

She allowed him to remove her foot off of Shyane because the real problem was Pedro. Had he not sent Shayne to Aria, she would've been moving on two uninjured feet. It was all his fault that Aria couldn't walk. They were willing to cooperate with him but he couldn't help himself from doing something unspeakable. She was capable of that too.

Her right leg was no longer perched on Shayne. She heard him cough frantically and run out of the office.
"Cyan." Nathan called nervously. He appeared in her peripheral vision, right in front of her firearm.
"Put it down." Nathan muttered.
He put his hands on top of hers and slowly lowered the firearm. Scared she was going to set it off at him by mistake, she lowered it all the way down and allowed Nathan to take it away from her. He unloaded the firearm, took out all the bullets in one quick motion and placed it inside his button-down shirt where she had no access to it.
"Are you okay?" he asked her.
She wondered why he had posed that question considering she had taken down two men by herself with no scratch. It must've been the DEC in him to be hundred percent sure that the members in his team were always safe.
"Come on." he said as he led Cyan out of the office.
They walked back to the lounge and Nathan picked Cyan's purse off the floor, where she had thrown it, and put it on her shoulder. They pushed through the crowd in the lounge, down the stairs,

past the dancefloor and they were finally out of the club.
Cyan dragged herself to the two cars they had left in the club parking lot. Scanning the area, she spotted their team three cars from the right. Aria was in the backseat with her bruised foot in Preston hands. He knelt in front of her, analysing her puffy and inflamed ankle. Attentive to Preston's actions, everyone else stood close, keen to hear what Press would say.
Cyan and Nathan approached the first Ford, where all the girls and guys assembled, in time to hear Preston say, "This is a bimalleolar ankle fracture. Her fibula and tibia are both broken."
"I'll call Doc." Jordan sighed as he walked a few yards to make the phone call.
"Is Preston a doctor?" Cyan whispered to Nathan.
"Yes. But not a medical doctor. His IQ is outrageous so we just treat him like one." Nathan replied.
Cyan breathed a quiet laugh.
"What happened, Aria?" Preston asked nervously.
"One minute we were talking to you over the buds and the next we couldn't hear you. Jay, Will and I ran out here to find the car door open and empty of you."

"He just opened my door and dragged me out." Aria answered tiredly.
"Who? Pedro?" Preston asked.
"Shayne." Nathan answered.
"The pervert Cyan was flirting with at the bar?" William asked.
Hearing the words "Cyan", "flirt", "with", "pervert" in one sentence made Cyan shiver. She wanted to correct William about how wrong his statement was but she realized that it wasn't the time and plus, she didn't have the energy to go at it with him.
"Yeah, him." Aria drawled.
"Pedro sent him to hold Aria as leverage. That way, we wouldn't take him in for all the product he is selling." Evan answered.
"I wish you hadn't let him walk." Aria said quietly.
"Are you kidding me?" Harper asked. "That prick was going to blow your brains out."
"I was so scared." Aria trembled.
This was the first time she let out tears after the whole ordeal. Preston pulled her close to him and pecked her on her forehead. Aria rested her head on his chest and seemed to calm down with the patting motions he was soothing her with.
"It's going to be okay." Preston whispered to her.

"At least we have a place to look." Evan pointed out.
"Will you go to the diner, Ev?" Nathan asked.
A confused expression masked Evan's face.
"Where will you be?"
"The Directors' requested an audience with me." Nathan reported.
"Why do they want to see you?" Evan asked.
"They didn't say but they probably want an update." Nathan answered.
"Already?" Harper asked. "They assigned this case to us hours ago."
"This case is different to many we have worked. The protocols are different." Nathan explained.
"Oh. Alright then. We'll stay with Aria and go over 'George Campbell' aliases and his apparently untraceable prison records. There's no way he is a living breathing human without a single trace." Harper said.
"There's no such thing as the perfect criminal." Evan agreed.
Cyan heard heavy thumps on the tarred road to her right. It was Jordan.
"Doc is on the way." he announced.
"We should probably get going." Nathan suggested.

They all jumped in the cars, four in each, just as they had travelled. They were almost in the same order they came in except that Preston wanted to be with Aria so Cyan ended up in the car Nathan drove. She was quietly unhappy with this arrangement because she was embarrassed to be in more of his presence after what happened upstairs.

Going over the events that transpired less than fifteen minutes ago, Cyan realized she valued control more than anything, that it was strange losing it to her anger. Instead of calculating the consequences, like she usually did, she just acted. Oddly, it felt freeing. Though, almost killing two men reminded her why she had those precautionary measures set in the first place. When she lost herself, she had the tendency of going overboard. That was one of the reasons why she kept some parts of herself in a box. Tonight, Nathan had to put her back in which was agonizingly mortifying.

The embarrassment bulldozed her into the backseat that Jordan had opened for her where it permitted her to at least sit down while she went over her actions. William took his place in the driver's seat leaving Nathan in the back with her.

They had quite an eventful night. Her brain was too clogged with tiredness to overthink their sitting positions so she just let any awkwardness she might have created in her mind to evaporate like alcohol in a teenager's liver.
William started the car, backed out of the parking lot and drove out of the club gate with Harper tailing him, behind the wheel of the second car. They drove back to the woods in silence. Cyan guessed that no one was in the mood to chat, which was a win for her because her eyes were about to collapse and the silence was just the catalyst she needed. She unzipped her gripping, thigh-high boots and internally beamed at the women who made up D12 who didn't allow a stiletto to get in the way of an eventful operation. Exerting pressure on Shayne's neck dismantled the sole and bridge of Cyan's foot pushing her to pull off the heavy shoes and throw them under Jordan's seat. She also removed her coat, because William had increased the heat in the car, leaving her with just her slip-on dress. Comfortable enough to sit through an hour drive, Cyan put her right leg on top of the other, set her head on the window and gazed at the wonderful night. Or morning. She didn't know what to call the

darkness of 03:00a.m. She stared at the blank canvas that was the sky and realized that although their night had taken a sombre turn, given that Aria had been hurt, there was also a touch of zeal in the air. It sunk in that they had found another piece of the puzzle.
Without removing her eyes off of the hypnotic sky that moved faster than sound, Cyan gave into the enervation of the night, gradually closing her eyes so that it could take her.
Almost in the abyss, she felt a warm build slide closer to her and shift her own body from the window to a soft nape that smelt of sweet berry. She was glad that her neck was in a better position because she had a feeling she'd have to answer to its stiffness in a few hours.
The last thing she felt were two sturdy arms encircling and securing her, stroking her hair while she surrendered to the night of the morning.

7. FRANCE AND GENEVA

"This place lacks a certain...*je ne sais quoi*."
Cyan wanted nothing more than to stick a fork into her eardrums to deem her incapable of

listening to William's complaints about how dingy Rock In Diner was. Judging by Evan's eyeroll to William's critique, she was pretty sure that he was one *'je ne sais quoi'* away from borrowing her fork and stabbing his own ears with it.
"These seats don't have the right fluff." William complained. "If a rat tried to nibble on these, his little teeth would break."
"Rodents have incisors that grow continuously throughout their lives. So, you don't have to worry." Evan replied flatly. "The rodent will live."
The three Agents were in Rock In Diner, sitting in a booth; capacity made for four, waiting for the opportunity to ask one of the current owners a few questions about the diner and perhaps look around for some clues. They were following the lead Pedro had given them the night before and they anticipated to acquire useful information from it. Cyan truly hoped that they hadn't wasted a trip because then working with one of her teammates, who made it undoubtedly clear that she was a waste of good air, wouldn't have been for nothing.
"Have you experienced fine dining in France? It's so eye opening." William gushed.
Evan stared at William fixedly.

"If you loved your life in France so much, why did you move back here?" he asked curiously.
William closed his mouth and cleared his throat. His silence shook Cyan because she expected him to jump at the opportunity to tell them how much croissants were better than scones. He clearly had his own secrets regarding why he chose to return home and it appeared he didn't want to share them.
"I have my reasons." he responded curtly and averted his eye to one of the menus in front of them.
For the first time since they entered the diner, Cyan hadn't experienced a moment of peace due to William's smart and condescending comments. It took Evan's inquisitiveness to finally shut him up. Cyan wasn't sure whether he asked that question with the intention of clipping William's lips or he was just being nosy. Either way, it didn't matter to her. She was just relieved she didn't have to hear one more tale about his amazing life in France.
Cyan remembered what Aria and Harper told her about his family. Specifically, how wealthy they were. It made sense why William had so many expensive memories all over globe. He was used

to luxury that sitting in the eatery they were in was clearly asking a lot from him. Cyan couldn't help but notice that he fidgeted every time he subconsciously leaned back into his seat, wiped his jacket when his scrawny fingers accidentally nudged the dinner table and glared around the place with so much contempt. He obviously preferred the fancy feat where the meals had less grease and more zeroes on the bill. Cyan understood that people like William didn't have the gene to appreciate life in its simplest form. They were sitting inside a heaty restaurant with the noise of oil sizzling and the smell of fresh bread dancing in the air. He couldn't comprehend the quality, the way the diner resembled the aeon of the Roaring 20s where such diners thrived in that era of American history or the jukebox attached to the wall on their right, reverberating unrivalled rock music. Cyan wasn't familiar with the American culture but she had to admit that the street names and number plates pasted around the diner took her back to a time that was inexplicably familiar. It could've been the American classic she had watched recently. Hairspray, it was called. The inside of the diner

looked a lot like the diners of that movie explaining the strong case of déjà vu.
A few minutes after they finally received a moment of peace, an old woman suspending a smile from cheek to cheek, eagerly approached their table.
"Hi there! I have been instructed by our manager to offer you a free meal whilst you wait for him. " she informed. "Can I take your order?"
"French toast with three cream-stuffed cherries, please." William ordered automatically.
The waitress's eyes widened, stunned by William's request. Her expression asked if William was aware of the fact that he was in a fast-food restaurant where they didn't serve fancy breakfast delicacies. She probably wondered what cream-stuffed cherries were. Cyan wondered that herself.
The waitress decided to respond to William anyway because she knew she was obliged to.
"I'm sorry, hon. No toasts here." she replied in her Texan accent.
"I wake up to disappointment every day." William lamented dramatically.
"Can I get you a juicy burger instead?" the waitress asked optimistically.

"He is a vegetarian." Evan intervened. "Plain fries will do. And if you could minimize the oil in the deep-frying pan, that would be great."
Cyan did not want the way Evan understood William to amaze her but it did. As strangely as she perceived it, the scene before her was surprisingly a familiar sight. Evan's response was a mirror reaction to Cyan's whenever Janine made any unrealistic demands to the chef. She would cut Janine off and order for them both to prevent any embarrassment on Cyan's part. Once, the two girls visited a Bohemian restaurant in the city of Prague during their restaurant-hopping excursion. Janine ordered baked potatoes with Caesar salad, except, she asked the waiter to remove all the main ingredients that made up the salad and deliver just the lettuce and the dressing.
Cyan ended up ordering Spaghetti Bolognese for the both of them that evening.
Her heart sank a little when she remembered her adventures with J. They were texting last night but Cyan could really feel the absence of her presence though they had been away from each other for only a short time. She'd have to call her today and update thoroughly on the details she was allowed to fill her in on.

"What about you darlin'?" the waitress asked Cyan.
"Six buffalo wings, a double stacked burger with bacon and a plate of chilly fries with extra cheese." Cyan ordered.
"Drink?"
"A glass of water, please." Cyan replied.
'Comin' right up." the waitress said as she collected all the menus that were on their table.
Waiting until the waitress was out of hearing zone, Evan asked, "What do you think of this place?"
"Nice." Cyan answered while simultaneously looking around. "Cute place, really."
"Do you think trading happened here?" Evan asked sceptically. "The walls look weak. They have no proofing. How do you trade drugs when everyone on the other side can hear you?"
"Things have changed." William reasoned. "The diner is not the same as it was twenty years ago."
"There is a door right there, near the ordering counter." Cyan observed. "Any chance that anything took place down there?"
"We should check it out." Evan suggested.
"I'm willing to bet anything that there is absolutely nothing in that room." William

responded. "Twenty long years have passed. If there was anything in in there, it's not there anymore."
"We just sit?" Cyan asked.
"No. But it's unwise to place all our hope that there might be something behind it. We have to accept the possibility that this lead might take us nowhere." he answered.
"If we don't find anything in this diner then yesterday's charade was in vain." Cyan pointed out.
"Trauma sits comfortably in our Organisation. You could go through so much of it with nothing to show for it in the end." William replied.
William had described the last six months of Cyan's life as if he had watched her live it. She almost burst out into humourless laughter at how accurate he put it.
About to shape the words to respond to him, William's phone began to vibrate and he immediately picked it off the table.
William murmured to his phone, "Oh, I completely forgot."
"What's up?" Evan asked him.
"My dad is attending the ADM thing in Geneva today." he answered.

Evan's head jerked up. "What? That's today?"
"It's today." William answered in a matter-of-fact tone. "I know because I've been travelling to Switzerland with my dad for the last couple of years after my parents separated."
"That sucks." Evan said shortly.
Cyan internally face-palmed at Evan's pathetic attempt to sympathise with William. Evan wasn't cold at heart. She knew that. The only explanation she could sum up was that he couldn't express himself adequately in situations that demanded consolation. He grew quiet or replied with short, curt phases such as, "That sucks."
Assessing William, Cyan noticed that he didn't seem to be bothered. His eyes were on his phone, fingers typing rapidly. She guessed that he didn't need any cheering up. Pity wasn't an emotion he was trying to evoke. And boys had their own ways of showing emotion. She had just forgotten, being that she had been away from a full team in half a year.
"There you go!" a man's voice exclaimed.
Cyan traced the squeaky voice to a man with a pitch-black, oily mohawk standing on his head. He masterfully carried three plates on his right hand and balanced a tray with their drinks on his right.

When the upper half of his knees made contact with the edge of their table, he put the tray of drinks down. Cyan retrieved her water and took a sip of the iced H2O. Evan followed Cyan's lead and took his own glass of orange Fanta.
William didn't order a beverage so the waiter took out his fries first and guided the oval white plate in front of him. He pushed Cyan's meal in front of her and she helped him push Evan's burger to him since he was sitting further from the man that was distributing their meals. When the plates no longer obscured the man that brought their food, Cyan recognised that their waiter was a short, stout man. He wore a stained, burgundy shirt with black dress pants and brown, worn-out loafers. He threw the plastic tray that held their plates on an empty neighbouring table and forced himself on William's side of the booth. Because Will wasn't expecting the waiter to push his weight onto his side of the table, he lost his form and banged his head harshly on the hard wall. By the end of it all, the waiter was breathing heavily and William had developed a deep scowl on his face.
"You must be...?" Cyan asked as she struggled to contain her laughter.
The man tittered. "I'm Jack. Jack the Manager."

"The food looks amazing." Evan thanked.
Cyan's buffalo wings were dripping of thick barbecue sauce, sitting alongside her towering, toasted burger buns that sheltered two juicy patties, crispy, golden brown bacon strips, fresh lettuce and melted cheese. Her cheesy fries attempted to steal the spotlight with their crispiness as they accompanied her burger on the side.
She wasn't certain whether it was because she'd only had goulash and Czech dumplings for the last six months or perhaps it was the fact that her stomach was growling loud enough to disturb the other customers but she was compelled to devour her plate. Against every being in her body, she took an elegant bite of her burger and allowed the ecstasy to travel around in her system.
"I thought girls were supposed to eat small portions. Like, little salads with feta and unsalted chicken." William commented.
"Will!" Evan chastised, appalled.
"I'm just asking." William shrugged.
Once upon a time, Cyan would've taken offense to what he said. Being scrutinised over what was in her plate wasn't exactly a feeling she welcomed with open arms. But she learned to make peace

with her need for indulgence once in a while. If it was a crime to eat, then William might as well have dragged her out of the diner in handcuffs.

"So, Jack. We've already introduced ourselves earlier as the SS-

"Oh! Yeah, yeah!" Jack interjected excitedly. "I can't believe you're in my diner."

"Yes." Evan replied slowly. "We just wanted to ask you a few questions."

"You're the same guys who chased the London Lawbreaker on the bridge!" Jack exclaimed.

"No. Those were our other teammates from a different Div-"

"Wait! How about that homicide guy that was caught for killing 6 women? That was you too, wasn't it?" Jack asked.

"Yes." Evan answered. "But we-"

"I'm actually embarrassed to say this but I have always wanted to send my application to the Special Service." Jack laughed nervously. "But you know, since you are here..."

"We wouldn't recommend you to our Organisation even if all you had to do was fry meat and pour carbonated drinks into plastic cups." William commented flatly.

Jack regressed as if he had been slapped.

"Can we focus, please?" Evan asked. "Jack, we need to know about the person who owned this diner before you. Can you tell us about him?"
"Oh, yes. Of course." Jack complied. "It was owned by a Vietnamese couple before they sold it to me."
"Okay. And when this couple sold this place to you, did they tell you how the restaurant was sold to them?" Cyan asked.
"They gave me a brief history, yeah. But I mean, I was just ready to sign the papers and kick them out!" Jack chortled.
"What did they say to you?" William asked impatiently.
"That this place was empty when they first visited it. No one was running it. They could hear the crickets chirping." Jack responded. "They heard through the grapevine that this place was run by some boys who participated in illegal activities. That's why they found it empty after three years of abandonment. Phuong and Thanh said they saw something in it and were determined to fix it up."
"Phuong and Thanh didn't purchase the diner from anyone?" Evan asked.
"No. They found it empty and occupied the

place.'' Jack answered. ''They were always afraid that the original owners of this place would come back to either reclaim it or ask for their profits since the restaurant was doing so well. But no one ever came." Jack answered.
"No one at all in the last five years?" Evan asked.
"No one." Jack confirmed. "Phuong called this diner her miracle. That's why she sold it to me at a great price."
"Did Phuong and Thanh ever tell you exactly what they were told about the boys that ran the diner?" William asked.
Jack hesitated. "I don't know. It's a morbid topic."
"We really need to know." William emphasised.
"Drugs." Jack whispered. "A fight club apparently. And I think wizardry."
"Okay, maybe not the last one." Cyan discarded. "What was that about a fight club?"
"I don't know. I think it means men fighting in some club." Jack answered innocently.
"The owners invite customers interested in making serious money to place bets over the men who are to fight each other that night." Evan answered. "Similar to gambling. It makes a lot of money for whomever is hosting the fights."
Cyan scrutinised the door she had noticed earlier.

If the claim of a fight club was true, then an underground room would've been exactly what they used. The diner was a small space with tables bumping each other therefore they probably had more room for their extra activities.
"Have you ever been behind that door?" Cyan pointed.
"No." Jack answered shortly.
"In the time that you've owned this place, you've never tried to see what was behind it?" Cyan asked again.
Jack inhaled a quick breath. "No keys."
"So? You couldn't find other ways to open it?" William answered sceptically.
"No. I haven't owned this place long enough to want to know what's behind the door." Jack answered.
"Now, Jack." Cyan cooed. "Something tells me that you're not telling us the truth."
As soon as they met Jack, he was a ball of fiery energy. But when Cyan mentioned the door, he became unusually subdued. That change of behaviour in such a short space of time suggested to Cyan that he was being dishonest. Jack had, in fact, opened the door. And Cyan was sure that he had a little secret behind it.

Jack gulped. "I've already told you what I know, okay? Okay."
His flushed face told them the opposite. Cyan had never witnessed someone so terrible at lying. She didn't even have to put effort in reading him to know that he was evidently hiding something.
He attempted to slide his way out of the booth when William grabbed his thick arm before his loafers touched the floor.
"Sit down." Evan ordered chillingly.
Goosebumps formed on Jack's arm and he quickly slid back into his seat.
"What are you hiding?" William asked.
Jack began to sweat. And not metaphorically. Pools of liquid were spread out on his forehead, ready to roll down his temple.
"Uhm, well, that would be-"
"I suggest the next words that leave your mouth be the truth." William threatened.
He reached into his denim jacket and retrieved a silver key. It was one of the inventions that Shannon, who headed the Organisation's Technical Team, created over a year ago. William was so adamant that they would need it at some point on their trip and he was right. Evan didn't think it was necessary but to shut William up, he

just agreed that he take it. Cyan knew he was silently thanking William for suggesting to carry it in the first place. She was too.
"This is what we call a Universal Key." William began. "It has sensors inserted inside it that translate the dead bolt and lock buttons formation from any door structure to the metal of the key. I won't explain further because your feeble mind wouldn't be able to comprehend this meticulous creation. I'll just simply say that this key can open any door. Anywhere."
He pushed it towards Cyan and nodded towards the door.
Cyan stood up, claimed the key and readied herself to unlock the door when Jack's sweaty hand grabbed her arm to stop her.
"Okay, okay! I'll tell you what- what's inside!" Jack stammered.
"Too late." William declined. "I'd rather see it than hear it."
"Wait! I'll tell you! Please!" Jack exclaimed.
"Quit screaming." Evan scolded. "You'll frighten your customers."
The more he yelled, the tighter his grip was on Cyan. It just made her believe that whatever was behind that door was not something she was

looking forward to discovering. Was he running his own fight club? Was he running an illegal salon? Or perhaps, he was gambling. He looked like a gambler.
Evan removed Jack's wet hands off of her and she proceeded to the mysterious door near the wall. When she stood across the door, she aligned the silver key with the keyhole for it to decrypt the lock button formations in the door. The key emitted a blue light that scanned the components of the door and flew into the keyhole as if the two were magnetized to each other. The key slipped itself into the door and Cyan turned it once to the right. She turned it again in time to hear a clicking sound. She depressed the handle and pushed the door inward.
She cast a glance back to their table to confirm with the guys that she had successfully opened the door. They nodded back, telling her to continue, while they sat with Jack.
She inclined her head in agreement, pushed the door wider and put one foot in front of the other. Soon after she stepped into the room, she was viciously knocked aback by an atrocious stench that consumed the space she had just entered. She stopped breathing immediately before the

smell clogged her nose. She had never missed the heavenly smell of cooked beef and fries more than in that moment.

The room was dark but there was a spark of light that emanated a few feet from where she was standing. It came from a dim lamp hanging off the ceiling by a long, torn cord, illuminating the area very poorly. It was slowly swinging back and forth, eerily, as though there was a supernatural force pushing it from one direction to another. Directly under the light was a steel table with two shelves that resembled the medical worktables found in the hospitals. While nothing graced the company of the second shelf, an object similar to a short knife sat above it. Cyan squinted her eyes to discern what was situated on the table but without decipherable results because both the light and the table were a significant distance away from her. That, and she had left her glasses yet again.

She was standing on a platform that led to a flight of metal stairs. She worked out that the only way she could see better was to descend the stairs and walk over to the table hence, carefully placing her foot on the first step. Just as she thought, the

flight of stairs shook because of the extra weight added to the already unstable staircase.
Cyan composed herself and instead of climbing down the stairs by solely placing her weight on one side, she moved to the centre of the steps in order to balance the unstable set of stairs.
With both feet on the steps, she heard an ear-breaking screech from them, similar to talons gliding down a blackboard. Cyan decided to ignore it to focus on her journey downstairs.
Fourth step down out of nine steps, she realized that the screeching was all she could hear. The familiar laughter of customers and crying of babies was completely shut off from her. The restaurant noise was a distant memory and Cyan wondered if the walls were soundproofed.
Focusing on going down the eighth step without dropping herself in the process, Cyan gained more momentum, securing better vision of the little table and what was on it. With one stair left, she swiftly jumped off it, looked back at the rattling stairs for a few seconds and walked a few feet towards the table.
She reached her destination and recognized that the small knife that she had seen when she was on the platform of the stairs was a scalpel. A

scalpel? Seeing the medical knife and medical table instantly made her nervous. As resistant as she was, she knew that she had to unblock her nose to confirm her thoughts.

She breathed in. Her nose was filled up again by the revolting smell that claimed the air and she blocked her nose again. She attempted to breathe in through her mouth. But the image of swallowing fetid air with foul particles in it put a plug on the suggestion.

Cyan wanted to drag herself out of the basement. Why had she volunteered to do this?

She knew that if she needed to specifically identify what the smell in the room was to reveal what was in it then she had to allow her pathways to open and put the luxury of fresh air aside.

She breathed in once again.

Bleach.

Right way, that created a flutter of panic in Cyan's stomach. She knew what a choking amount of bleach meant; dead bodies. Thinking about the medical knife and the tragic dullness she was currently in; she was afraid that it all made a little too much sense for Jack to be a murderer. Feet planted on the stone floor, she dreaded going any further. She didn't know what she was going to find. There could've been an unknown lingering in the darkness. If she was to die down here, who was going to know?

With all these thoughts speeding like a race car, the voice in her head reminded her that she could handle it and if anything happened, the boys were upstairs.

She wanted to take a deep breath to brace herself but she understood that that wasn't an option so instead, she just scanned the underground place again.

To her left was another room. All that was visible to Cyan was a brick arch that contained a deep hole of darkness inside. She felt for her flashlight in her pockets to obtain a clear visual of what she was about to walk into. Tapping her jean pockets expectantly, Cyan couldn't feel any protuberances in her pants and she remembered that she had left it and her phone upstairs. She groaned at her mistake but realized that she had no other choice but to feel her way into the other room; which was the last thing she wanted to do considering she was the closest thing to a germophobe. She invited courage and dragged her feet to the brick wall that created an archway into the next room. She unwillingly placed both her hands on the wall

and began to move with it as her guide.
Six steps later, her right hand no longer felt any brick, revealing that she had reached the end of the wall. With an inch of a step, she set both her feet into the room. She couldn't see much of anything but she came to the conclusion that if she was fully in the room, her eyes would help her see what she couldn't have from afar.
She took a few more steps in.
The stench of bleach was stronger in this room as compared to the one she had left. And there was another scent intertwined with the bleach. Another strong, concentrated smell that she couldn't quite put her finger on.
Where exactly was she?
She felt around the wall for a switch of some kind. There had to be one somewhere here. Her hands searched the wall for something softer than brick. Hope kept her going until she reached the corner of the archway wall. Like a rogue painter creating an abstract piece, she waved her hands all over the wall for a light switch. Her fingers began to crack because of the friction her hands were experiencing with the brick but luckily, they had hit something hard with a smooth surface and she realized that she had found the light.

Before she flipped the switch, exhilaration to use her eyes again got the best of her and she bounced excitedly near the switch without thinking ahead of what might happen if she jumped around in the dark. That caused her to trip over an object she wasn't aware of and slamming her face into a hard surface. Her head spun from the impact but that wasn't nearly as staggering as the queer textures she tasted in her mouth. She coughed and splattered uncontrollably, what she thought were strands of hair, as if her life depended on it and attempted to steady herself by gripping onto the same hard surface that she bumped into for balance. For a nanosecond, she found her footing, and she was grateful to whatever she held onto because it gave her stability. However, she quickly let go because whatever was on the surface she held onto was pricking her palms and fingers. And it was also wet.

And warm.

Wait. Was it moving?

What on earth did she just...?

She tried to retreat briskly, back to the other room, but her behind bumped into yet another surface. The difference was that this surface

wasn't as hard as the first and it made a small noise once Cyan made contact.
Cyan jumped like she had been electrocuted by bolts of ferocious lightning and screamed the air out of her lungs. Her vision was now in line with the flicker of light in the first room and it allowed her to sprint back to the other room. Her heart was pounding hastily and for someone who claimed she wasn't easily scared by anything, she was quite disappointed in herself.
She didn't know what was in there. What she experienced was open to interpretation and in her opinion, that was a more petrifying predicament.
Cyan staggered back in efforts to leave the basement. Her feet pushed her towards the door in order to leave the basement. She walked with her back towards the stairs because she didn't want anything to sneak up on her while she was leaving. She realized that it was another bad idea among the few that she had made in the last fifteen minutes because she bumped into yet another hard surface.
She shrieked and hysterically smacked what she had snuck up on her.
"Cyan! It's me!" a male voice shouted.
She stopped to look at who it was and she felt a

relief so powerful that it overwhelmed her.
"Evan." she whispered as she put her head on his shoulder.
Evan scanned her to see if she had been injured in any way.
"I'm fine." Cyan noticed.
Evan acknowledged Cyan's response and let go of her arms. His nose scrunched up when the smell found a way into his nose and searched around the room. Cyan could tell that he was confused by what this place really was.
"Bleach?" Evan asked.
"Do you have your light?" Cyan asked.
He took out a small, black flashlight from his denim pocket and switched it on.
Besides the grey chapped and cracked walls with mould growing in them, there was nothing interesting to go over in the first room, so they moved into the second space to confront what had terrified Cyan.
They stepped into the room.
Cyan guided Evan's flashlight to her left where she attempted to feel for the switch. It was also the same area she had an unpleasant encounter with a hairy, mortifying creature.
Evan threw his light upon the unknown they were

trying to reveal.
Cyan gasped and took a step back.
"Is that...?" Evan breathed.
"I-uhm." Cyan stuttered. "You see that too, right?"
"Yeah." Evan answered slowly as he cocked his head to the side. "I'm afraid I do."
Evan's flashlight shed light on a thick, hairy man leaning against the graffitied wall with fear masking his chubby face. He wore a black waist coat, without anything else inside, revealing all the tattoos that covered his entire body from his neck to his chest and arms. Cyan couldn't tell their story, because they were overlapping onto each other, nor did she want to because she was still trying to wrap her head around the discoveries they had made. The hairy, mortifying character was indeed just a hairy man attempting to blend in with the wall.
Cyan remembered that there was another surface that she bumped into. She turned around and Evan turned around with her. The flashlight revealed a petite woman leaning against the painted wall, possessing luscious, black hair, multiple piercings on her face and jet-black lipstick. She wore a black jumpsuit, material resembling spandex and thick, black heels that

didn't belong in their current century. She also had tattoos on her face all the way to her arms, just like the man behind them. And just like him, Cyan didn't waste time trying to understand the art on her features because she was too stunned to believe that the creature that caused her soul to leave her body with fear was the small woman standing in front of her.
A thought occurred to Cyan that they might have been held in the basement against their will. But Cyan noticed their full, rosy cheeks, face covered in make-up, perfectly ironed clothes and disagreed with the thought. This was also aided by the chairs, stretcher tables, a few stencils, green soap, and different chemicals in little jars that surrounded them.
"Tattoo parlour." Cyan and Evan said simultaneously.
"Would you like one?" the man asked shyly.
"What? No." Evan replied in exasperation. "Owning a tattoo parlour underneath a restaurant is illegal and very unsanitary. Are you aware of this?"
"Jack wanted us here." the woman answered quietly.
"And you just allowed Jack to store you down

here? In the dark?" Evan grilled the tattoo artists. They both shrugged nonchalantly.
Cyan groaned. "Time to go."
They all left the brooding darkness that was the diner's basement and escorted Jack's illegal artists to one of the cars they had travelled in, waiting for LPD to arrive and take them to the station. Because a health code violated by the diner, Evan assigned Will to instruct all customers to stop eating immediately and clear out of the diner. They were all confused when William asked them to put their burgers and milkshakes down, as they had the right to be, but they all stood up calmly at the sound of Will's voice and created a calm stampede with all their belongings out the door. The plan was to clear out everyone before the LPD cruiser arrived to prevent panic. It seemed to work because within fifteen minutes, the tables that had been occupied by families, couples and friends were empty with only half-eaten food and half-full beverages as an indication of their presence some time before.
Evan stood by the car that confined Jack and the tattoo artists as a guard when they heard the familiar police siren shriek loudly as it drove into the diner's parking lot. Two men and a woman

jumped out of the vehicle; the man and the woman dressed in the police regalia and the other man in a swamp, green suit, holding a notebook, a rectangular recording device and an old-fashioned camera.
Evan opened the Ford door and officially handed the diner's management to the custody of the two officers, who squeezed all three of them at the back of their cruiser. Cyan couldn't make out much of what Evan was saying to the policeman and policewoman, due to staying behind in the diner, but she knew he was explaining what they saw underneath the restaurant to them. The man and woman seemed to understand, jumped in their cruiser and drove away.
Evan turned his attention to the third man who was still standing by the entrance and beckoned him to follow him inside the diner. The man followed behind Ev as he guided him to the door that had led Cyan and Evan to their strange discovery.
"As I told the officers, the manager was running an illegal tattoo business that is in violation of the Health and Safety Policies." Evan explained to him. "You'll find what you need down there."
The health inspector nodded, took out his

flashlight and stepped into the basement.
Once the health inspector was out of sight, Evan sat down at their booth, on the side that William sat before.
Cyan sat across from him.
"Can you believe we came here looking for George Campbell's past life but instead, we busted a diner manager and his illegal friends?" Cyan asked.
"I wish I had known that when we were driving all the way here to check permits." Evan said dryly. "Pedro's lead was a waste of time."
Straight away, Cyan's stomach caved in and her throat constricted. Nausea crept on her like a long, lost ghost and she felt the urge to vomit.
"Are you alright?" Evan asked worriedly.
"We ate in an unsanitary restaurant." Cyan heaved. "I mean, what if they tattooed the meat? I think I saw-"
"You didn't eat tattooed meat today." Evan clarified.
"Oh my." Cyan gasped. "What if we did?"
"Hey, hey. Relax. You didn't." Evan reassured.
Cyan leaned back into her seat with her face to the ceiling.
"Our day can't get weirder than this." she said.

Evan sighed. "I don't know. I think it can."
Intrigued, Cyan asked, "What do you mean?"
"I'm a little worried." Evan announced.
Cyan sat up.
"About what? Are you okay?" she asked.
"I'm fine." Evan answered.
Cyan stared at him expectantly.
"Have you noticed that Nathan has been acting...strangely lately?" Evan asked.
"I don't know how I would notice something like that considering I've only been in Leicester for less than two days." Cyan expressed.
"I just thought you would since you know..." Evan trailed off. "You know him very well."
"I didn't pick much. Why?" Cyan asked.
Evan took an uneven breath and looked at Cyan carefully, contemplating whether it was the right decision to let her into his mind.
He eventually gave in and broke the silence.
"I think Nathan is hiding something." he revealed. "Concerning the case."
Evan was right. He did find a way to make the day worse.
"What made you reach such a conclusion, Ev?" Cyan asked.
"I can just tell." Evan responded shortly.

Cyan scoffed. "You've got to give me more than that, Evan. What, like you're using your weird, supernatural best friend connection to tell whether he is sabotaging this case?"
"No. It means that I've known him for a very long time and noticing whenever he is being dishonest is as easy as wearing my badge and showing up to work every day." Evan retorted.
"Well, I know him too. And he would never do what you're accusing him of." Cyan returned.
"I'm not accusing him of anything." Evan responded with agitation in his voice. "But I noticed something. And I wouldn't be doing the team or the case any good by ignoring it."
"Let us assume that your allegations are true." Cyan said. "What have you seen that has confirmed them enough for you to tell me? Instinct can only take you so far."
"The date today. What's the date today?" Evan asked.
"Are you seriously changing the subject?" Cyan asked incredulously.
"I'm not." Evan refused. "What is the date today?"
"I don't know, Evan. October 23rd?" Cyan answered in frustration.
"It's October 22." Evan corrected.

Cyan expected more information after that but Evan remained silent and eyed Cyan.
Waiting for something more concrete from him, Cyan registered that Evan's silence was to provide enough room for Cyan to catch on to what he was thinking. He hadn't asked his question casually because he already knew the answer. He had asked to evoke a certain memory in her. The only problem was that Cyan was still beyond clueless to what Evan wanted her to know.
"It's October 22. And?" Cyan asked.
"Nathan has been unusually talkative, which is strange as you know, because he has a pensive personality." Evan explained.
Cyan sighed. "He does that when he is lying. He uses that as a counterbalance so that no one notices that he is not being honest. At least that's what he thinks it does."
"And yesterday. He was more than willing to sacrifice his reputation to find out more information from Pedro. That is not a decision he'd make if it meant creating a domino effect for his team."
"I noticed that too." Cyan responded reflectively. "He knows that the Organisation is strict about that kind of thing."

"And in the parking lot, he told us that the Directors' requested an audience with him." Evan recalled.
"Yeah, he said that such cases have different protocols. Or something like that."
"Think back to the date, Cy. What is today?" Evan asked intensely.
She began to think harder. The date was familiar yes, but she couldn't quite put her finger on it. She knew it had something to do with SSU's cultures and traditions but every time she tried to remember; the thought slipped away like water in her palms.
In an instant, her mind transported to her memories earlier in their day, when William told them about where his dad was today. The meeting in Geneva. And swiftly, her memories of the day-long holiday were suddenly unlocked and the pieces fell into their places.
"Today is the ADM." Cyan remembered. "The Annual Director's Meeting. All the Directors from all the SSU branches meet today for a yearly debrief."
Evan remained silent while Cyan figured it out.
"Nathan told us the Directors wanted to see him today." Cyan put together. "But if they are all in

Geneva..."
She didn't want to finish that sentence. That would only make Nathan's actions real and true. And she didn't want to think that he was insane to do anything insanely stupid.
But he was already doing something insanely stupid by lying about his whereabouts. Either he knew what he was doing or he was genuinely unaware that his lie to visit the Directors today clashed with the fact that they weren't in the country.
"He wouldn't ever sabotage this case." Evan defended.
"I don't want to believe he is." Cyan said.
"I think he is trying to solve it. But there is a force stronger than our mandate that is pushing him to crack it no matter the cost." Evan said. "Until we find out what that is, no one can know."
Before Evan finished his sentence, the opaque diner door swung open and a flustered William walked through, swiping his hands together due to the freezing weather.
"Know what?" he asked as he sat himself down on his side of the booth, next to Evan.
Cyan and Evan were quiet for a minute. They couldn't tell William their findings because that

would distract him and their other teammates that he would've told from their main operation.
"Jordan has been sneaking tequila shots into his room in the middle of the night." Evan blurted.
"What?" William gawked. "The footsteps I hear in the middle of the night are his? I don't have a sleeping schedule anymore because of him?"
"What? Jay?" Cyan gasped with sufficient amount of exaggeration to make Evan's lie believable.
"Uhm, yeah." Evan replied.
"It's about time something is done about it." William suggested firmly. "We can't have a drunkard and a sleep-disturber on this team."
"Well, uhm, what is your plan?" Evan asked curiously.
"Do you know where he keeps his stash? We could just take it all out and throw it all away." William said.
"Probably in a secret compartment." Cyan chortled. "I don't think you'll ever find it."
Cyan's words left William stunned and breathless for a minute. His small eyes narrowed and his eyebrows furrowed downwards, deep in thought. Cyan wasn't sure what she had said that provoked William to thought but she instantly regretted she did. She understood that if William took Evan's lie

too seriously, peace would only be a term they knew only the definition of and so, Cyan urged Evan with her eyes to do something before William came up with a destructive decision to confront Jay about the alcohol shots he didn't have.
"Say that again." William instructed.
"Say what?" Cyan responded confusedly. "That you'll never find Jay's stash?"
"No." William mumbled. "About the secret comp-"
Without warning, William took out a small knife from his denim pocket, stood up and stabbed the leather cushion he was sitting on with Evan. With it, he tore the cotton right out their booth seat.
"Dude!" Evan yelled. "What the hell? I'm still sitting here!"
"Move, then!" William yelled back.
Evan, annoyed, pushed past William and went to stand near Cyan's side of the booth.
"Man, stop! You can't go ripping out every chair that irritates you just because it's not soft enough!" Evan reprimanded.
William didn't reply to that. Instead, he continued vandalising the seat and when he removed all the cotton out of it, he threw his knife onto the table. He stepped out of the booth and knelt on its right

side, analysing it profusely. He put his hands underneath the red seat, hands moving aggressively, feeling for something. Almost immediately, his hands stopped and he looked towards Cyan and Evan with his eyeballs halfway out of their sockets. He began to feel again and stopped once more.

He stood up again and knelt in front of the seat. He put both his hands on either side of the booth and pushed it backwards.

The seat moved.

William then pulled it back towards him and pushed it upwards. The upper cushion was separated from the wood that stabilized it and within the seat, was an empty space, similar to a box.

Cyan exchanged stupefied stares with the two boys. Evan walked toward the box seat, kicking all the cotton out of his way with Cyan following closely behind.

"How did you-?" Evan asked.

"My friend and I used to hide each other's game buddies in such chairs back in France." William explained. "When Cyan said the words "secret compartment", it unlocked a memory."

Cyan took a look inside the seat that was also a

box. She didn't know what she was expecting to find but she knew she wanted to see more than an empty container. There was nothing in it except a small piece of tattered paper.

"Come closer." William instructed.

Cyan listened and dropped her height to kneel next to him while Evan bent his knees to see more clearly. William pointed to a large marking in the centre of the box that Cyan hadn't seen when she was still standing.

"Marking." he noted.

Markings were carved all around the chest with different drawings, just like a vandalised toilet door. But Cyan's eyes rested on the large marking that William's finger pointed at.

"TS+GC+CJ." William read.

"What is that supposed to mean?" Cyan asked.

"Initials." Evan answered. "What's that?"

Evan asked his question referring to the piece of paper that Cyan had noticed earlier.

She picked it up. It was torn and tattered so she willed her fingers to handle it delicately. Opening it, she noticed that it was indeed a photograph, worn out by the years of entrapment. A photograph of three young, handsome boys, who sat in the very booth that they had destroyed,

smiling at the camera. The boy at the left was the only one who wasn't smiling because his attention was captured by his two friends, eyes full love and affection.
Cyan held the photo up close to her eyes.
"Are these the boys that owned the diner?" Cyan asked.
"That's the only explanation that makes sense." William replied.
"Well, these boys look very familiar." Cyan deduced.
"Let me see that." Evan said as he took the photograph from Cyan.
Within seconds of having the photograph, he developed the same expression William had before he took out the knife from his pocket.
"I don't know if I'm-I'm seeing right." Evan stammered in a low voice.
William registered Evan's voice and remained silent. Cyan could tell that he was nervous about what Evan was about to say just as she was.
"The boy on the right," Evan pointed. "That's Director Swat, isn't it?"
"What?" William exclaimed.
He snatched the photograph from Evan and tried to match the resemblance from the pre-existing

forty-year-old Director that was engraved in his brain. He examined the photograph as if he was going over answers for a spot test.
"You've got to be kidding me." he whispered.
Cyan took the picture from William to see for herself. She thoroughly scanned the boy at the right.
That was Director Thomas Swat. One of the most important figures on their Special Services Organisation Director's board. Unlike all the Directors who were difficult to approach, he was always the easiest. Time was the one thing that he gave freely to all the soldiers that sought him, making him the Divisions' favourite official. It was strange seeing him again, especially 20 years younger on a worn photograph, underneath a red, leather seat. Confusion was beyond what Cyan's mind was experiencing.
She switched her attention to the next boy who was in the middle. His eyes were bright and his straight teeth were out on full display. She immediately recognized who he was. It was the same smile that she saw on the photograph that Dave showed her back when they were still at Retro Café in Prague. These were the same pearly whites that she had seen two days ago.

"It *is* him." Cyan surmised quietly.
"Whoa. I can't believe that that is Director Swat." Evan breathed.
"No. I mean, yes. The boy to the left is Director Swat." Cyan blubbered. "But the boy in the middle. I recognize him. That's Minister Clement James."
Stunned to silence by the revelation, the only noise Cyan could hear was the sound of the busy roads outside. The two boys beside her couldn't form the words to accurately respond to what had been discovered.
"So, the boy on the far left is-" Evan began.
"TS+GC+CJ." William repeated. "GC."
"The boy on the far left is...George Campbell?" Evan asked incredulously.
"It looks that way." William responded.
"They were all friends?" Evan asked.
"Are they still?" William asked.
"Considering that George had Clement's son abducted, I'd express a hard no." Evan responded.
Cyan huffed. "Then what happened between them?"

8. REVELATION

Commander Joseph Alexander Henly was the First Field Marshal of the Special Services Unit in the year 1993. He worked in the Leicester Police Department for 10 satisfying years before he came to the realization that conforming to a corrupt system was not how he planned to live the rest of his life. His passions and desires to make the world a better place were misplaced in the five-storey building, ushering him to quit the force and start his own. He didn't have any capital or support from the city of London but financial security was nothing compared to the life-sized dreams he was favoured with. He persevered and drew up the first SSU building plan in the month of February, months after he resigned. He completed the building in the month of December, enjoying the fruits of his labour with his family during the popular holiday. He encouraged his old partners from the LPD to join him create a muscle that would serve and protect their people. Because as a team, they rose like an eagle with nothing but strength and determination.

Or could it have been, as a team they conquered everything with the power and determination of the eagle?
Nathan couldn't remember how the tale went. They were taught to memorize the story of Joseph Alexander Henly in the first month of their Academic year to help them understand their SSU history. Joseph-Alexander was a hero. Without him, soldiers all around the world wouldn't have had the honour of wearing the SSU badge. Without him, the eradication of high crime rate in the entire world wouldn't have been possible. Without him, the world wouldn't have been a safer place.
Nathan ridiculed the fairy-tale just as he did when heard it in his first class. Their First Field Marshal was portrayed as the perfect manual for what an SSU Agent was supposed to be. An unrealistic character imposed on them with no real background about his life. He was sure that Commander Joseph's accomplishments were all prodigious and extraordinary but there had to be more than that about him. Nathan remembered asking one of his seniors if there was real story

behind Joseph Alexander. His many accolades must've come with an experience.
Conrad relayed that from what he was told by his own Supervisor, Commander Henly went through pain and suffering that surpassed the satisfaction the edifice brought, which to Nathan, was an accurate representation of any passionate officer building a force from the ground with nothing but will and faith. He also told Nathan that Commander Joseph's black and blue eagle, Diamond, was his wise council. He managed to overcome all that was thrown at him because he emulated how fierce and determined Diamond was. She taught him her ways.
Staring at Commander Joseph-Alexander Henley, who had been moulded into a tower of bronze, Nathan mused at what he had achieved amidst all that he went through. He managed to tackle his difficulties and push for one of the greatest police forces in the world. One Nathan couldn't be prouder to be a part of. He couldn't imagine the brand of strength he possessed.
He wished it for himself.

Nathan was not at the Headquarters. The Directors did not summon him. As it happened, he was, in reality, at the Academy looking for a very important paper that would link most of the dots to a few questions he had. He could've told his friends what he was planning on doing but if he was caught sneaking into the offices of the higher-ups, he didn't want any of them to go down with him.

His plan of action was simple. Today was the Annual Director's Meeting, meaning, Headquarters and the Academy were almost empty. Students were given a holiday because most Supervisors accompanied the Directors to Geneva, leaving the cleaning staff and a few Distress Gatekeepers behind to hold down the fort in case there were any emergency calls. All he had to do was sneak into Donna's office, quickly scan it for what he was looking for, collect it and leave the school without being spotted.

And that was it. That was his plan. Simple like extracting lemon juice from a very juicy lemon. He felt quite confident about it. He just wasn't sure why his palms were so sweaty and why his shoes suddenly fell a size down, gripping his feet to the ground. He was stuck in the corridor of the pink flowering trees, allowing the falling blooms to use him as a transit until they reached their final destination. Perhaps, they were punishing him. They were well within their right. He was a Division-Expert-Chief, for crying out loud. As an alternative to acting like a stranger and sneaking into his second home, he could just talk to Donna and request for what he needed. He knew she would always help.

Except, he didn't want to have to explain anything to her. He wanted to figure this out alone, making his first plan the only viable one.

Nathan gathered himself, shook off any doubts or any fear of the consequences and willed himself to take the first step.

Before he could execute is plan, two young boys walking towards each other in his direct line of vision near the first castle interrupted him. He immediately took cover behind the giant trees so as not to be picked out. So far, no one knew he was here and he wanted to keep it that way.

"This assignment is killing my will to live." the first boy groaned.
"That's too bad. Sent and delivered on my end." the second boy boasted.
"Congratulations." the first boy replied flatly.
"I could help, you know." the second boy proposed. "For a price."
The first boy suddenly showed interest. "What do you need?"
The second boy blushed. "I like Lisa. And I know you two are quite close. So, I was hoping you could put in a good word for me."
"I can do that." the first boy agreed.
"Do it today because I have plans of sneaking into the girls' dormitory tonight while Miss Donna is away in Switzerland." the second boy said excitedly. "I want to give Lisa the poem I wrote for her."
"A poem, Oliver? You're so whipped." the first boy teased.
"Whatever, Noah." Oliver dismissed. "Do it and I'll help you."

"Fine." Noah responded. "But we have to go to the cafeteria first. I want to grab one of those Belgium chocolates they store in the pantry."
"You know those are kept for the teachers, right?" Oliver replied.
"I'm aware." Noah replied.
"Alright, then. Let's go." Oliver ushered.
And by that remark, the two boys ran excitedly in the direction of the second castle on the far side of the school to look for chocolates. Nathan was glad that he witnessed their little exchange because they released a piece of vital information that worked wonders for his benefit.
Donna wasn't around. That meant Nathan could get in and out without the fear of being caught by her. That gave him enough confidence to take the first step towards the grandiose building that rested between the two castles that flanked it. Through the closed shutters, he could tell that the activity inside was quite low which urged him to open the transparent door and walk in assertively. The central building between the two castles was an immense infrastructure for the academics explaining its skyscraper nature. In the room he

was currently in, there was a long aisle in the middle that led to a grand stairwell that parted after two flights, winding into two different directions to the classrooms. Four tables were on either side of the long aisle with desktops, scattered stationery, phones and files of each student perched on them. On each desk, a receptionist would be present, handling the daily running of the school.

He was silently grateful that the hall was empty because the last person he wanted to explain his presence to was the school receptionist.

He focused his attention to the bank of grey elevators on his right that extended from the foyer area to the beginning of the staircase. He walked toward the middle elevator and pressed the button that would take him upstairs.

A nostalgic thought entered his mind the minute he did so. It was in his first and second Academic year that their professors strictly instructed them not to use the elevators when going up to the classrooms but to use the stairs instead. That way, they would secure a fair distribution of blood circulation for extra energy in order to participate effectively in their lessons. Growing up and learning the small Organisation secrets, Nathan realized that that wasn't the reason. The real reason professors didn't want students to use the elevators was because they didn't want to share them with noisy and sweaty teenagers.

The elevator doors opened.

Nathan stepped in and pressed the circle with the number thirty engraved on it.

The elevator doors closed.

That was the essence of growing up, Nathan supposed. You didn't understand a plethora of affairs when you were younger. But as you grew older and had your fair share of the experiences, the fog cleared up and you saw a little better. One of the prime examples of this change in his life was realizing that his grandmother kept secrets from him. He was an Agent-in-training and one of its main lessons was learning how to sniff out suspicious behaviour. It didn't hurt that Nan was his closest family, making it easier to pick on certain habits she exhibited when she thought he wasn't aware.

Nathan always thought it was strange how she would catch the dawn to collect the mail outside and take it to her room. Nan was not getting any younger and Grandad had passed. She had hired helpers to do almost everything for her but every time the mail came in, she managed to lift herself off her bed very early in the morning, subject herself to the implacable weather outside and collect the mail. He didn't think much of it until when he was at the age of nineteen, one of his Directors showed up to his house unannounced to have a chat with his grandmother. At first, he thought that the Director wanted to talk to his grandmother about his revolting behaviour outside class. He had had a steamy make out session with one of the youngest teachers in her office before one of the Supervisors walked in on them. Therefore, he almost wet his pants thinking that his actions had given him the axe. But it didn't seem right that one of the highest-ranking officials of their whole Organisation would visit his home for an issue so beneath him. To find out what Director Swat truly wanted, Nathan stood where none of them could see him. He knew it

was wrong but there was no other way to find out what was really going on.
The adults exchanged pleasantries and Nan pulled out the letters she had collected that morning from her suit pocket.
On three occasions, Director Thomas Swat showed up to his home to have a "chat" with Nan. And on all three occasions, Nathan wondered the kind of chat they claimed to have without any meaningful words exchanged. It was enough to pique his interest and he attempted to find out more.
A few weeks before he graduated from the Academy, he visited home to see his Nan. When he arrived, he called for her until Betra, her helper, explained that she left for the market with her friend, Sally. He figured it was the perfect opportunity to check her bedroom, for his peace of mind. He would casually look over some of her things to see if she was hiding anything from him. Maybe, he'd find some of those letters she hogged. If he could read one of them, he'd understand what the meetings with his Director were all about.

When he walked into her enormous room, he didn't have to trash the place to look for a clue as to what it was that she was hiding. On her wooden headboard, a stack of letters addressed to Nathan from a "GC" were perched neatly against the wall. She must've collected them that morning.
He didn't have a chance to grab any of them because only seconds after he had laid eyes on the letters, his Nan erupted into the room with so much excitement to see him after the months he had been gone.
Hearing the name, George Campbell from Pedro the night before lit a bulb in him so bright that it blinded him from the inside. The letters were always at the back of his mind and he couldn't help but believe there was a correlation between the sender and the man Pedro described, however weak.
Visiting the Directors was a lie that he had made up on the spot in the parking lot so as not to explain his crazy, almost unreal, theory. His own friends wouldn't believe him. There were a bunch of letters that his old grandmother gave to one of

his Directors almost three years ago. Envelopes that could possibly have held a cheque that helped maintain and improve the school.
If he was going to get it wrong, then he'd do it without anyone knowing. Though, he had a strong feeling that it was more than just a long shot because he always trusted his instincts.
The elevator doors slid open to the thirtieth floor and his sketchers made contact with the black and white chessboard floor. This part of the building was completely different from the plain section downstairs. This area was reserved for Directors who preferred to work directly with students. Thick arches stood on both sides of the corridor walls, built around the windows that overlooked the castles, depending on where you were looking from. Every five metres, there was a sophisticated chandelier attached to the ceiling that added a certain importance. Nathan quietly moved down the corridor, passing the lamps that were attached to both sides of the walls and the immaculate design of the cream paint. He counted four doors on his right and reached a shiny, oak door with a golden knob.

He took out an L-shaped metal bar with a hexagonal head out of his jean-pocket and one of the girls' bobbies pins he found lying on the kitchen counter. He placed the shorter end of the wrench on the lower part of the keyhole and turned it to the right. With the wrench in place, he inserted the bobby pin a few inches above to pick the lock. He gently pushed the bobby pin backwards and then upwards to unlock the door.
The door didn't open.
He took a breath and tried again. He applied more pressure to the bobby pin this time and moved it in circular motions.
The door still didn't open.
He applied more pressure to both the wrench and bobby pin hoping the pin wouldn't break from all the force he was applying to it. Before Nathan could think about finding another solution to opening the door, he heard a click. He turned the golden knob to the right and the door unbolted.
He let out a breath of relief and made sure no one was in the corridor so as to briskly step in the office without being noticed. He quietly closed the

door behind him and faced the cosmic task that was ahead of him.
The office's regular and clean space made it very simple to search for what he wanted without any difficulty, pacing his pounding heartbeat.
Where was he to start?
He went around to the giant desk and dragged the drawers open as quickly but as quietly as he could. He didn't see any white envelopes in any of them except a half-full bottle of whiskey in the last one. He rummaged on the desk; underneath the calendar that acted like a blanket for the desk, the stationery, the files with the SSU eagle on them and underneath the telephone.
There was nothing.
A file cabinet was adjacent to the desk. He went through its cases searching for a white envelope with his name on it. He couldn't find anything except more SSU files with Diamond stamped on them. There was a bookshelf near the door and he ran across the room to check there. He approached it but his hands froze. There were so many books; from John Milton, Charles Dickens and F. Scott Fitzgerald, similar to the collection

that he had displayed back in their own debrief room. His hands went through the books, opening them briefly, shaking them for an envelope to fall out. None of the books or the shelf surfaces he had checked had given him a single hint as to where he could find the letters so he moved on to the couch. He bent his large fingers, morphing them into the right size to fit into the crannies of the couch for any piece of paper.

Nothing.

He checked under the couch.

There was nothing.

Exasperated, he turned back to the desk hoping to have missed something on it. He then noticed the large screen attached to the wall behind the desk that he hadn't seen when he walked in. He ran towards it and felt for anything that remotely resembled a piece of paper. He didn't know what he expected to find in a television screen hammered to the wall but he just wanted to try. Of course, he was met with nothing but a bunch of wires.

When he reached the conclusion that the search was making him delusional, he took a breath and

scanned the room. Something he should've done as soon as he stepped into the office. He caught a glimpse of the screens, the desk, the file cabinet near the window, the shelf stacked with books, the couch against the wall and chair sitting at the back of the room against the door.
The door.
The door he was directly facing was a different door from the one he entered with. It was painted a dark silver that blended in with the walls, which explained why he hadn't seen it in as soon as he walked in. His heart began to pound. The possibility of finding something excited him.
His tall legs guided him to the door and he removed the chair that was blocking it and put it aside. He took out his L-bar wrench from his jean pocket and felt for his bobby pin.
He couldn't feel it.
He pushed deeper into his pockets to see if it was hiding in the nooks and crevices of his cotton pocket and when he still felt nothing, he searched for it on the floor. It would make sense if it had fallen. He bent his knees to have stronger eyes on the floor and swiftly surveyed the area around

him for the tiny black pin. As hard as he squinted, he couldn't find it. He then surmised that he could've left it at the door. He felt relieved because he knew it was the most probable place he could've left it. Returning to his normal height with a lighter heart, he turned around in the direction of the front door to go and collect the bobby pin.

Nathan’s relief was short-lived when he came face to face with a tall, pale woman. Her dirty blonde hair flew around her face with just a few strands to create the bangs that covered her forehead. She wore high shoes with a pair of ripped jeans and a tank top. Her red-painted lips were curled upwards with scorn while her drawn eyebrows furrowed downwards with confusion and anger.

"What are you doing in my uncle's office?" she asked.

Nathan's breath was stuck in his throat. Up until this moment, he had calculated his steps carefully. Everything had gone well and no one had spotted him. Just when he was so close, he was caught with the gun in his hand.

"Donna, it's not what you think." Nathan said as he tried to maintain a cool stance. Wasn't Donna supposed to be away in Geneva? Nathan mentally kicked himself for listening to those two boys instead of finding out if she was really gone for himself.
"Really?" Donna scrutinised. "Because from where I am standing, it looks like you're snooping through my stuff."
"I just wanted to see you." Nathan lied. "So, I just waited in... here."
Donna chuckled humourlessly. "You could never lie to me even if you tried your absolute hardest, Caldwell. Plus, my picked lock is telling a story of its own."
"The perks of growing up together, huh." Nathan sighed.
One of the reasons he didn't want to approach Donna about what he needed was because she knew him too well. His Nan and her mother were close friends and in turn, they became friends themselves. They ended up attending the same military Academy and graduated in the same year. He had known her half his life which should've

reminded him that Donna would rather throw herself in a shopping spree on her day off rather than go to an annual meeting with a bunch of old dudes.

"Sit." Donna ordered.

Nathan was taken aback that Donna wasn't more upset with him than she should've been but he just listened to her and sat down. She put her shopping bags down and sat on the chair across from his. She opened the last drawer, took out the bottle of whiskey he had seen earlier and two glasses in a compartment under the desk that he hadn't known existed.

"You keep alcohol in your office?" Nathan scolded.

"You don't?" Donna asked curiously.

"Donna-"

"Quiet." she ordered.

As Division Expert Chief, he had become accustomed to take orders and not to receive them. That was why sitting across from Donna annoyed him extremely. But he wasn't sure why he was surprised. Those were the dynamics of their whole relationship. She talked, he listened.

And besides, he did sneak into her office. The least he could've done was indulge her until he felt less guilty.
The sound of a calm waterfall projected into the room. Donna poured that whiskey into the two different glasses. She poured more into one of them and pushed it gently across the desk to Nathan.
He glanced at it and back at Donna.
"Go ahead." she suggested.
"No." Nathan refused. "I'm on duty.
"Well." Donna uttered and took a sip of her own glass.
With the couple of days he was having, Nathan supposed taking one sip wouldn't hurt. He lifted the glass and introduced it to his lips. He allowed the room-temperature Scotch penetrate his lips and flow down his system. He took another sip. And another. And another until he eventually took the last gulp and emptied the glass. Donna poured more whiskey into his glass and this time, he devoured the whole glass in one swig.
"Now, do you want to tell me what's bothering you?" Donna asked.

"No." Nathan responded curtly.
"Nathan-"
"Don. I don't want to talk about it." he asserted.
"Fine." Donna sighed. "Will you at least tell me what it is you invaded my space for?"
Nathan contemplated on whether to tell her or to continue the search of the letters on his own. He realized that he couldn't go far without Donna's help, being, she knew where everything was in this office. So, he ended up telling her what he was looking for. He vaguely explained why he needed what he needed, why it was such a matter of importance all the while profusely apologizing for sneaking into her office. After internalizing Nathan's information, she stood up from her chair and strutted to the door that Nathan tried to open before Donna caught her. She took out a small key from the back pocket of her denims and placed it in the keyhole.
The door squealed open and she walked into the room. Nathan had no idea what was behind it, whether it was a basement or a secret passageway that led upstairs because the second Donna walked in, she slammed the door behind

her. He could hear a lot of boxes being thrown aside and he assumed that it was some kind of a storeroom.

Approximately two minutes later, Donna came out holding a medium sized box.

Nathan sat up.

Donna threw it on the table, appropriately in the centre between the two of them and threw herself back on the swirly seat behind her desk.

Nathan keenly opened the box to find stationery, little toy cars, SSU guideline books and files with the name "SWAT" stamped on them. He took everything out of the box while Donna opened each file to see if there were any letters pushed inside.

Nathan was about to empty the box when he heard Donna read, *"To Annie Caldwell."*

He immediately stopped what he was doing and stared at the familiar white envelope that was in-between Donna's tattooed, ring-filled fingers.

Some part of him didn't expect to find anything when he began this search. But some part of him knew he had to try. He was glad that he listened to the latter conscience.

Donna handed it to him and he eagerly took it from her. He checked the back to double check if he had the initials right of the first letter he saw. GC.

Opening the letter, he had no guesses as to what he would find. Or what it would say. Or reasons why his grandmother would hide letters and hand them over to Director Swat.

He removed the prison stamp that sealed the opening of the letter and took the folded paper out.

He unfolded it.

Empty. The envelope was emptier than Jordan's brain when he was asked to name all fifty American states.

"Where the hell is the letter?" Nathan asked, agitated.

"M-maybe Uncle took it? Or your Nan gave Unc an empty envelope." Donna stammered, confused herself.

"This is such bull!" Nathan bellowed. He dug his hand into his silky hair. "You mean to tell me that I held on to the idea of these letters, lied to my

Division and drove to London just to open an empty envelope?"
"Nathan, chill." Donna calmed. "You said there were letters, with an s, right? Meaning, there has to be another one somewhere around here."
Nathan exasperatedly threw the envelope on the table and joined Donna in the search for the other one.
If it was even there. The idea of the author of these letters being connected to the same guy Pedro described last night was fading away like a good dream. Maybe it was a long shot. Not maybe. It was definitely a long shot. What was he even thinking? It was as if he was led by an amateur version of himself that never thought things through before executing his plans.
Though he was close to resigning this search, he wouldn't have forgiven himself if he hadn't seen it to the end. That was why he still continued to look through the files until he reached the end the box. His hands felt for something.
A folded paper.
The reason they hadn't seen it was because it was hidden underneath one of the box's flaps, folded

in quarters for it to fit. It was intentionally hidden. Nathan pulled it out to see a crumbled and creased envelope that had been evidently opened and refolded many times.
It was addressed to Thomas Swat. Nathan's heart sank and felt intrigue simultaneously. None of the letters they had found were addressed to him. He wondered if he saw visions the day he snooped in his grandmother's room and found a letter addressed to him on top of a stack of other letters. But he decided that it didn't matter now considering he couldn't find them anywhere. He was currently concerned about the letter addressed to Director Thomas from this GC character. He prayed with all his might that all he had done wasn't in vain.
"This letter is addressed to your uncle." Nathan informed Donna.
Her head jerked up from the files it was submerged in. Confusion and dread were the only emotions masked on her face. She swallowed hard and shook her head.
"Open it." she instructed.

Nathan's phone made a ping noise within his bomber jacket indicating a message. He ignored it and focused on unwrapping the letter that had been squashed by all files imaginable without ripping it. He managed to straighten the envelope enough to pull out the note that was inside it. He unfolded the A4, lined paper to see a letter with words that stretched across the page from the top to the bottom. Nathan noticed that first half of the letter was written in soft, cursive letters as compared to the second half of the letter that was written abrasively.

He began to read:

"Dear Thomy,

It has been a while.

You no longer visit me.

I understand. You are a busy man. Your Organisation doesn't run itself, I guess.

I would wish to see you again and talk things through. Perhaps, I would see matters from your perspective and understand why you and CJ left me to rot in this dump.

It takes me back to the days we owned the diner. To the days the world belonged to us. You, CJ, and

me. I always believed we could do anything and everything we set our minds to.
And we did. The diner was a success for many reasons, a few of them being your amazing cooking and planning skillset, the other being my economic background and CJ's charm to invite new diners.
Those were admittedly the best years of my life. And I think about those days a lot. Because there is nothing fiercer than our memories that allow me to escape the darkness that constantly chases me. And I find myself begging my mind to transport me to the days when we were just boys, to give myself a break from reality.
Sometimes I smell your ravioli and at other times, I hear CJ's laugh.
The silence that follows reminds me that I'm all alone.
I mean, we didn't see eye to eye but you've never once come to visit.
It's futile to even write this letter because I know you will not respond, just as you have the past twenty letters. But may this one serve as a reminder of just how much how much you

betrayed and let me down. I would write the same letters to CJ, if only the thought of merely writing his name down did not make me physically sick. Prepare to see me. And, to possibly hate me.
With all the love in the world,
Geo."
It wasn't a small bomb that was dropped by reading this letter. It was more of a nuclear reactor that destroyed almost and anything and everything in its vicinity and miles beyond that. Nathan couldn't read Donna's expression, not because her face was void of any but because there was too much going on within her that he couldn't pinpoint what it was she was truly feeling.
"When was it written?" Donna choked.
"There's no date." Nathan replied softly. "But judging from this outdated prison stamp, I'd say almost ten years ago."
"You don't think Geo is responsible for my uncle's death, do you?" Donna cracked.
"Your uncle died six months ago, Don." Nathan answered softly. "I doubt it's connected."

"So, what does that letter mean?" Donna asked urgently.
"Well, it means that your uncle was friends with George Campbell and someone named CJ long ago. Clearly something terrible happened between them." Nathan analysed. "I wonder why George hates CJ so much."
"Nathan." Donna sighed.
Donna seemed distressed as if a pile of bricks had been dropped on her head.
"What's wrong?" Nathan asked worriedly.
"I know who CJ is."
"How? Who is he?" Nathan asked.
"CJ was my uncle's closest friend. They used to see each other all the time before he passed." Donna recalled. "Uncle would call him 'CJ' when he thought no one was around and call him 'Clement' out in public."
Nathan couldn't believe it. "Clement? As in Clement...James?"
"CJ." Donna confirmed.
The revelation was quite heavy for Nathan, triggering him to sit back into his chair. He hadn't expected this especially after they questioned the

Minister almost four times, asking him if he knew anyone in his past or present, who would try and harm his family. Either he was absolutely clueless that his former friend had been released from prison or he was hiding something himself that was bigger than bringing the perpetrators who kidnapped his son to justice.
Nathan suddenly felt angry. They went around in circles attempting to find this murderer when it someone James knew all along.
"My uncle was murdered six months ago. Lucas James was abducted two days ago. Tell me now that George Clooney isn't on a revenge tour." Donna contested.
"It makes sense that George went after James' son. But I don't understand how you think he went after your uncle when he was killed on SSU grounds, Don. How on earth would George have had access?" Nathan asked in disbelief.
"Nathan, Jan Jalesmycie shot my uncle with a Glock that he grabbed from the officer that held him." Donna expressed. "What if his plans were orchestrated by George?"
"Donna, Jan Jalesmycie was deemed criminally

insane." Nathan argued. "He was caught breaching Headquarters' security and the only way he thought he could escape the mighty force of all the Agents was shooting everything and almost everyone around him. He fired those shots because he had nowhere to go."
"He fired those bullets because my uncle was in the vicinity." Donna argued back. "Why do you think he snuck into our Organisation in the first place? It wasn't to buy a cookie, Nathan. He was a mercenary."
Deep down, Nathan was on the same page as Donna. The events that transpired on the worst day of SSU history were all too confusing and strange. It just seemed wrong to undergo an effective investigation when they had to worry about the innocent lives that had been lost that day, including their families, as well as certain Agents that left because of how devastating the incident was.
Bringing it up now, especially after everyone had tried to somewhat move on with their lives and forget about that day was the same as poking a poisonous snake. The new, resurfaced information

could've potentially set the Agency back and that was why Nathan fought with Donna. Unlike a strong personality such as herself who was determined to find out what really happened that day, most of the other Agents and outside victims that suffered the worst effects of that day couldn't bear any more leads. They just wanted to forget.

That was why getting it wrong was not an option.

"Fine, Donna." Nathan resigned. "Come back with me."

"What? No." she refused. "I can't leave."

"Yes, you can. We'll investigate this. And we'll prove that George was behind it."

"Jalesmycie's case and the James' case are separate. You know we can't mix the two." She replied.

"There is a potential connection. So, we'll work with that. Come on, say yes." Nathan pleaded.

"Fine. I'll drive back with you." Donna agreed.

"Great." Nathan replied.

"Sure." Donna answered as she clicked her tongue.

Nathan internally sighed. Just like Evan, Donna

had a way of subconsciously telling on herself when she was thinking of something unpleasant. It was usually about him.
"What?" Nathan asked apprehensively.
"What do you mean "what"?" Donna asked cluelessly.
"Just say it." Nathan sighed.
Donna chuckled. "I heard Cyan came back."
Nathan should've seen this one coming.
"Yeah." Nathan answered. "Dave wanted more women in our Division."
"Of course, he did." Donna said sourly. "Chasing after her and completely forgetting that she abandoned the Agency when it needed its soldiers the most."
"Don't do that."
"Do what?"
"Don't be reckless with her feelings." Nathan reprimanded. "That day didn't just affect you."
"I didn't say it did. But I stuck it out. I stayed after someone important was stolen from me." she replied angrily.
"Donna, people deal with things differently. Cyan felt it was best if she left." Nathan defended. "She

had a hard time."
"We all did Nathan! We all had a hard time!" Donna exclaimed. "But, right. I had forgotten. You always take her side."
"Oh, come on, Donna. Grow up. This has nothing to do with sides." Nathan retorted.
"Of course, it does. You're too in love with her to see that each and every time there is a disagreement, you always support her."
"There's no such thing as loving someone too much, Donna." Nathan denied.
"Tell that to your rosy cheeks." Donna taunted.
Was he blushing? His face *did* feel hot.
"I know you would rather die than have Cyan be nicked by a mosquito." Donna joked. "I get it."
"Yes, Donna. I love her. With every inch of my being. I would do anything and everything for her because without her, there is no me." Nathan declared. "Happy?"
"So, why are you so sad?" Donna asked.
"I'm not, Donna." Nathan sighed. "It's just..."
"Just what?" she pushed.
"She doesn't trust me with her heart anymore, okay?"

"You were the one that ended things with her. You did what you had to do and quite frankly, I say good riddance." Donna said snidely.
Nathan remained silent.
Donna sighed.
"Do you want her back?" she asked.
"I'm afraid I don't have the words in me to express how much." he responded.
"Then fight. For her. And everything you built and that you are yet to in the future." Donna reached for Nathan's hand. "Stop feeling sorry for yourself. Man up and chase after what you want."
Nathan chuckled. He appreciated Donna's attempt to cheer him up. She could be an amazing friend when she really wanted to be.
Because he knew how much time and energy he could use going over his current status with Cyan, he immediately removed the thoughts out of his mind before he landed himself in a stagnant state of anxiety.
In that time, his phone rang.
"Before we go back, you have to leave any attitude you have towards Cy right here in this office." Nathan instructed.

He pulled his phone out of his pocket.
"Aye, aye Captain." Donna responded.
"I'm serious, Don."
He read Jordan's name on the caller I.D and swiped up on the emoticon that answered the call.
Donna shrugged. "So am I."
Nathan rolled his eyes. He put his phone on his ear and answered the phone call.
"What's up?" Nathan answered.
"Hey Nate. I'm at LPD going through some prison records and the craziest thing is happening." Nathan heard Jordan mutter.
"What's going on?" Nathan asked.
"Clement James walked in wanting to drop the case." Jordan mumbled.
"What?" Nathan asked incredulously.
Jordan replied to that but because he was mumbling, Nathan didn't get much of what he said.
"Jordan. I didn't get any of that." Nathan said confusedly. "Why on earth are you whispering?"
"Because!" Jordan whispered aggressively.
"George Campbell has Clement James at

gunpoint!"

*****

"Do you think he is home?" Evan asked.
"I don't know." William replied unsurely. "I mean, could he?"
"Did we think this through?" Cyan asked.
They were in the middle of an empty plain with no other structures in sight except a house that stretched for miles claiming the area. A bar gate separated the mansion from Cyan and where the boys were, obscuring them from receiving the full view of what was inside. From what she could see through the little spaces of the brown gate, the house was perched confidently on a hill, looking down on whomever passed to admire. Brown paint was coated all over the plain house making it the only colour describing it. It reminded her of ancient castles in the countryside that didn't need excessive embellishments to stand out. It was majestic in its simplicity.
A long, dusty driveway emanated from the gate area to the house, sizing up a three-minute walk. On either side of it was one of the greenest and

most perfect lawn Cyan had ever seen. A few silver birch trees were positioned sporadically on it, shielding certain parts of the mansion. Where the driveway ended near the entrance of the mansion, Cyan noticed water that took the colour of any object it met as it flew downward from the babies' mouths into a small body of water. In front of the cocoa house, ghost-white baby statues sat around a pond in different poses, acting as fountains by pouring water in the small reservoir. Long pathways, similar to the length and width of the driveway, emerged from the pond to the rest of the garden in different trails as if an octopus was extending its limbs away from itself to other areas. The long sub-driveways led way to hedges that were delicately trimmed, forming symmetrical walls that boxed lime-green grass, sculpted and trimmed into the letters of "J". Cyan assumed it stood for James and was impressed with precision and articulation of it.
"It's too late for doubts." William responded to Cyan.
"Coming here just seems..." Cyan trailed.
"Impulsive?" Evan filled in.
"Yes. It feels impulsive." Cyan agreed. "Not to mention, if Dave finds out we visited Minister

Clement James' property without appropriate protocol, he won't be happy."
Evan's eyes moved in the direction of the Minister's house.
"It *is* a reckless idea." he said simply.
"Then why did we drive two hours to Benscliffe?" Cyan asked.
"Aren't you a little curious about how our own Director is tangled in all this?" Evan asked. "Yes, Lucas is equally important. But what were Swat's affiliations with George? Did they work together? Were they still friends? Did they still keep in touch? Or they parted ways and lived on two different sides of the world?"
Cyan had to admit that the only person who had the answers to those questions was Clement James himself. And seeing this investigation through had unlocked some boxes that couldn't be closed again.
Evan's last statement had provoked a thought. One she didn't want to express out loud. One either of the boys didn't want to express out loud as well. Knowing that George Campbell was after Clement James, what were the odds that he went after Director Thomas Swat six months ago? She refused to believe that the devastating blow they

experienced on the 17th of May as an Organisation was due to a man pronounced criminally insane. There had to be more to it. There just had to be.
"Clement wasn't straight with us before. Why would he be straight with us now?" Cyan asked rationally.
"Easy. If he makes it difficult, we'll make sure LPD issues a warrant. We will take him in for official questioning and search his house." William responded. "Not only is it humiliating for the Minister of Public Works to be in police custody but it also forces him to talk."
"Fair point." Cyan replied.
They unanimously decided to descend from their Ford, march over to Clement's gate and find a way in.
Cyan's phone, however, interrupted their process as it began to ring. With one foot on the rocky ground, she pulled it out of her out of her pants' pocket and turned the screen to face her.
Her smartphone announced that Preston was calling her.
Cyan cocked an eyebrow. Not that she hadn't expected him to give her a ring but Cyan didn't remember plugging her phone number into his phone. And if he was calling, what was it

regarding? If it concerned the case, Cyan thought Evan would be the first point of contact.
"Hello?"
"Cyan! I'm so glad I reached you!" a familiar, female voice exclaimed.
"Aria?" Cyan asked dubiously. "Why wouldn't you be able to reach me? And why are you calling with Preston's phone?"
"Because I assumed Evan told you not to answer my phone calls since he purposefully decided not to answer mine." Aria responded. *"You wouldn't suspect me calling if I used Preston's phone."*
Cyan stared at Evan whose eyes were already on her with confusion.
"Why would he do that?" she asked slowly.
Within a second, his expression effortlessly switched from uncertainty to realization tangled with resignation. He was obviously up to speed about who was calling and why. A piece of information Cyan was determined to find out.
"Well, I've been blowing up Evan's phone, desperately trying to reach him so that I could inform him that Ms. Julie is causing a ruckus over here." Aria reported.
"Uhm, Julie?" Cyan asked unsurely.
Evan's head went up to the sky, down at his shoes,

at the area around them all the while maintaining a blank face.
"Julie is at the house?" William asked. He turned to face Evan who was standing on his right.
"Didn't you end things with her?"
Evan remained quiet.
"Cyan, put me on speaker, please." Aria exhaled.
Cyan obeyed Aria's request and removed the phone off of her ear and tapped the option on her screen to put her phone on loudspeaker.
"You're on speaker." Cyan reported.
"Evan, I love you. So, so very much." Aria began urgently. *"But breaking up with someone requires constant clarity. Skills you seem to lack considering Ju-"*
"Where the hell is he?" Cyan heard an unfamiliar voice shriek. *"He thinks he can leave me? For her?"*
"Julie, Evan is not here!" Cyan heard Harper yell back shortly after. *"We are in the middle of an important investigation right now. You need to leave."*
"I need to leave?" Julie asked in a menacing tone. *"I must leave after giving half a year of my life to him? Only for him to drop me like a hot trash bag for some Division 5 vagrant? What was it about*

me that he didn't like, huh? I'm hot. I'm attractive, I'm beautiful, I'm aesthetically pleasing. He was lucky to have met me!"

"Lucky is a very strong word." Harper returned. *"Either way, please get your silly, narcissist behind out of our house and argue with someone who actually gives a damn. Evan is one of my best friends and you will not talk about him like this in his territory. If he wanted to leave you for Andile, maybe you should ask yourself why. I already know the reason but I suggest you take a good look in the mirror and I guarantee you, you'll see what we all see."*

The silence Cyan heard was so still that she could hear pins drop down to the last octave. Evan's silence was the loudest. Because in the predicament he was in, Cyan expected him to panic and find ways to either reassure Julie or to remind her that it was truly over. Instead, all he did was stare at the phone, bulky arms folded over his chest with a neutral expression covering his face.

Cyan heard a huge thump on the other side of the phone and an extremely loud door slam.

"Ugh." Harper groaned loudly. *"Why can't Evan tell this lady the truth? Now we are stuck cleaning*

up his mess."
"You're still on speaker." Aria whispered sheepishly.
"I would've said it to his face." Harper replied flatly.
"Very true." Aria agreed. *"Anyway, I'm glad Harper managed to escort Juliana out because I think I have a lead."*
"What did you find?" Evan spoke for the first time. Cyan chortled inwardly. She made a mental note to never a get into it with Evan. He wouldn't give her a reaction that she could work with.
"So, Jordan travelled to LPD in order to scan George Campbell's physical records because I did not have them on the Organisation's Database. We went through trials, depositions, indictments and we came up empty. All we know is that he was held in HM Prison, Leicester. Cell 29J." Aria began.
"Let me guess. He used an alias." William said.
"Yes, he did." Aria agreed. *"His lawyer encouraged him to use an alias on his records for anonymity. Meaning that George Campbell may not be our guy's real name which might makes things harder."*
"What about the evidence they used to arrest

him? Isn't there a mobile phone or something we could trace back to him?" Cyan asked.
"Jay said that there is just one block of cocaine and the money they found with it was donated to an upcoming police academy. I asked him which one but he hasn't responded. He just went MIA." Aria responded. *"But speaking of mobile phones, I went over mobile activity in and out of the prison on the day George was released in 2013 and came up with nothing. As I was doing this, I noticed that three towers in a twenty-mile radius registered a burner phone just two hours after George was released from prison."*
"You were able to find a burner phone used four years ago in such a large area at the exact time?" Evan asked in shock.
"My skills impress me as well." Aria boasted.
"She did all that whilst stretching her broken leg on the ottoman under the influence of antibiotics in a tank top, shorts and a gown." Harper chipped in.
"Okay, Harper. That is too much information." Aria whispered. "*But yes. I triangulated the phone and two numbers popped up on my screen. They disappeared as fast as they came meaning that GC disabled the phone as soon as he was done with*

it."
"And this data is from when he was released four years ago?" William asked.
"Yes, that's correct." Aria responded. *"Fast-forward to today, an alert from the same tower popped up on my monitor. Different burner and different mobile account. There is also a record of text messages sent back and forth but I'm waiting for Shannon to give me authorization to use the software."*
"So, what makes you think that that is our guy?" Evan asked.
"Because I concentrated in on the two landmarks that the burner phone pinged. I showed them to Preston and he oriented the map, calculated the bearings and did his math calculations. Two addresses popped up." Aria reported. *"Saxon Street and Benscliffe."*
Cyan, Evan and William stared wide-eyed at each other.
"Did you say Benscliffe?" William asked squeakily for clarity.
"Yeah, Benscliffe. George used the burner phone from that location just yesterday." Aria confirmed.
Cyan involuntarily glanced at Clement James' mansion. If George called from their current

location, could it have meant that was he here with an agenda? Cyan's nerves became more rampant. What was the state of the house at the present moment? What if it they were standing outside a bloodbath and impulsively driving almost two hours was their chance to uncover another potential murder?

No. The Minister couldn't be dead. Outside George, he was the only one who had the information they needed. And his son? His wife?

"You don't think..." William asked with his eyes in the same direction as Cyan's.

"Hold up. Did I miss something? What's in Benscliffe?" Harper asked.

"James." William responded. "That's what's in Benscliffe. He lives here."

"We are actually outside his house." Cyan informed.

"You're where?" Harper asked in disbelief.

"It's good that we are here because we might be dealing with a potential 10-54." Evan jumped in before Harper went on a rave.

He felt is phone vibrate in his pocket and immediately took it out. When he looked at the screen, he furrowed his eyebrows.

"Or maybe not." Evan whispered without

removing his eyes from his screen.
"What's wrong?" Cyan asked.
""George is at LPD."" he read. *""Had Clement James at gunpoint.""*
Aria gasped.
""Jay deescalated hostage situation. George in custody."" Evan finished. "Message from Nathan."
"No way." Harper laughed humourlessly. *"There is just no way. He was able to hide himself this whole time without so much as a paper trail. And now he is in custody for an offense as reckless a hostage situation in a police station? Does anyone else think that George is smarter than that?"*
"There's obviously more." William agreed pensively.
"I don't know what's going on over there but we have to go." Evan instructed hurriedly. "Wiliam, scan the mansion. Now."
"On it." William agreed as he took off in the direction of the gate.
Cyan brisk-walked to the passenger seat of the vehicle while Evan rushed to the front seat. He punched the button to start the car and quickly put it in gear. Cyan fastened her seatbelt.
"Aria, we are leaving now. I'll talk to you later, yeah?"

"Wait!" she exclaimed. "Shannon just gave me the green light to access George's text messages."
Evan drove out of the forestry area to the tarred road.
“What do they say?” he asked.
There was a moment of silence that passed before Cyan and Evan heard anything from Aria.
Just as Cyan was about to ask Aria if she was still on her phone, she heard Aria read “*"I want him to know about me. He is my blood. Prepare to see me. Geo."*”
Geo.
Cyan stared at Evan whose eyes dug holes into the road he was driving.
His blood?
"Do you think this message has anything to do with what is currently happening at the police station?" Cyan asked.
Evan didn’t answer.
Instead, he pushed his foot downwards on the accelerator and sped in the direction of the police department.

9. NALA

17 MAY, 2017
SIX MONTHS AGO

Cyan always loved the colour green. It was a shame she couldn't wear it often considering her wardrobe mostly consisted of blues and blacks. But whenever she had the opportunity to dress the way she wanted, she would search for something green because she loved the way her skin complemented the colour. She appreciated how it represented life, one thing that she often witnessed the loss of more than she needed to. She always had loving disagreements with Nathan about what the colour stood for. She believed it was the breathing aliveness of all entities of life. He argued that it was the colour blue that represented life, which Cyan agreed was accurate to some degree. Though, she believed that the existence of it was different. Blue was the beginning of life and green represented the continuation of it. Being born wasn't a choice anyone made but carrying on when the odds were stacked against you was what Cyan believed required true strength.

That was the reason she wore fern that day, in a low-cut top with an open back and flared sleeves. Flared sleeves she felt someone drag downwards in a frantic motion. The pressure that it had on her arm did not have as much of an effect as the yelling of her name in her ear. She even felt the splashes of wet residue she surmised was saliva in her right hearing side, snapping her out of her stillness.

She didn't remember how long she had been frozen. Two seconds. Three seconds. Five minutes, perhaps. It was too long a reaction taking into account that she had heard five consecutive gunshots only a few miles away from her. In any professional case, her firearm would've been in her hand, senses alert and proficient. But in this setting, where she was in the Headquarters' kitchen helping Blas and his catering staff with snacks for the Open Day, she didn't think she would need it rendering her numb.

Cyan's initial thought when she heard the violently

loud disturbance the first time was why the senior students in charge of releasing the fireworks did so too early. She paused shoving the lettuce in the bird-shaped bread and stood on the tips of her toes to look outside the window adjacent to the wall. No fireworks. The sky was clear as ever, no cloud in sight. After double-checking the blue airspace for any firecrackers she probably missed, she stood in her position behind the counter with confusion settling in her mind like a new tenant. When she heard the sound for the second time and the third, she quickly untied her apron and charged towards the transparent sliding doors to follow the noise. Before she reached them, she heard the noise for the fourth time, shocking her immediately in her tracks. It took the fifth noise for Cyan to realize that she wasn't hearing fireworks but deafening gunshots discharged from a Glock 17C Generation 4.

The sound should've been familiar to her as she could recognize the sound in her sleep. As well as the fact that it was used frequently by Agents daily.

That could've explained why she took too long to react. She was so used to the sound that she was desensitised to it.
There was something about that day in May. She was so out of her work element, consumed by the beautiful atmosphere and the fact that she didn't have to worry about anything besides inserting the right toppings on Blas's pizza.
"Cyan! Cyan! Cy!" she had heard a voice scream her name.
She felt someone pull her top, shaking her to wake up from the still state she was in.
That was when she finally regained her sense of mind, all the commotion that was happening around her filling her ears with such ferocity. From Agents running and pushing past, leaving the kitchen to Medical Aid running across the fields pushing stretchers.
The scene unfolding in front her was too real. And confusing. There had been a shooting on SSU grounds? How? Who? Why?
She figured she didn't have the time to find out because she had to find her siblings and take them to a safe place.

She burst out of the kitchen, straight into the commotion of Agents escorting parents and children inside the headquarters. She looked for Nala and Omari within the crowds that were herded inside the giant edifice but didn't see any pitch-black curls or a black crew cut on two twelve-year olds. It then occurred to Cyan that Mari had left with Dave to play games on his game buddy in his office so she knew he was safe. But where was Nala? Cyan remembered her younger sister asking for her permission to leave with a group of tourists that was planning on visiting the Corridor of Blooming Flowers near the entrance gate. It quickly came back to Cyan that she had agreed to that and she ran towards that direction.

Sixth gunshot.

Cyan sprinted and pushed people out of the way to get to her sister. But she probably didn't have to. Whomever was giving the tour obviously removed everyone and took them to safety. The hope almost slowed her down but she kept going. She just had to see for herself that Nals was out of the danger zone. She had to have her hand in hers to

know that she was okay.
Nearing the Corridor, Cyan's eyes found Chad, one of the Agents who volunteered to show around some of the touring groups. Maybe he had seen her sister. She wanted to run to him and ask him if he had seen Nala but his shirt soaked in blood stopped her from doing that. Because he ran across the fields with urgency, Cyan noticed that he wasn't injured in any way.
The blood wasn't his.
It made Cyan sick to her stomach. That meant his blood could be anyone else's. It could've been-
"Cyan!" she heard someone call from behind her. Her heavy-breathing boyfriend stopped in front of her, eyes full of panic.
"Cyan. Are you okay?" Nathan asked as he physically checked her for any injuries.
"I'm fine." Cyan replied with a ball in her throat. "Nala. I can't find her. Help me."
Nathan began to run, hand on Cyan's back ushering her forward. Not that she needed the motivation to find her sister but Nathan did that when he needed Cyan to calm down. And oddly, it worked every time.

Just not that day.
They neared the Corridor of Blooming Flowers, her heart beating faster and faster as they approached. The commotion she found in the fields when she was still in the kitchen was unlike the commotion she found under the flowering trees. The corridor seemed to be the centre of all the chaos that was taking place. The noise, the medical stretchers and all the wailing and weeping emanating from that beautiful hall.
"Nala!" Cyan called out above the noise. "Nal!"
"Nala!" Nathan called.
It wasn't until she called for the second time that she heard a woman screaming. She shrieked at the top of her lungs that it shook Cyan to her bones.
"Uncle!" the woman continued to cry.
Cyan and Nathan followed the noise. They ran into the corridor and that was when Cyan saw him, limb on a stretcher with bullet in his neck. She heard Nathan take in an uneven breath. He didn't expect to walk into what they did; Donna in tears and snot, her body huddled on top of her uncle's limb one on a stretcher.
"Go to her." Cyan ordered Nathan.

He hesitated for a moment but understood that his childhood friend needed him because her uncle had been killed.
Cyan continued running, the warm wind carrying her tears as it blew past her. She was now terrified. The scenes in front of her had sent ice down her spine. She couldn't count the number of medics in her view because they were crawling under the trees like ants on a hill. On the ground lay still bodies snuffed out of life, some alive but injured and others beside their loved ones that had been incapacitated.
She began to feel fury. What the hell had happened here and who was responsible? Why did she let Nala out of her sight? She could've been cutting sandwiches with her. Why wasn't she with her?
As she was beating herself up, Cyan's eyes met Chad again, back under the trees, rocking a body back and forth. Because Chad's back was to her, she couldn't see who it was because of the direction he was kneeling. She briskly walked over to him because it seemed as though he needed some help. Plus, she had gathered the strength to

ask him if her sister was in his tour group. She just wanted to find Nala.

Cyan stopped.

The body Chad was rocking back and forth wore hot pink Addidas sneakers with white sequence glitters pinned all over them.

Cyan bought those same sequence shoes for Nala after she relentlessly begged her.

Cyan swallowed her tight throat. She bolted over to her fellow Agent to see voluminous black curls in his arms, blood flowing on the ground as if a rock had been removed from a waterfall stream. Chad looked up at her from the ground, where he was, with tears and sorrow in his eyes. He opened his mouth and shut it. He opened it again and the words barely came out of him. But Cyan heard them.

I'm so sorry.

Cyan didn't hear anything else after that. Cyan couldn't hear anything else after that. Her world had shattered into a million different pieces, plummeting towards her and scathing every part of her skin. She felt as if her heart had been sliced by a knife and her veins hauled in different

directions like a puppet. Cyan didn't have any control of her body but her weakened knees found their way to the grass beside her baby sister. Her hand shook as it travelled to the gunshot wound on the left side of her chest, scared to worsen what had already taken place. Instead, she shook her sister frantically, hoping she would open her big, brown eyes and look up at Cyan.
"Nala." Cyan whispered. "Nala, wake up, honey."
She shook her again and again and again.
"Nala." Cyan called on her sister desperately when her eyes didn't show so much as a flutter.
"Nala. Come on." she sobbed. "Nala."
And again.
"Nala. Wake up."
"Cyan." Chad called softly. "The bullet penetrated her heart. I'm sorry but she-"
"Shut up!" Cyan shouted at Chad aggressively. "My sister came here to watch the birds and the flowers! She didn't come here to die!"
She continued to shake Nala, cupping her face, opening her eyes and pushing her hair backwards.
"Nal! What the hell? Wake up!" Cyan cried. "Nala, please!"

Her sister didn't move one inch.
"Nala, no. No." Cyan wailed, her head on her sister's shoulder, one she had always cried on.
"Cy." she heard Chad call her. "They have to take her."
"No." she whispered. "No."
Suddenly, she felt her hands on her waist, dragging her away from her sister.
"No!" Cyan shrieked. "Leave me alone!"
She couldn't see clearly because the tears clouded her eyes but her vision was clear enough to tell her that a medic lifted her sister, put her in a cadaver bag and was in the process of closing it.
"No!" Cyan cried as she tried to shake free from the hands that were holding her. "Leave her alone! Nala!"
In that moment, Cyan had no idea what to do with herself. She wanted to punch something, hit it to let out everything that was happening within her. It was as if her heart was sinking further and further into a darkness she couldn't comprehend the more the medic closed the bag. All she could do was scream.
And she did.

She screamed.
And screamed.
Nala.
My baby sister.
Nal.
Don't do this.
It was when they took her away on a stretcher that she sunk her head into whomever was holding her. She didn't know who it was and she didn't care. A piece of herself had been ripped away from her without her approval.
She held onto whomever was caging her until her mind eventually shut down and she lost consciousness.

******

The feeling of solving a case always lifted a weight off of Cyan's shoulders. She felt lighter than a cumulus cloud and for some time, she would soak in her achievements. Investigating and solving a mystery was intensely draining and mentally strenuous that when it was all over, in those few moments before she received a new case, air was

breathable again. The excitement of laying her head down to rest consumed her and relief kept pouring out of her with no limit.
Seeing George in custody did not feel like that. In truth, seeing him through the clear window seated on his metal seat behind the metal table caused Cyan's nervous system to react. It couldn't have been this easy to arrest him, she thought, let alone keep him in the interrogation room.
His arrest was simple, she'd heard. She hastily arrived at the police station with Evan after leaving William at Benscliffe. They were told by some officers that George was compliant and more than willing to be plugged into custody.
Near the water fountain by the front desk, Cyan found Jordan regurgitating the events that had transpired to Nathan and Donna who seemingly, had just arrived as well. Cyan managed a double take when she witnessed Donna standing a few feet away from Nathan.
Why was she here? Her office was two hours away in London. When did she arrive?
Cyan couldn't think of any reason except that perhaps she had new information regarding the

case. Cyan resolved that she would find out her reason for being at the police station at a later stage. In the meantime, she would try and avoid her in hopes of not engaging in any awkward conversations.

Being in the Leicester Police Department more times than she could count, Cyan knew where the interrogation room was located and decided to walk down its specific hall to assess the state of George's arrest.

She entered the last room in the hallway to her right. It was spacious room covered in dark paint with a window owning a very long exterior on the other side. There was a door adjacent to the wide window that would've led Cyan inside the second room but she remained in the first. She walked in to two officers chatting silently. They acknowledged her presence by smiling and nodding towards her and she did the same to them. Once she had taken in her environment, she focused her attention on the window.

Behind it were these penetrative blue eyes that did not allow any emotion to escape out of them. They were surveying the room until they stopped

and rested on the window with great nonchalance. They drilled holes into the opaque glass that Cyan was convinced George genuinely didn't care about his whereabouts.
Most police stations adopted a Clear and Release tactic. The purpose was to undo the feathers of the accused before questioning. The more time they spent alone before the investigative process, the more anxiety set in, causing them to lose composure and sing the truth. The window aided in this behavioral tactic because the accused seated for questioning was behind a one-way glass. He or she couldn't see outside of their reflection. Usually, the person inside the Interrogation room believed that there were other eyes on him he couldn't see and this further helped with receiving the truth.
In George's case, placing him in the Interrogation room made no difference because he had no feathers to be ruffled. He looked too nonchalant, without a care about his current surroundings and he seemed too calm for someone who had just held the Minister hostage. This prompted Cyan to look at him closely.

An advantage of the window was that Cyan or anyone on other side of the window could see what was in the plain room clearly. She was free to analyze him thoroughly and she noted that there was something that was incredibly and eerily unique about the man in the other room and yet so familiar. He reminded her of powerful business moguls whose postures did not lower or curve, carrying the weight generational wealth on their backs.

George Campbell wore a navy-blue suit that did not spot a single crease, a chalk-white shirt that popped out evenly and neatly out of his blazer, a crumpled, satin handkerchief that revealed part of itself from the left pocket of his suit jacket and cufflinks bearing a striking resemblance to real gold that Cyan considered looking twice just to make sure.

His hair, which caught Cyan's attention when she first laid her eyes on him, was a net full of grey strands. It didn't tell his age because he looked relatively young for a man in his forties, but Cyan guessed he changed its colour to a grey-white. The colour was rich, the hair full of life that Cyan couldn't imagine the man in front of her looking like anything besides how he did. He had some unique features besides his hair that she couldn't help but notice; his nose for one. All around it were freckles scattered over it. They spread out across his cheeks, some reaching both his ears. His cheekbones sat comfortably on the upper part of his face, bone structure sharp as a knife, shaping his face.

Cyan was stunned to say the least. What was a man like that sitting in a police station due to his own doing? He seemed so put together that a prison slum was the furthest place from where he was supposed to be. Taking all this into consideration, Cyan began to worry. What was the endgame here? Was he planning on bombing the place? What damage did he want to do inside that he couldn't do outside?

Before her mind raced further, Cyan heard the door open.

"The Minister is fine." she heard a very familiar voice behind her. Cyan turned around to attach the voice to a face.

"Yes, Director Xavier. I understand that very well."

Dave O'Connor expressed.
Behind him walked in Jordan, followed by Evan, a stout man who she remembered as Sergeant Bruce and lastly, Nathan.
"We have him in custody at the moment. He hasn't been questioned yet." Dave answered into his phone.
Nathan walked over to Cyan near the window and stood beside her whilst the other boys engaged in a very low conversation with the Sergeant a few feet to her left.
"Well Sir, the Minister and his family are in protective custody. He is being questioned as we speak." Dave answered into the phone as he walked towards the last wall of the room.
Cyan thought back to when they left William at the James household. He had managed to send his family over to Protection. Cyan let out an inward sigh of relief. This meant that Susan and Lucas were safe. They weren't touched by George Campbell.
"What are you thinking about?" Cyan heard Nathan ask her as he bumped his shoulders softly with hers.

She had been a bit quiet, taking in everything that was going on around them.
She answered, "Well, I'm thinking about how about our murderous psychopath in the other room."
"I'm thinking about it too." Nathan responded gravely. "All this energy we use to deal with these criminals makes feel peckish."
Cyan snorted. It felt wrong given where they were but she couldn't help it.
"Peckish?" she repeated.
"I mean, I wouldn't mind sitting down for a meal." Nathan said.
"Should we sneak out and get some wings?" Cyan laughed.
Spicy chicken wings were always Nathan's comfort food. He always had them when he was in a stressful situation or whenever he was happy. The familiarity of them always removed him from a bad mood or maintained his good one. Cyan found it funny because that delicacy seemed to make him happy in ways that she never could.
"I say we should. We should just leave this place and drive to the restaurant and hide there whilst

we wait for something to eat." Nathan joked.
"We should take Sergeant Bruce's cruiser. If we activate the blue siren, it'll get us there faster." Cyan added.
"Good thinking." Nathan chuckled. "In fact, I drove there two weeks ago and apparently they brought back that chocolate cake you love. So, we might need more than a siren. Maybe a convoy."
"Wait, what? You mean to say that I can go to Awesome Chips and order the Divine Decker Dessert Promise Cheese Cake?" Cyan chortled with excitement.
"Yeah." Nathan laughed. "You can order the Divine Decker...Cheese Promise Dessert. Or whatever it's called."
"Oh." Cyan mused. "I cannot believe it! Chocolate cheese cake. It is the perfect ending to any meal."
"Uhm no. Chocolate sucks. Don't get me started on cheese. Now, if you infuse those two together-disastrous." Nathan refused.
"You can't hate chocolate cheese cake if you haven't tasted it." Cyan reasoned. "And they don't use your traditional gouda and cheddar. It's a mixture of fresh cheese, some ricotta cream

cheese and cottage cheese. Just imagine sitting in a coffee shop, having a slice in a small saucer with beautiful view, accompanied by a cup of strong expresso. I just-ugh! All this talk of cheesecake is making me salivate." Cyan fantasized.

"I'd hate to be the end of the fork you use." Nathan mocked.

Cyan gasped. "Shut up!" she laughed as she playfully nudged Nathan.

"Your love for it confuses me." he said once he regained his balance.

"You wouldn't understand because you have no taste." Cyan returned.

Nathan laughed. "I do have taste. I just hate confectionery."

'Would you like to explain the difference? Because there seems to be none." Cyan giggled.

Nathan laughed and rolled his eyes. "Whatever. I'll taste it just to show you that the world of sweets and chocolates has no place on this planet."

"I think you'll love it." Cyan said. “You just have to give it a chance.”

"Maybe. Maybe not. But I'll make a deal with you." Nathan suggested.

"I'm listening." Cyan replied.
"If you are right and I like the double decker, then you have to allow me to take you to dinner." Nathan suggested.
Cyan breathed a laugh. "And if you're not a fan?"
"You would have to convince me, right? And what's a better way to do that than to take you to all the cafés until we find the one I do like?" Nathan said.
"That could take forever." Cyan replied.
"I don't mind forever." Nathan said smoothly.
"Alright, alright, alright." Dave interrupted urgently.
"Jay," he called. "I need SSU eyes on the Clement James questioning. Would you?"
"Yeah, yeah. Sure." Jordan answered on his way to the door.
Dave rested his eyes on Cyan for a brief minute.
"Nice to see you again, Cy."
"Hi Dave." she responded.
"What are we going to do with him?" Evan asked referring to the man in the interrogation room.
"I have a feeling direct confrontation won't work." Dave answered. "We can't go in there demanding

for answers."
"What is our goal?" Cyan asked. "Do we want a confession? Or do we want to find out why he is really here? Because I'm certain that he wouldn't mind telling us what he did how and he did it."
"None of our typical interrogative methods will work on him." Sergeant Bruce chimed in. "He is still running on the adrenaline from that little stunt he pulled earlier."
"He is expecting us to barge in there and flood him with questions. And he will have an answer to every single one." Nathan explained. "Our best bet is to give him some more time. His adrenaline will wear off and he'll get bored."
Cyan digested what was said and it made sense to her. George was expecting them to attack. But only, they had to do it when he least expected it. And that was not to attack at all. Everyone else around them seemed to agree to this suggestion given the nods and the mumbles of agreement, a wave of silence hitting them as it sunk in how great of a task the man in the other room really was.
"Where is he? That bastard! Where is he?"

Cyan heard shouting.
The next few events that happened in the following minutes of that day were too immense for Cyan to comprehend. They were too immense for anyone in that room to comprehend. Cyan was always used to plot twists and theatrical work which was usually exciting, but on that particular day, she wished she had never shown up to the police station with Evan. Against her own will, Cyan remembered every detail of the twenty minutes that altered their lives, starting with the way Minister Clement James stormed into the interrogation room they were all in.
The wooden door was impelled open.
"Don't tell me to calm down! Don't you dare! Where is he?" Clement yelled.
Jordan was right behind a towering, pale man that owned a bold, glimmering head and a belly so large his suit pants started below his stomach. He stomped all the way to the second room of the accused, suit jacket flying in the air from all the wind he was collecting and without a second, he pushed the door open until it slammed the wall behind it.

"No, don't go in there!" Cyan heard the Agents and the policemen around her shout.
It was futile, in her opinion, because the tomato-colored man was seething so much, saliva foamed on the side of his mouth that no amount of warning could've stopped him.
"You son of a-!"
Cyan sprinted to the blue interrogation room as did the rest of the others did to stop a potential assault. When her foot touched the ground, a chill ran down Cyan's spine. She wasn't sure whether it was temperature in the room or whether her sixth sense was warning her about the impending events. She believed it was the latter because in front of her were former brothers who hadn't seen in each other in over ten years with anger brewing in their hearts that with one push, all contents would spill over.
George wasn't startled by Clement's ruffled nature. In truth, he didn't even blink. He didn't look up. He concentrated on his reflection that if Clement James wasn't shouting on the top of his lungs, Cyan would've been certain that George hadn't heard a word that was being said.

Clement slammed his hands on the metal table and shouted, "Look at me!"
The saliva that had formed a cloud on the side of his mouth, escaped in anger and his veins had stretched from his temple to the beginning of his cheek resembling a rope.
George remained unfazed.
"Minister, please calm down." Dave implored as he attempted to deescalate the situation.
Clement ignored Dave and continued, "You take my kid and then you point that thing at me? What did you think was going to happen, huh? You thought you were going to get away with it? I own this city! You can't threaten me in my own city!"
George's eyes moved slowly from the window to a disarranged Clement but his mouth remained clipped shut.
Clement began to laugh manically. "Quiet? That's what I thought. You don't have a reason to be a sociopath."
George sniffed. The air was pure without any detrimental particles flying around so Cyan was confused why George was motivated to contract his nose. Cyan realized that it was an attempt to

appear indifferent in hopes to irritate Clement. The Minister was too angry to notice this and fell into George's trap.
"Tell me why you took my son!" Clement shouted again.
Everyone around the two, former friends stood in studded silence. Dave, who previously warned the Minister to calm down, shrunk in his thousand-dollar suit as the speech left him. Nathan, Jordan, and Evan stared at the scene in front of then as if it came out of an action movie and the officers eyed the scene as of it was the first interesting exchange that has ever happened in their station. Nobody could stop a play that was already rolling.
"Answer me, dammit!" The Minister yelled again.
Clement James breathed in and flared his nose. He wiped his face with his hand in order to smooth all the anger apparent on his face. He couldn't stand still. His chest was moving rapidly up and down that Cyan could almost feel the amount of effort Clement put in order to breathe at a normal rate.
George cocked his head to the side and measured him from the bald patch on his head to the heel of

his shoe with distaste in his eyes.
"You have a fleck on your right temple." George spoke for the first time. "Take care of that, will you? It's not a pretty sight once it throbs.
"Good grief!" Clement yelled. He felt for his temple. "That's where you positioned your pistol!"
George shrugged nonchalantly.
Clement let out a big breath."
"My son shouldn't have been a play in your silly game."
"Game? It was a necessary cause of action." George replied simply as he fixed the handkerchief on his chest pocket.
"Necessary?" Clement screamed. "My son, Geo! Lucas is my son!"
George chuckled gently. "Your son? That boy is practically an orphan if he has a father like you. He should spend time with his Uncle Geo and maybe then, he'll know what a father figure really looks like."
"You're sick." Clement said quietly.
"Don't worry about any mental disabilities you may think I have. Your core focus should be watching every word you say to me because as

still as I am, I'm a hungry lion surviving on revenge." George replied.
"Don't tell me you're still mad about that money we took ten years ago! That was not an excuse to harass my family!" Clement shouted.
"I couldn't care less about the money you stole from me ten years ago even if it aided me to breathe." George said in menacingly low voice. He stared daggers at Clement James. "You took so much more from me when you sent me to jail for more than a decade."
Clement's expression resembled realization of an era ago, a time that he had long buried. His grey eyes widened and his mouth moved rapidly as if he was shivering. He looked away from George, analyzed those of them that were standing around as spectators and averted his eyes to the tile floor.
George smiled a small smile. He crossed his right leg over his left leg.
"You were the one who sent that anonymous tip to the station about our diner." George said confidently
Sergeant Bruce gasped dramatically.

"You were the one who threw me in a pit to rot for rest of my life." George continued. "Everything we worked so hard for found home in the trash, as if it had never existed."
"We had no choice." Clement muttered.
"You had a choice. Thomas had a choice." George contested. "And you both made a decision."
"You used Thom and I, Geo." Clement expressed daringly.
Cyan noticed the young man from years ago express what he felt he could never have said back then.
"We didn't want to sell drugs in our diner. We didn't want to clean dirty money either. We just wanted to sell good food and make money for our families the right way. You took that opportunity away from us."
"You didn't have a problem using the money." George mentioned sardonically.
"Because I had to pay for my brother's medical bills!" Clement cried. "You knew Cliff spent his entire life in a wheelchair and my parents couldn't afford his expenses anymore. You knew that when you left me out of the shares once you calculated

that I wasn't spending enough time at the diner. You knew that I was struggling and you still decided to take advantage of me. I decided that I wouldn't be abused by you so, yes. Thomas and I stole all the money from the diner and set you up. We made sure you were working late that night and I only had to walk down the street and ring the police that illegal activities were being run on Saxon Street. I did that and I don't regret it." Clement said.

George stood up abruptly and went toe to toe with Clement.

"That was always your problem, CJ." George reprimanded. "You and Thomas. You were both weak. All you knew how to do was enjoy the money that you didn't lift a finger for. Your brother's illness will never be an excuse for the lazy kind that you are. My own wife was pregnant with my so-"

For the first time in the confrontation, Cyan noticed a tinge of raw emotion on George's face. He wasn't pretending. When he choked, he showed a sadness, a melancholy he carried in his heart for years.

"My son." George said quietly.
And even though Clement showed extreme hatred for George, he shared his sadness.
"I wasn't there when her soul left her body giving our son his." George breathed. "And that is why I despise you. Not because of the money. Or the decline of our business. But because my own son doesn't know about me because of you. When he looks at me, he sees a monster instead of a father trying to love him. I had no impact on the man he is today. All because of you."
Clement stared at the floor as if there was heavy metal on his neck keeping his head in that direction. He couldn't look at George because, perhaps, he understood what George said to be true. The guilt was apparent in the way he stood, hands hitting against his thighs nervously. Cyan looked at George who still stared at Clement, eyes unfaltering.
"Geo." Clement approached cautiously, like a hunter securing an impala in the middle of a desert. "Tell me you didn't do it."
George sat down.
"George, tell me that you didn't do it." Clement

begged more urgently.
"Do you believe in hell?" George countered quietly.
Clement didn't answer.
"Damaged souls travel there to suffer eternal punishment for the wrong they committed here on earth." George explained. "That's where Thomas Swat belongs. Someone had to do it. It was my responsibilty."
Cyan felt her body rapidly decrease in heat. She wasn't sure if she had heard correctly so she went over what George had said again. He said, verbatim, that it was his responsibility. He sent Director Thomas to hell. He had him killed.
The next few seconds were a blur for Cyan but when she recovered back to reality, she found her body weight pressing George Campbell to the ground. She heard a collective of voices shout her name, boots thudding towards her in order to pry her off of the accused but that was the least of her worries. Strong hands lifted her off George and placed her on the ground. The owner of the strong hands made a mistake by believing that she would stay still because Cyan ran back to attack

George as soon as her feet hit the ground. She felt the same hands that dragged her, pounce her waist. Cyan was writhing, crimson braids leaving her tight ponytail and clothes creasing from the hurdling she was doing.
"Cyan!" she heard Dave shout. "Cyan!"
"Let me go!" Cyan yelled back. "Let-me-go!"
The plain room was now in a frenzy. The police officers of the station rushed to stand between an electrified Cyan and a stunned George while Nathan, Evan and Jordan tried to calm Cyan down by explaining to her why they needed to keep George alive.
Cyan didn't care about all that. Nothing justified keeping her sister's killer alive. In fact, she needed to kill him, snuff out the life in him and watch his last breath blend in the atmosphere around them. She reached for her Glock in her right holster but Nathan was faster than her. He pulled it out before Cyan could get to it and unloaded it. That only fueled Cyan's fury causing her to push through the barricade of her friends to take care of what she had started. Instead of pushing through, she fell into Nathan's arms, who caught

her just before she slithered her way to George Campbell.
All her efforts to make her way over to him were futile and that was the moment Cyan began to bawl and scream.
"You're the reason my sister is not here anymore?!"
George stared at Cyan, wide eyed, hand serving as a stopper from where the blood poured out from the wound she had inflicted.
"I don't understand what you're talking about." George responded angrily and confused.
"You didn't just take Director Thom’s life that day." Evan explained with sadness in his eyes.
"You murdered young men and women. Children were buried as a result of your vendetta."
"Nala was only twelve years old! She was only a girl." Cyan wept. "You took her from us! My mother lost a daughter, my brother lost a twin and I lost a sister because of you! You-"
Cyan tackled Nathan's body to get to George but she wasn't strong enough to. He still held her, tears and snot flooding his white shirt. Either he didn't notice or he didn't care. His main focus was

on Cyan, doing whatever it took not to let her go and kill George himself.

In the entire twenty-seven minutes that they had been stuck in the interrogation room, Cyan hadn't seen a tinge of authentic emotion on George's face. Now, his face dropped with sorrow, an emotion that seemed to match him completely, as strange as it sounded. He was no longer angry but downcast, eyes aging a thousand years, rings falling into place under his eyes.

"You're lying. It was just Thomas that day." George denied viciously. "I don't touch children."

"My sister is in a casket under the ground because you sent a faulty mercenary!" Cyan screamed. "My sister whose hope was to watch the flowers and the birds that day ended up losing her life because of you. Once he lets me go, you better run."

"I didn't know-I-"

"Shut up!" Cyan yelled as she tried to jump over Nathan.

"Cyan! It's not worth it." Evan said. He stood in front of her behind Nathan. He held her face in his palms. "It's not worth it. I know the pain is intense

right now. But I also know that Nala wouldn't want you to avenge her in a way that would compromise how she sees you."
Cyan placed her head on Nathan's shoulder and began to cry openly. All that anger transformed itself into pain and all Cyan could do was shed tear after tear. She felt a hand stroking her head and assumed it was Evan's because Nathan's were on her waist. Evan's words were enough to stop her on her quest for violence and keep her in one place.
"I too know what it's like to lose someone." George confessed.
"Screw you." Jordan snapped. "You don't know a damn thing."
"I know what's it's like to have somebody you love ripped away from you with no warning. To live in a darkness that recreates itself no matter how many times you try to escape. To live in world where your heart ceases to be the home for the people you love because they no longer exist." George lamented.
Cyan breathed hard. She couldn't stand looking at the man who murdered his sister but everything

he had said was true. All of it. He had lived through a pain that caused him to understand hers.

"I took away somebody important to you, I see. I would like to offer my remorse, especially after you looked after somebody dear to me." George apologized.

Cyan removed herself from Nathan's embrace.

"I didn't look after anything of yours." she spat.

"You did." he replied firmly. "My son. And that is why I regret taking your sister's life."

"I've never met your son." Cyan replied confusedly, anger temporarily stalled by George's allegations.

"He is who he has become because of his friends." George continued. "He is nothing like me because he was raised in love by his grandparents."

Cyan involuntarily looked up at Nathan, whose face was masked with confusion, to find out if he had the slightest idea of what George was talking about. He was clearly in the dark as well so Cyan faced George again to acquire more answers.

That was when she saw it.

It suddenly hit Cyan why George looked so familiar. His eyes. She had seen them before. Those piercing, blue orbs that perforated Clement earlier. Those were the same eyes she stared into every time she looked up to talk to the one she believed was her soulmate. The same eyes she fell asleep looking at when they shared the same bed. The same eyes she fell in love with before he had said anything to her on the first day they met. These were the same eyes that resembled the sea on a sunny morning when all was peaceful and you didn't want the time to move. She could pick those eyes in any room full of people. She could pick those eyes anywhere.

Cyan shifted her focus to Evan. She didn't know what prompted her to do that, but she did. Perhaps, it was to confirm what she had thought she realized. Or maybe, she just wanted to witness Evan's reaction when his best friend's world was turned upside down. Her eyes were blurred with the tears but from what she could see, he stared at Nathan as if he was just going to pull him in and hug him. Sorrow took shape in his almond eyes.

She looked at Dave, whose eyes were on the floor, his teeth clenched with anger in his mouth and Jordan who looked everywhere else in the room but Nathan and George, tears pooled in his own eyes as he tried his best to return them back to whatever valve they escaped from.
She caught a glimpse at Clement James. His attention was on Nathan, taking him in as if he was someone he hadn't seen in eons due to his own doing. He roughly averted his stare and faced the wall.
Everyone in the room seemed to catch on to what was happening except Nathan himself who could not comprehend what George was trying to say to them. To him.
George stared directly at Nathan. "I used to send letters to his grandmother but I'm sure he never received any of them."
Nathan's attention was captured.
"I failed him, Levi." George muttered to himself.
"How do you know my name?" Nathan asked aggressively.
George swallowed.
"It was-my wife's. My wife's name was Levi."

Nathan's face turned pale but he remained silent. "She always wanted you to have that name." George said in a low voice. "She said that she would give it to you. I guess she did."
"What are you saying?" Nathan choked quietly.
"I'm sorry you had to find out this way." George swallowed. "My name is George Charles Caldwell. I'm your father, Levi."

10. CASE CLOSED

Evan didn't know whether it was the dying pollen or the cold air outside that was causing his sinuses to respond. It was overcast outside, clouds gathering in the airspace to mourn the disappearance of the sun. All the trees stood empty and alone, the fog covering their nakedness and the entirety that was the outside. The temperatures had swiftly decreased from the hot weather they had experienced that day. Not that he was anywhere near surprised. The weather couldn't be trusted to stay in one season. The team had arrived three hours ago from the police department. If Evan mentioned the word 'team', he would be using the term quite loosely. Jordan, Dave and Evan returned to their house without Nathan or Cyan. After George, the man under law enforcement's eye, revealed that he was Nathan's biological father, Cyan stormed out of the interrogation room. Nathan attempted to follow her but Dave stopped him from going after her and did so himself. He came back exactly three and half minutes later with news that he couldn't find her. He didn't know where she had rushed off to.

Nathan carried a titanic load on his shoulders. His ex-girlfriend's sister had been brutally murdered by a man who claimed to be his father. Evan couldn't imagine what he was going through and that is why he understood it when Nathan stormed out of the interrogation room and disappeared himself.

Evan moved himself out of the way, giving him space to leave. What words of comfort would be effective enough to numb his best friend's pain? He was not qualified in such situations. Plus, he didn't think it was necessary. Nathan wouldn't listen to a single word. Evan knew he wouldn't.

After the eventful day, Dave, Jordan and Evan drove the forty-five minutes back home in silence. It was the longest Evan had his foot on the accelerator, the woods moving in a slow blur.
As soon as they arrived at the entrance of their house, the three men were greeted by a string of questions by their teammates who worked from the house, none of which Evan knew how to answer. This resulted in him walking past Preston, William and the girls, throwing himself on their grey couch in the living room.
"What's his problem?" he heard Harper ask.
Dave didn't respond but beckoned them to the other couches where Evan was. He asked everyone else to sit down and explained what had transpired at the police station. Evan had zoned out of the conversation when Dave began the narration.
His mind began to think of important locations Nathan would've visited if he had a bad day. His mother's grave was usually the first place he'd go but he knew Nathan wouldn't go there at this time.

Sometimes, he went to the Organisation to clear his head. But Evan knew that he wasn't there either.

Nathan needed time. Cyan too. Time would mend their hearts.

Evan laughed internally. He didn't even believe that himself. His older brother passed when he was five and he still felt the pain every waking day. Emmanuel died peacefully, in his sleep after a long battle with bronchial cancer. He spent his last days travelling, helping charity organisations dealing with his condition and spending time with his friends. He managed to disallow death from controlling him. Evan loved that for him.

It still didn't stop him from understanding Cyan's pain, though. Death of a sibling. Some part of you died with your sibling, leaving you emotionally vulnerable and alone.

"Evan!"

"Huh?" he responded.

He didn't know how many times he had been called but based on Harper's expression, he might have been called more than a few times.

"Are you okay?" she asked.

Evan slightly nodded.
"Dave said George gave you something before you left." Harper asked. "What was it?"
Just as they were about to step out of the interrogation room on their way to their vehicle, George asked Evan to wait. He didn't want to but he did anyway. George pulled out the silk handkerchief that decorated his suit pocket and pushed it across the metal table. Evan stared at it dubiously before he looked back at George.
"I will understand if he never wants to see me again." George had said. "But perhaps, he can learn more about where he comes from and who he is."
Because Evan didn't want to stay in that room any longer, he grabbed that handkerchief and stormed out.
"His legacy is the handkerchief?" Preston asked confusedly when Evan was done repeating what had been said to him. "I don't really follow."
Evan took it out from his Jean's pocket and placed the silk cloth on the table. He opened it up to reveal a small, silver key.

"A Kwikset key." Preston identified. "Common for opening knob doors. That's a house key."
"I'm not sure why George would leave this for Nathan." William spoke for the first time. "He has no desire to know him."
"We don't know that." Aria countered.
"Are you serious?" Jordan asked incredulously. "He is a criminal. Nathan is Division Expert Chief of an International Organisation. He is not going to want that man in his life."
"You grew up with your father around, Jay. Nathan did not. You wouldn't know what he wants." Harper challenged.
"All we are saying is that it doesn't make sense if he ran into his arms." William retorted.
"Your father's infidelity on your mother was the reason their marriage was ruined and yet you spend more time with him." Aria snapped. "Does any of *that* make sense?"
"How the hell do you know that?" William barked.
"You're not as slick as you think you are." Aria retorted.
"Guys-'' Preston started

"Preston, if you finish that sentence, I'll smack you with my crutch." Aria interjected violently.
Preston pursued his lips and sunk into the chair he was sitting on.
"I'm tired of William opening his mouth before he thinks. He walks around here as if no one has feelings." Aria continued angrily.
"I state facts." William returned.
"Who asked you?" Aria asked sourly. "Would it kill you to be sensitive?"
"I don't think I need to remind you that George murdered Cyan's sister. What do you think will happen when Nathan accepts George into his life? It would be the end of that relationship." William replied firmly.
Aria struggled to sit up on the chair because of her broken ankle but the crutch she threatened to beat Preston with helped lift herself up an inch.
"Cyan's feelings are suddenly important to you?" Aria asked menacingly low. "Where was that concern when you insulted her every chance you got?"
"That's not the point." William responded gruffly.

"Then, what is? Because if it is to tell us the obvious, we know!" Aria yelled.
"Aria!" Dave called.
"Nathan and Cyan are somewhere out there heartbroken and we don't know where they are." Aria said sadly. "We don't know what to do."
"Okay, everybody take a minute." Evan intervened. He stood up from his couch and went over to Aria's side to calm her down.
He knelt by her side, whispered the words "Be strong", kissed her on the forehead and returned to his seat.
"Fighting with one another at a time like this is probably the dumbest thing we've ever done as a team." Evan rebuffed. "Nathan will make his decision. It is our job to support him as his team and most importantly his friend. Cyan needs our support as well. She is a member of this team and we will stand by her. The decision the two of them will make concerning their relationship is their business. We'll focus on ours."
Everyone in the room agreed.

"Our job is not finished." Evan continued. "George's men are still out there and we don't know what they are doing."
"Geroge's men are mercenaries so probably killing people for money." Harper said sardonically.
"How do we find those guys?" Jordan asked.
"Mercenaries are incredibly difficult to trace. That's why they are always hired."
"It's highly likely that George hired Jan Jalesmycie to carry out his mission the same way he did with the men that kidnapped Lucas. If we find how he contracted Jan Jalesmycie, we can possibly source out how he found the other two." Preston suggested.
"Don't criminals just find each other? How are we supposed to know how they met?" Jordan asked sceptically.
"It looks that way but criminals don't just meet." Aria answered. "They communicate."
"Where are you going with this?" Evan asked.
"Are you guys familiar with the Dark Web?" Aria asked whilst pulling out her laptop from underneath her seat.

"Vaguely. I know that it's part of the internet that's hidden unless you're using a certain browser." Harper answered.
"Correct. It can only be accessed using a browser called Tor. That's where all the shady business deals go down. Including leasing contract killers." Aria explained.
"So, just like Ebay but more dangerous." William surmised.
"If you'd like to put it that way then yes." Aria agreed. "Contract killers used to sell their services to the highest bidder back in the 1900s. But with modern technology, mercenaries have their own accounts and profiles on the Dark web. They use pseudonyms for their emails and usernames making them anonymous. They install blockers to deter any traceable advertisements and encrypt their profiles."
"I've never caught on to the whole encryption thing." Dave confessed.
"The concept is known as cryptography." Preston began. "Whoever decides to hide their information from any internet user can do so by using mathematical formulas solved only by an

algorithm. This will transform plain text into cypher text, a key formulated by the user being the only tool that can decrypt the data."

"So, you're saying that the owner of the account locks it, preventing anyone from viewing the content. But they have a key, a password, that can be used to unlock the account." Harper deduced.

"Precisely." Aria answered. "The general make of the website is pretty standard. The name of the service, job descriptions, visual testimonials and contact information. But the individual account details for specific mercenaries are not public. You have to go through the initial stages of the screening to acquire the key that unlocks the private account."

"What is the name of the website you think George used?" Evan asked.

"Hire A Killer." Aria responded simply.

"Classy." Dave replied flatly.

"If I understand correctly, the only way we can catch this mercenary is if we go through the website to find him." Jordan repeated.

"Yes." Aria agreed.

"But you said there was a screening process to see if the one accessing the account is serious. And I'm assuming that it is payment for the service upfront." Jordan responded. "A kind of deposit."
"Correct and correct." Aria answered. "But I can hack through the encryption. Give me a second."
Aria narrowed her eyes and began to hit the buttons on her keyboard rapidly. Evan felt a sense of pride. In most cases, Aria's technical skills provided the team most of information they needed. They solved cases because Aria could get to what they couldn't.
"Hacked their backdoor." Aria announced, eyes still on her laptop.
"What does that mean?" Harp asked, attempting to keep up with what Aria was doing.
"She managed to hack the main control of the website." Preston answered.
"There are so many contract killers here. I can't narrow it down if we have next to zero information about the people we are looking for." Aria complained.
Dave groaned loudly. He abruptly stood up from the couch and walked over to the kitchen counter.

He placed both his elbows on the granite and dropped his head in his palm. Extremely quiet sounds came from him as if he was muttering and mumbling to himself to insanity.
Evan stared at him. Something about the sound of his voice triggered him. It sounded tired and drained, as if there was an entity holding his shoulders down and he couldn't get back up. His attention wasn't the only one that was caught because he heard the noise of the laptop keys simmer down.
"What's wrong?" Aria asked Dave.
Dave remained silent.
"David." Preston pushed.
"Jan Jalesmycie is alive." Dave blurted.
"What do you mean by the word 'alive'?" Harper asked in confusion.
"It means that he didn't die on the 17th like everyone was led to believe." Dave muttered.
"I don't get it. Why were we told that he was shot?" Jordan asked incredulously.
"That part is true. He was shot but he didn't take his last breath. He went into a coma." Dave

explained. "We all thought that he was dead. He suffered a fatal wound. But when he woke up-"
"The Directors decided to make everyone believe that the killer who almost destroyed our home was six feet underground." Harper finished.
"They were just concerned that telling everyone he was really alive would spread chaos throughout the Organisation so they decided to kill him in the eyes of the public and the Agents to manage the predicament. That way, everyone would move on peacefully and the SSU would be a safe place to be again." Dave recited.
"What was the real reason?" Evan asked.
Dave stared at Evan.
"Why were we lied to?" Evan asked again impatiently.
"When he woke up, Jan Jalesmycie expressed that he was afraid of being deported back to Poland. Their judicial system isn't kind to international criminals so he begged for a deal. He would tell us everything he knew about who sent him in exchange for some kind of mercy." Dave explained.
"What did he tell you?" William asked.

"Director Xavier agreed to the deal and Jan Jalesmycie's word vomit began. He told us that that there was a man named George Caldwell burning to get his hands on two, well-known men. He was contacted on a website with instructions under two pictures of Clement James and Thomas Swat with no real back story. He was to assassinate Clement at the Activism Campaign in February and sneak into the Organisation and kill Director Thomas shortly after.
He managed to get the job done with Thomas but failed with the Minister.
There were no threats on the Minister's life after Director Thomas's death so, we relaxed.
It was radio silent until Clement's eleven-year-old son was kidnapped three days ago. We knew who it was. That is why the most proficient Division out of the whole Organisation was assigned to the case to find the George character before we had another murder on our hands." Dave explained.
"You made us investigate this case when you knew who the killer was this whole time?" Aria asked in frustration. "Why didn't you give us that

information to find him? It would've been a lot faster."
Dave remained silent.
"That would give away that the man we were looking for was Nathan's father." Preston surmised.
"Had he learned the truth then he wouldn't have taken the case. And even if he was forced to, his head wouldn't be on straight. He is the DEC. He had to remain focused." Dave explained.
"You prioritized finding this man over what this would do to Nathan. You do understand what this has done to him, right?" Evan asked shaking with anger "His life has been shaken!"
"I understand that but-"
"Do you?" Harper asked sadly. "Because you had this information and you still recruited Cyan to be a part of this team to work this case. She was investigating her own sister's murder and she didn't even know it. Do you have any idea how heartless that sounds?"
Dave slumped down on the living room couch.
"It wasn't my call. The Directors really wanted this man found." Dave defended quietly. "I'm really

sorry to you all. I didn't have a choice. They told me that if I didn't assign this case to my team, they would find another Supervisor to take over. Permanently. I didn't want anyone, besides me, watching over you so I accepted it. I knew this crap would screw with Nathan's head and that was why I brought in Cyan. I thought she would be able to cool him and make him feel better in ways that we could not.

And as far as Nala goes, Cyan deserved to find the truth. She has always wanted it. It was just a shame that she had to find out this way."

"You did the best you could." William said.

"He's right." Aria agreed. "You were put in a horrible spot."

"Jan Jalesmycie said that George was specifically searching for expertise, location and experience." Dave said. "That should help narrow the search."

"It does." Aria replied.

She began typing on her keyboard, faster, as a person with newfound knowledge would.

"When it comes to location, George would look for any mercenaries unknown to this country but

convenient to get his demands and payments through." Evan said.
"Russia has the highest number of mercenaries but George wouldn't go there because that is the first place we would look. He would reach out to the smaller countries such as Estonia or Latvia." Preston added.
"Plugging in that now." Aria responded.
"As far as experience is concerned, he would look for someone with twenty years maximum in the game. He wouldn't want any mistakes." William aided.
“He would also look for someone who lives a very quiet life. That way, nothing is traced back to him.” Jordan added.
"I think I found them.” Aria announced. "Victor and Magnus Hansen. Two brothers from Denmark. Their account has a bullet stamp signifying that they were booked for a job."
"Send this information to Conrad." Evan instructed. "He will assign the arrest to a different Division."
"Sent." Aria responded.
"Case closed."

*****

Cyan woke up early the next morning before the sun started its daily rotation. Many stays at her grandparents' house engraved that habit in her. She hated it at first. Who wouldn't? Sleeping was just as important as breathing and it was a criminal act to disturb it. However, she learned to appreciate the early mornings. She realised that she loved to start the day before the actual day started.

She dragged the heavy fleece off of her and took a once over of her old room.

It was a tiny-sized room, just as she had remembered it, with a small bathroom and a shower. Her chipped wooden dresser sat directly across her bed and on it, were some of her old facial and body products that she had left behind before departing for the Academy. Every summer she visited, she would always find them sitting on her dresser like mahogany apart of the table.

She still couldn't believe that her mother didn't clear some of her old belongings after all this time, especially, since she used Cyan's old wardrobe as a second pantry for extra groceries. Each holiday, she found the strawberry-scented body lotion sitting on her dressing table, collecting dust. Why didn't Cyan just throw it away?

The thought pushed her out of her bed and she marched all the way to her vanity. She grabbed the bin that was kept underneath it, huddled all her old property into her elbow and shoved it all into the blue trash bin.

There. That was much better.

The walls of the room were a mix of light and dark brown wallpapers that Cyan and her younger sister stuck to her walls after her public exams. They also added posters of their favourite stars all over the room. James Bay. American Mouth. Robert Pattinson. Cyan couldn't forget that afternoon even if she tried her hardest. She laughed so hard with her sister that day until her jaw hurt.

Her feet took her to that very wall of her favourite posters and she ripped them off the wall. She stuffed them into the trash bin with her old lotions and placed the bin at the foot of her bed.

Every detail about being home reminded her of her sister and she didn’t need the reminder of one of the best days of her life. It was a sharp pain at the core of her heart that she couldn't cure. One she couldn't physically or mentally rip out of her chest. It was a pain that would stay with her forever until she was in her own grave. Perhaps, that was why it took her 6 months to visit her family. She didn't want to feel the burning sensation of the wound again.
All the mental turmoil exhausted her so Cyan threw herself back onto the unmade bed. She didn't do it graciously resulting in piece of plastic glass hitting her arm. Cyan scrubbed her arm where the blood rushed to and determined to search for what had attacked her. When her palms felt something solid inside her sheets, she picked it up.
It was her little mirror.
It was one she always kept above her bed on her headboard such that each time she woke up, she would look at herself and repeat affirmations to every morning.
"You're smart. You're brave. You're beautiful." she

would say to herself. This always lifted her spirits and made the path she had to walk that day brighter. It became habitual after her family relocated from Swaziland to the United Kingdom. They had left their father behind because he didn't want to change with them. He wanted to stay in Mbabane where he knew everything and everyone.

It didn't change her parents' relationship.

For a time. They were perfectly in sync until the distance became too much to bear with the communication on their father's end being insufficient. Cyan's father was an old head. Technology was a nuisance to him. Anything new. Anything different.

This affected Cy to a degree because she didn't really know her father. She didn't remember him after some time which shook her soul. She used running as a means of distracting herself from those thoughts that intruded her mind from time to time.

Assessing where she was in her life now at twenty-three, all signs pointed to her excelling in everything that she had been doing.

But digging deep into herself by looking into the little mirror, the young girl who struggled so much growing up stared back at her. The same girl who lost someone valuable at such a young age locked eyes with the young woman who had lost another member of her family. Her crimson braids were all over the place, her eyes red and puffy from all the crying, her right hand throbbing from where she had punched the criminal back at the police station in the face and her feet hurting from running to Euston Street, that was miles away, to catch a bus home.

She didn't remember which bus she ascended or which route she took to her mother's house. All she remembered was being in her soft embrace and weeping until all that came out were dry tears.

She remembered confiding in her mom about what had been happening in her life; how Dave approached her asking her to go back to the Organisation, how they investigated the Minister's case, how they found out that George brutally murdered a man named Geoffrey, whose only mistake was being a pawn in George's game and

Director Thomas Swat, whose neck was pierced by a bullet released under his orders.
Lastly, she told Patrice that her daughter's life was taken by a lunatic who was currently held in custody. Nala was only caught in the crossfire.
Cyan's mother broke down. The tears fell from her eyes but no audible sound came out. She just shivered and began to wash plates that were already spotless.
From that time, Cyan didn't remember much of what happened until she opened her eyes the next morning.
"Omari, if you're going to lick that spoon, you might as well finish the vegetables in your plate." Cyan heard her mother scold from the other side of the door.
"Mama, is Cyan still sleeping?" Omari asked.
"We don't want to wake her up. She had a really rough day yesterday." Cyan's mother responded.
"Please, Ma. I'll just peek to see if she's awake." Omari pushed.
"Okay." Patrice gave in. "Bring that plate here before you go."
Cyan heard small footsteps hit their wooden

floor, travel to the kitchen and move towards Cyan's bedroom.
She hadn't seen her little brother since she arrived home so she quickly lifted herself up from her single bed and opened the door. On the other side stood a twelve-year old boy with a crew cut and inquisitive brown eyes. His skin was so warm and tan that she could see the blood rush to his skin from smiling too much. Cyan couldn't believe that her baby brother had grown so much. And he wore spectacles now? What other growth spurts had she missed?
''Cy!''
Omari ran to his older sister. Cyan scooped him up and hugged him so tightly that she creased his clothes. She kissed him dearly, telling him how much he had grown and how much she had missed him.
When she thought that her younger brother needed some air, she put him down and knelt across from him that they were at the same eye level.
"How are you?" Cyan asked excitedly.
"I missed you." he said quietly. "Why were you

gone for so long?"
Cyan felt her heart break.
"I missed you so much more, my love. I'll never leave again, okay? I'm here forever." Cyan assured Omari.
"Are you sure?"
"I've never been more certain of anything in my life. Your big sister is here." she replied.
She kissed his forehead knowing that she meant every word. She took her brother's hand and they entered the sitting room. She switched on the television and urged Omari to sit down and watch some cartoons whilst she went to the kitchen to see if her mother needed assistance with preparing the breakfast.
"Morning, Mummy." Cyan greeted.
"Morning, my baby. How did you sleep?"
"Like a log. Why didn't you wake me up? I could've made breakfast." Cyan asked.
"Cyan, please. Sit down." her mother instructed.
Cyan pushed out a chair from the kitchen table and plonked onto the wood.
"Sausages and veggies?" she noticed from the remains of Omari's plate in the sink.

"Hmm." Patrice agreed. "I thought you'd want a nice, hot breakfast after yesterday."
Cyan's stomach growled as if on cue.
"Smells good." she replied sheepishly.
"Don't worry. The food...is...now...ready." her mother said in between breaths as she dished the food into their white plates.
Her mother carried both plates to the kitchen table where Cyan was seated and placed them on the chipped oak. The smell of fresh eggs in the morning filled her nose and her stomach growled even more. It sunk in that she hadn't ingested anything for the past twenty-four hours. That was why she probably felt weak and drained. She was just glad that the plate in front of her was full of her favourites; carrots, greens, eggs and crisp bacon.
"You still like your eggs scrambled with charlottes in them?" Patrice asked.
"Yep." Cyan smiled. "Thank you, Mama."
Patrice kissed her daughter on her forehead and took a seat across from her daughter. Once she relaxed into the dining room chair, she stretched her hand towards Cyan and she knew what that

meant.
Cyan clasped her hand with her mother's.
"You're saying grace." Patrice announced.
They both closed their eyes.
"For what we are about to eat, may the Lord make us truly thankful. Amen."
"Amen."
Cyan suddenly felt a whirlwind of emotions.
Praying with her mother instantly calmed her. It consoled her. She remembered the times when her mother prayed on her behalf when she wasn't strong enough to do it on her own. She remembered all the times that her mother used forehead kisses as a means of silencing the racing thoughts in her brain. And all the times that she cooked for her and took care of her.
Cyan wanted to burst into tears. What if running away from home wasn't the answer? What if being with her family was the cure she needed to numb the pain?
Being here reminded her of Nala. It reminded her that she couldn't take of care of her and the guilt that entrapped her became too much for her to bear. That was why she left for Cesky Krumlov for

a different scenery. If she left all that reminded her of her sister, then she wouldn't feel choked by it all. Life would be worth living.
At least that was what she thought. She just didn't realise that the more she strayed away, the weaker she grew, the more hurt she felt and the more she abandoned those she loved. In the six months, her brother's growth had streaked and she didn't want to miss any of it anymore.
Any thought of returning to Prague disappeared with the wind.
"I'm sorry, Mama."
Patrice looked worried. "For what, baby?"
"I'm so sorry, Mum." Cyan wept. "I'm sorry that I just disappeared when Nala died."
"It's alri-"
"No, it's not." Cyan sniffed. "It's not alright. I left you here all alone. I won't leave again. Please believe me."
Cyan's mother smiled at her and gripped her hand firmly.
"I was not alone. God was here with me." she responded. "You dealt with her loss the best way you could. There is no formula to grieving. And

what did I say about worrying about me? That's not your job."
Cyan nodded.
"Plus, how can you leave? You have a certain someone here for you." Patrice winked.
"Ma."
"Chii?" she asked.
Usually, when her mother switched to their native language, passion exuded in whatever she said. In this case, she asked what caused Cyan to call on her name in that tone.
"Did you not hear me?" Cyan asked confusedly.
"His father is the reason I'm crying this way."
"What does that have to do with him?" Patrice asked with cauliflower in between her teeth.
"I'm not going back to that house." Cyan resolved.
"Why?"
"Because I can't." Cyan answered.
Patrice sighed and Cyan realised that her mother was about to use the soft voice.
"Cyan. Have you ever heard the saying that goes, 'The sins of the father are not to be laid upon the children.'?" Patrice asked.
"It's actually the opposite, Ma." Cyan corrected.

"The sins of the father are to be laid upon the children. By William Shakespeare."
"I changed it because the original is stupid." Patrice replied passionately. "It's not Nathan's fault that his father is a disgusting and despicable human being. It's not his fault that Nala is not here today. That young man was brought up in love by his grandparents. That is the Nathan that you should be seeing. Not blaming him for the death of our beautiful girl."
"I'm not blaming him." Cyan denied.
"Some part of you is." Patrice contested. "And I can't fault you, honey. But appeal to your heart. He just found out that a man that he has been yearning to know his whole life is a psychopath. How do you think he is feeling?"
Cyan's mind hadn't travelled that far. Nathan went through mental breakdown because of the man that was absent from his life. Finding out that he was a killer was enough to drive anyone insane. She admitted to herself that she might have been judging Nathan harshly for a mistake he didn't make. And knowing him, he was feeling guilty for a sin he didn't commit.

And naturally, Cyan felt sad for Nathan.
Of course, she wasn't being unreasonable by not wanting to see him. Was she?
She wasn't sure. Perhaps, she had no actual reason to be upset at him. His only crime was being a son of a murderer.
Cyan understood that she had to go back to that house.
"I hear you, Mama." Cyan agreed. "I'll go back."
"Once you're done eating, there is hot water on the stove. Bath quickly. You can find extra clothes in my wardrobe and make sure you look neat." Patrice instructed.
"Ma, I'm 23." Cyan groaned. “I’m going to dress well anyway."
Patrice shrugged and continued.
Cyan focused on her own eggs. She mentally went through her mother's closet to see what would fit her body. She wondered if her mother still had that skirt she had saved for Nala when she was all grown up.
The weather was quite chilly so maybe she would pair that with some tights underneath the skirt, her mother's oversized cardigan and a jacket over

that.
At least when she went to make her position on the team permanent, she'd look neat.

11. HOME

“Pres! Would you please make a cup of coffee for me?" Aria yelled from the living room.
"When you break both your legs then maybe I can assist you!" Preston chortled from the kitchen.
"Seriously? That wasn't funny." Aria responded dryly over Preston's belly laugh.
"Okay, I'm sorry." Preston said as he tried to find his composure. "How many sugars do you want?"
"6." Aria replied confidently.
"Put two sugars, Preston." Evan corrected, who was seated on the couch in the living room adjacent to the kitchen.
"I need as much energy as I can get. The pills are making me so drowsy and I don't think I'll be awake for the whole trip." Aria replied.
"You don't have to." Evan said. "You'll sleep on the plane."

"Plus, you become jittery and too energetic when you take in too much sugar." Preston noted.
"Don't forget the bigger problem; diabetes." Jordan chimed in, who was also in the living room.
"And heart disease!" Harper shouted from upstairs.
"Okay, okay." Aria gave in. "Two sugars it is."
In that moment, William walked into the room from the direction of the debrief room.
"I can't find my laced shoes." he complained.
"What?" Jay exclaimed in false confusion. "What do think happened to them?"
"I'm not sure." William grumbled.
Jay sipped his red tea. "I wonder where they are."
"What am I supposed to wear to the March Of Fallen Heroes?" William asked in panic.
"Will, you cannot wear those shoes." Preston said. "My great-great-great grandfather was alive when those things were manufactured."
"You can borrow my dress shoes. How about that?" Jordan suggested. "Your renaissance shoes clearly disappeared mysteriously."
Will nodded in agreement and threw himself onto the couch next to Evan.

"Where did you put his shoes?" Evan mouthed silently to Jordan.
Jordan just chuckled and sipped his tea.
"We are wearing our SSU uniforms so it's strictly polished dress shoes. Not shoes from the Cold War." Aria jumped in.
"Understood." William resigned. "What time are we leaving again?"
"In about ninety minutes." Evan responded. "We have to leave early for the hangar. We will meet the Directors in Switzerland."
"I'm not sure what I should wear to the party afterwards." Harper contemplated as she descended the stairs into the living room where everyone was.
"Something decent." Aria mumbled.
"Obviously, Aria. I'm not going to show up with no clothes on." Harper answered. "When have I not dressed accordingly?"
"Well..."
The room was filled with negative sounds with the notion that disagreed with Harper's stance on her way of dressing.
Harper gasped. "Even you, Jay? You think I dress

like a street walker?"
"Uh...n-no. Y-you don't at all. I mean..." Jay stammered.
"Pick your words wisely." Evan advised in a low voice.
"You know what? Whatever." Harper sulked.
"You'd look good in about anything you wear, okay?" Jay said nervously. "Everyone in here is just bitter because you put effort into how you look. That's all."
"And that's how you get yourself out of the doghouse, ladies and gentlemen." William chuckled.
"I have to. Who else am I going to dance with tonight?" Jordan replied as he winked at Harper.
"I'm just going to that after party for the food." Aria announced. "The catering is always spectacular. I wonder what they'll have this time. You know what? I don't even care. I'll eat anything they serve."
"I might pull one of the Directors to the side and propose a state-of-the-art laboratory to them. We will be able to test any matter of any case on our own and hire our personal coroner as an

Organisation instead of relying on a third party." Preston stated excitedly.
"I hope you're all not forgetting why we are really going to Geneva. To mourn for the dead who passed on the 17th of May." Evan reminded. "The after party is to celebrate their lives."
"Is Nate coming?" Aria asked quietly.
Evan didn't respond for a long time.
"No." he answered shortly.
"Why isn't he? We are all supposed to be there." Aria replied nervously.
"Imagine having to attend a march for the dead because one of your parents caused it." Evan reasoned. "He feels guilty."
"How is he?" William asked.
"As expected." Evan replied shortly.
"What is he doing up there? He has been in his room ever since he got back last night." Harper asked. “He hasn’t once left his room.”
Evan sucked in his teeth.
"Uhm..." Evan stalled.
"You rarely use hesitation forms, Evan." William noticed. "Your speech is almost flawless."
"Is there something going on?" Aria asked

worriedly.
"After Nate came back last night, he was pretty messed up. He was in very bad shape." Evan started. "We talked and he made me promise to keep quiet about something."
"Evan, we don't understand riddles." Harper chastised.
"Nathan wanted to wait until after we all left for Geneva to say goodbye." Evan announced.
“Oh.” Aria responded calmly. “He is going to his Nan’s? When will he be back?”
Evan didn’t answer that question.
“He usually goes after every case. That’s where he is going, right?” Preston asked.
“That’s where he is going, yes.” Evan responded. “He’s just not coming back.”
"What? Is that what he is doing upstairs? He is packing?" Jordan asked incredulously.
Evan nodded silently as if the words were stuck in his throat.
There was an uproar of noise.
"Wait, are you serious?" William asked.
"What do you mean he is packing? Packing what?" Aria asked.

"Evan, I can't believe you waited until this moment to tell us this. This is news you could've told us hours ago!" Harper complained.
"Maybe it's not what you think, guys." Preston attempted optimistically. "He could be packing the new clothes he bought from that thrift shop we went to into his closet."
"Preston, you have an IQ of 170. Of all people, you should understand that if you're removing a set of clothes from a place you originally travelled from, it's called unpacking." Evan corrected. "I know you don't want to believe it but I tried to talk to him. Nathan is as stubborn is a mule. He doesn't know how he can stay when he feels he has caused so much pain."
"But he didn't!" Aria contested. "It was that psychopath that ruined everything!"
"That psychopath is still his father." Evan finished. That seemed to silence everyone in the room.
"He wanted to leave after we all left. He knew that he wouldn't be able to do it if he stayed to say goodbye." Evan continued.
"So, why are you telling us now?" Will asked curiously.

"Because this is a promise I can't keep." Evan answered. "I'm hoping that we can all convince him to stay. He is the best DEC we'll ever have and I don't want him to be eaten by something that has nothing to do with him."
"Does Cyan know?" Jordan asked.
"No. And I don't know if it will be worth telling her. I mean, she might not want to be a part of this team anymore." Evan answered.
In that moment, the team heard the entrance door shut loudly and footsteps from the side of the entryway near the glass window. The thigh high boots that hit the tile floor belonged to Cyan who now stood in front of the team. She was elegantly dressed in a short black skirt that followed the direction of her curves, a white cardigan and a black leather jacket.
She looked brighter, better in a way. It could've been the way her eyes went back into position after they had bulged the day before. Or it could've been that her clothes were no longer creased and all her braids ran down her back.
She smiled a small smile to everyone.
"Cy." Aria called softly.

She stood up to greet her but crouched as if she was going to sit back down on the couch. She stood up again and took baby steps towards Cyan. Cyan looked fine. Great, in fact. But Aria did not know what state she was in mentally. How would one look if they found out devastating news about a family member in the worst way imaginable? Aria didn't know what to do. She wasn't sure if hugging Cyan was a good idea, though it was something she desperately wanted to do.
Cyan walked all the way to where Aria stood and put her arms around her. She leaned into Aria's embrace and rested her head on her shoulder for what seemed a while. Suddenly, Cy began to feel warm. The temperatures outside were terrifyingly low for the Fall but being in a familiar place melted the ice that had begun to form around her.
They let go of each other and Aria tucked a braid that flew astray from the other braids behind her back.
"Hi everyone." Cyan waved. The same way she had done when she first arrived.
"Are you alright?" Harper asked as she stood to embrace Cyan.

Cyan nodded her head yes.
Her eyes shifted to the flight of stairs as if they were a great wall she had to climb. The person she wanted to see wasn't down here only meaning that he was up there. Only twelve stairs stood between her and the section above but her body language showed that she was inviting strength just to climb them.
"He's in his room." Evan answered Cyan's silent question.
"Thanks." she expressed softly.
She glanced at the stairs one more time and started on her journey up the house.
It didn't take her very long to reach the landing but it did feel like a lifetime especially with the whispers that reached her from the living room.
"Do you think she overheard us speaking?" Jordan asked.
"When did she get here?" Preston whispered.
"Will she be able to talk to him?" William asked.
"Honestly, I don't know." Harper answered truthfully.
Cyan almost paused on the stairs to ask what the rest of the team was talking about. It clicked that

perhaps they wanted her to talk to Nathan after what happened at the police station. She could definitely do that. She was planning on it anyway. A conversation with him was obviously overdue to discuss the elephant in the room as well as possibly make her position on the team more permanent.

If that was what the issue was about, why were they whispering?

Cyan reached the top of the stairs and proceeded into the hallway.

In the days that she had lived in this house, she had never been in Nathan's room. She didn't know where it was. But she did remember Harper directing her in case she ever needed to speak with him and he wasn't in either the Debrief or the Gadget rooms.

Third room to the left, Harper had said.

Upon walking up to Nathan's door, Cyan found it slightly ajar. She knocked on his door and stood outside his room so that he could let her in.

In a way, she was dealing with the death of her sister. Somewhat. She visited her family and it rejuvenated a part of her that she thought had died with Nala. Cyan had shoulders to cry on, people she could cry to.

Unfortunately for Nathan, it wasn't the same. The only family he thought he had kept a devastating secret that had shifted his universe. Besides his grandmother and his friends, he had no real family that would tell him that everything would be okay. He was in a very fragile state and that was the exact reason Cyan had to speak with him. She had to tell him it wasn't his fault. That he had nothing to be sorry for; he had a family here.

After she went over her speech mentally, she realised that she was still standing outside. She knocked again on his oak door and there was still no response.

Cyan squeezed her eyes through the little space that the door didn't cover and noticed that Nathan was sitting on his bed, facing the window with his back to her. She couldn't see much of him except the white sweater he was wearing and some white cotton shorts.

Cyan wasn't sure if he had heard her knock but she didn't really care. She didn't wait for him to answer but instead, pushed the door open and

walked into his room.
Her boots were pretty loud on the laminated wood but Nathan still didn't turn around. This confirmed that he was purposely ignoring anyone who attempted to speak with him.
She walked towards the edge of the bed, to where he was sitting, and positioned herself next to him.
His head whipped to her direction and his puffy eyes widened in surprise.
"Cyan." he called quietly.
"Hey." Cyan greeted with a smile.
“Hi.” He responded. “What are you-how did you…?”
“Oh. Uhm, I took a bus to my mum’s yesterday.” Cyan answered.
“Oh.” Nathan replied.
“Yep.” Cyan clicked her tongue.
Silence fell over them.
This gave Cyan time to notice how clean his room was. Way too clean. Shelves, where his property was supposed to be, were spotless. His walk-in closet, that was half open, was almost empty of all his clothes and shoes. The side of his dresser that stored his comic books was vacant.

Where were his things? She meant to ask that out loud but the words remained in her throat because she had the feeling she already knew the answer.
Instead, she asked him where his anime comic books were.
“I’m taking them with me.” Nathan answered.
“And where is that?” Cyan asked.
“Back home.” He replied.
“You’re visiting your Nan? When will you be back?” Cyan asked curiously.
“Cy…”
“Cy what?” Cyan replied irately. “I didn’t know visiting meant packing all your belongings.”
Nathan clipped his mouth and stared at the ground.
"You don't have to be here." he said without looking at her.
"Well, I'm here. So, hi." Cyan responded tersely.
Nathan raked his cotton-silk hair that had grown a few inches in the day that Cyan hadn't seen him.
He stood up from the king-size bed and marched over to the other side of the headboard and procured some of his rings and chains and placed

them on the bed.
"The Directors are releasing you from the Organisation. The criminals have been caught and are yet to be sentenced so you're free to go." Nathan informed monotonously.
"Well, I want to stay." Cyan replied quickly.
Nathan nodded.
"I want you to stay as well." Cyan added.
"That's not possible." Nathan replied shortly.
"Why is it not possible, Nathan?" Cyan asked.
"In case you haven't heard, my father is a good for nothing criminal. He caused so much pain to the people I love and I can't imagine looking at them in the eye knowing what he did." Nathan responded in a low voice.
"What he did. What George did." Cyan emphasised. "Why are you carrying a burden that's not yours?"
"He is my father, Cyan." Nathan responded.
Cyan stood up wanting to march over to Nathan but her left eye noticed his black duffel bag stuffed under his dresser. That must've been the luggage he packed his belongings in.

Cyan crouched to the level of the dresser and pulled the bag from underneath it. She zipped the bag open and unpacked the sweaters and sweatpants that Nathan had originally packed in the bag.
"Cyan!"
"You're not going anywhere." Cyan ordered firmly.
"Cy-"
"Don't you dare call my name!" Cyan exclaimed. "You're leaving? The team? Me? Who do you think you are?"
Nathan took a deep breath.
"That day affected me too but you don't see me running away!" Cyan continued.
"Running away?" Nathan repeated incredulously. He crunched his teeth to regain his patience. "Would you hand over my bag, please?"
"No." Cyan replied stubbornly.
"You've been doing so well without me, Cyan. Every time I'm in your life, I just cause you pain." Nathan explained. "I can't stand making you unhappy over and over again."
"So, you're going to abandon the life you've built because you feel sorry for yourself?" Cyan asked

in an appalled tone. "You're just going to be what- a nobody, after you leave?"
Nathan clenched his teeth in order to calm himself down.
"Leave this room right now and give your fruitcake of a father the power." Cyan pushed. "Do it."
Nathan began to huff and puff.
"I'm sorry, am I making you mad?" Cyan asked sardonically. "Because if I am then great! Hyperventilate and wheeze. Do whatever the hell you have to do!"
"I don't know what you're trying to achieve here." Nathan responded as he grabbed his clothes from where Cyan had thrown them and stuffed them back in his bag.
"That's right." Cyan urged. "Get mad, Nathan. That way you can admit the real reason you're leaving."
"Oh, really? And what would that be? You seem to know so much." Nathan challenged.
"You're remorseful for what your father did. But a bigger part of you is afraid that all you'll live up to is his legacy. You're afraid of not achieving more than you have right now because knowing that

George is your father could potentially reveal characteristics about you that could make you hate yourself. And that's what scares the heck out of you. That we will see outside of who you are." Cyan explained.

Nathan couldn't breathe with anger.

"Are you done?" he asked.

"No." Cyan responded with just as much agitation. "No, I'm not done. You are angry because your whole life, you've always yearned for a father. You were depressed about it and it turns out that he is not what you pictured. He is the complete opposite. And you don't know how to deal with it."

"You hit the nail on the head." Nathan responded gruffly. "You want to analyse me and make me feel like crap even more?"

"You are running away from your emotions. Not from this team. And that is what I want you to realise so that you don't fool yourself as you walk out that door." Cyan explained. "Don't you get it? You're allowed to be angry at your father. You're allowed to throw things and punch the wall. Do that for Pete's sake instead of leaving those who

truly care about you!”
"Cy..." Nathan whispered.
"Do it!” Cyan cried. “Scream!”
Nathan let out a deep roar, one that came from the depths of him, covering the entirety of the room they were in. He threw the duffel bag at the wall and covered this face with his palms. His knees gave out and he fell to the ground.
"Every time you look at me, you see my father, don't you?" Nathan asked in between tears.
Cyan was silent for some moments.
"I thought I would." Cyan admitted. "But all I see is you."
Nathan shook his head, his hair moving in all directions.
"Your sister is not here anymore because of someone I'm affiliated with. No matter how many times we deny that fact, it'll always be true. George Charles Caldwell still remains my blood, Cyan." Nathan whispered. "How can you even stand to be in the same room as me?"
Cyan removed her boots and threw them on top of Nathan's duffel bag and knelt where Nathan was.

"Look at me." Cyan said to him.
Nathan's eyes remained on the ground.
"Look at me." she urged again. This time she put her fingers under his chin and turned his head towards her.
She smiled at him.
"I want children in the future." she giggled.
Nathan stared at her in confusion.
"Don't get me wrong, I still want to enjoy my youth but if I was blessed with a bundle of joy with your beautiful eyes, I wouldn't be against the idea. Let alone being half the man that you are, I would do a backflip." she expressed.
Nathan chortled.
She put her soft hand in his.
"Unless there was another version of you present with either your father or Jan Jalesmycie when those people were killed then I don't understand why you're feeling guilty." Cyan reassured.
"You had nothing to do with Nala's death or all the other deaths that your father is responsible for. You helped me look for my little sister and helped get everyone including Donna to safety.
Your father had his own agenda he wanted to

achieve that had nothing to do with you. You are not going to assume his sins. I won't let you."
"Won't being a DEC be difficult?" Nathan whispered. "What if I don't have it in me to lead anymore?"
"George was a criminal when you were made Division Expert Chief and he'll forever hold that title. Don't give him that power; to dictate how your life works from inside a cell."
Nathan sighed and he sat down against the footboard of the bed. He pulled Cyan by the waist and sat her down on his laps.
"I don't know how I can apologise for Nala. Psychotic father or not. She was everything to you, your mother and Mari." he apologised. He put his head on her stomach.
"I'm so sorry."
Cyan pecked him on the cheek.
"She always loved you. She thought you were very cute." Cyan reminisced. "I realised this when she told me about the time you went to the amusement park without me."
"We tried looking for you. But she said she couldn't wait to jump on the rides and buy cotton

candy." Nathan remembered. "She was strong-willed."
"That she was. And beautiful. Bold. And very young."
Nathan squeezed Cyan tightly.
"She is watching over me. Over all of us. Watching every move I make, telling me that I'm the cool older sister." Cyan laughed softly.
Nathan chuckled. "She is making the face too."
Cyan chuckled too. "That face that was the literal definition of the term 'unbothered'. She wasn't easily impressed. An old soul."
They sat again in silence. Only this time, it was the comfortable silence that Cyan was always used to. The silence that they used for resting, and after the shouting they did at each other, they really needed it.
"Are you going to unpack the clothes in that duffel bag of yours?" Cyan asked.
Nathan nodded.
They stayed that way; Cyan on Nathan's lap, Nathan in Cyan's arms, until they had forgotten all the trauma they were both going through. They were both tired and, in that moment, they rested

in each other's embrace.
In his arms, Cyan felt very familiar as if they were at a place she hadn't visited not because he hadn't longed to do so but because she had lost the directions on the way.
She had found them somehow, she didn't care how; she was just glad to be back home sitting near a hot furnace shutting out the freezing cold.
"Yes." Cyan filled the silence.
"What?" Nathan asked curiously.
"I agree to your deal. I agree to a lifetime of cheesecakes with you." Cyan agreed.
"Do you think this is a wrong time to ask you to take me back?" Nathan asked Cyan.
She tilted his head to face hers.
“I mean, I expected roses and confetti but I will settle for an empty duffel bag.” Cyan replied.
"Cy. " Nathan said in a low voice. “I'd do more than roses and confetti if you let me. So much more. Favour me with your love again and I promise to hold you tightly when the ground beneath our feet loses balance. Be with me in everything until I'm just a memory.”
For the first time in six months, Cyan and Nathan

kissed passionately. Butterflies sprung into Cyan's stomach and it made her kiss Nathan more. They were so in sync, each movement mimicking the other perfectly.
"Mm-hm." she agreed.
"I'm so in love with you." Nathan whispered.
"This is as good as it gets." Cyan joked.
Nathan chuckled.
"I love you." Cyan responded.
"...esss!"
Nathan paused.
"Did you hear that?" he asked.
He effortlessly picked Cyan from his lap and gently set her down on the bed. He stealthily walked over to his bedroom door and opened it quickly. On the other side of the door, the rest of the team piled on top of each other, ears plastered on the door. All of them except Evan, who seemed to be the only civilised among the seven.
Because Aria was the shortest, she was stationed in front. Her whole body must have been resting on the door when Nathan opened it because she lost her balance and stumbled into his room. He caught her before her straight teeth met the

ground.
"Are you alright?" Nathan asked her.
"Yep." she answered sheepishly as she stood up straight.
Jordan, Preston, Harper and William faded away in embarrassment, backing away from the door and dispersing to different areas of the house.
Aria, who wasn't fazed that she was interrupting an intimate moment, made eye contact with Cyan, who was still sitting on the bed, and signalled a hidden smile.
She stared at Nathan and asked, "We are walking to the hangar in twenty minutes, right?"
"Yes." Nathan smiled.
It took everything in Aria had not to jump and hug him.
"Okay, then." Aria smiled. "Bye."
"Bye, Aria." Nathan laughed.
Once she was out of view, he shut his door.
He walked back to his bed and gently removed Cyan's leather jacket and hung it on the coat rack that stood in the corner of his room near the window.
As if they had one mind, they both lay down on

the puffy bed spread, all the air dissipating from under them.

They faced each other, Cyan's hand in Nathan's hair and Nathan's hand engulfing hers.

"I didn't know the Organisation was hosting a March Of The Dead." Cyan noted.

"They sent last minute emails this morning on the SSU Platform. Since the criminals in Denmark were caught, the Directors saw it fit host a little celebration." Nathan explained.

"How nice of them." Cyan expressed.

Her hand traced Nathan's jawline softly.

"You hate parties." Nathan chuckled.

"Because they keep me out too late." Cyan reasoned. "But I'll go to this one. It would be a good way to honour and say goodbye to everyone."

"We can always sneak out and find a cotton candy place." Nathan suggested.

"That sounds like a plan." Cyan excitedly. "And maybe we can find a coffee shop. I remember you said your mom loved hot croissants."

Nathan chuckled softly. "She had this thing for them with vermicelli, apparently. The taste

fascinated her.”
"Cotton candy and croissants. Tonight. It's a date." Cyan announced.
Nathan checked his watch.
"We have exactly seventeen minutes before we have to leave this bed and get moving." He noted in DEC voice. “And I want to spend each and every second looking at you."
They kissed again, softly and deeper, reintroducing themselves to each other again.
When they pulled apart, Cyan pecked his nose and made herself comfortable in Nathan’s soft nape, absorbing his heat until she felt warm again. The coldness that she had felt inside because of her tragedy had melted into a liquid, flowing like a waterfall into a small lake.
Knowing that they could fight battles as long as they were on the same side, Cyan and Nathan held each other tightly, breathing the same air.
Nathan set his watch aside, in hopes that he wouldn't be tempted to check how much time they had left before they had to travel to Geneva.
He discarded the concept of time and relaxed in Cyan’s embrace.

He held onto her and she held onto him, until they both closed their eyes.

12

Made in the USA
Columbia, SC
02 June 2023